THREE-LEGGED HORSE

2.00
JP

Also by Ann Hood

SOMEWHERE OFF THE COAST OF MAINE
WAITING TO VANISH

Bantam New Fiction is devoted to novels with contem-
porary concerns. Publishing some of the most exciting
voices at work today, these titles are available wherever
quality trade paperbacks are sold.

BANTAM NEW FICTION

THREE-LEGGED HORSE

ANN HOOD

A BANTAM TRADE PAPERBACK

BANTAM BOOKS
NEW YORK • TORONTO • LONDON • SYDNEY • AUCKLAND

For Bob

THREE-LEGGED HORSE
A Bantam Book / September 1989

*Grateful acknowledgment is made for permission to reprint lyrics from "The
Way You Look Tonight." Music by Jerome Kern and lyrics by Dorothy Fields.
Copyright 1936 T.B. Harms Company. Copyright renewed. International copy-
right secured. All rights reserved. Used by permission.*

Library of Congress Cataloging-in-Publication Data

Hood, Ann, 1956–
  Three-legged horse / Ann Hood.
    p.   cm. — (Bantam new fiction)
  ISBN 0-553-34732-2
  I. Title.
PS3558.0537T48 1989
813'.54—dc19   89-266
                                                                  CIP

Published simultaneously in the United States and Canada

Bantam Books are published by Bantam Books, a division of Bantam Doubleday
Dell Publishing Group, Inc. Its trademark, consisting of the words "Bantam
Books" and the portrayal of a rooster, is Registered in U.S. Patent and Trade-
mark Office and in other countries. Marca Registrada. Bantam Books, 666 Fifth
Avenue, New York, New York 10103.

PRINTED IN THE UNITED STATES OF AMERICA

FG   0 9 8 7 6 5 4 3 2 1

Acknowledgments

For their inspiration and advice, I would like to thank Lloyd and Gloria Hood, Melissa Hood, Bob Reiss, Glenn Russow, Elly Abelow and Gilda Povolo, Garret Weyr, Gail Hochman, and of course, Deb Futter.

PURE MUSIC

For Abby, it was not the applause that she loved. Or the way that audiences seemed to focus on her whenever she played her violin. In fact, those things embarrassed her. The thing she loved was the playing. The feel of the wood under her chin, the instant when the bow first touched the strings and the music began.

Three-Legged Horse was playing at Groucho's in Providence, a cavernous place filled with college students and locals. Everyone drank draft beer, and by the end of the night people usually ended up dancing on the tables. Outside, a cold January rain fell, and Abby's head buzzed with the sound of it on the roof mixed with traffic from I-95 and pool balls crashing together in a back room.

Sean asked her, "Ready?"

Doug leaned into the microphone and said, "Hi, we're Three-Legged Horse."

The outside noises began to fade for Abby and all that existed was her violin and her music. The band always started off with her playing a few bars of a Mozart violin concerto before they went right into something the audience recognized, like "Leather and Lace" or "Diamonds and Rust." The "love duos," Doug called them.

Abby tucked her violin under her chin. For an instant, her eyes settled on her twelve-year-old-daughter, Hannah, who sat at a front table sipping root beer. She drank daintily, with one pinky extended straight out. Lately, Hannah had been pretending she was a mysterious French girl. Watching her, Abby imagined that Hannah was fantasizing that the root beer was a glass of red wine and that Groucho's was a cozy cafe on the Left Bank. Hannah used to be her biggest fan, but since she'd started junior high, she tried to be cool, aloof. Abby wished Hannah would look up, give her a smile.

But she didn't. So Abby lifted her bow and stroked the strings. Sometimes she watched the audience's faces change as her music filled the room. She would see eyes turn toward her, beer mugs freeze in midair as the notes cast a spell. But tonight, Abby just wanted to close her eyes, to block out those faces. As she played, she was no longer a mother, a wife in a crazy marriage, or a fiddler in Three-Legged Horse. She was, instead, pure music.

When the first song ended, Abby opened her eyes. Everything seemed harsh compared to the peaceful beauty she'd felt as she'd played. The faces that looked back at her had an eerie cast from the white bar lighting, and Abby felt like she'd just landed on a different planet. She shook her head slightly, to shake off that feeling. Then she focused on Hannah. Her daughter never failed to make Abby feel centered, even when she sat, like now, oblivious to everything around her, head buried in *Arsen Lupin*. For ten years, Hannah had sat in bars and restaurants, ski resorts and hotel lounges, listening to Three-Legged Horse. It had long ago lost its appeal to her.

"Wait till she really gets started," Doug said into the microphone.

A man in the back whistled, a long, low catcall.

"You're out of luck," Doug said. "She's married."

Hannah looked up then and rolled her eyes.

"Well," Doug added, "kind of."

The audience laughed. Abby felt their eyes on her and she blushed.

She had been a performer forever, but still the attention embarrassed her. One of her earliest memories was plucking out "The Itsy Bitsy Spider" on the violin at Sardi's after her parents' opening night on Broadway in *The Little Foxes*. She remembered being hoisted onto a table draped in linen and littered with wine glasses and ashtrays, the rustling of her petticoats as she moved the violin into position, her mother, Deirdre, urging her on, calling, "That's my kid up there! Come on, kiddo. Knock 'em dead." And she remembered the way all the grown-ups had stopped talking when she'd played, how everyone had stopped to stare at her, and how right after she'd finished, she'd burst into tears.

Years later, when she had been Hannah's age, she had played onstage at Lincoln Center. Her mother had made sure that people threw pale pink roses at her feet. "Always pale pink. That way they'll see them and think of you," Deirdre had advised her. When she was fifteen and started running away from home, Abby used to play her violin in parks and subway stations around Manhattan, keeping her violin case open and watching as people dropped in coins and crumpled bills. Those people had hardly ever looked at her. They'd kept their eyes downcast as they walked quickly by, then retreated to a distant corner to listen.

That was how she'd met her husband, Zach. Playing in Washington Square Park, trying to make money for food and rent. But he had walked right up to her. He'd looked her in the eye.

Abby shook her head again. She did not want to start thinking about Zach. There had been no word from him since November, when he'd sent her a dozen bunches of violets, the way he did every year for their anniversary.

On the day they'd been married, he'd shown up at her apartment after six months away from her, traveling in Europe, looking for inspiration for his art. When she'd opened her door he had not said anything except, "Let's get married." "When?" she'd asked him. "Right now," Zach had said, holding out a tiny bunch of violets. Her wedding bouquet. They had stood in line at City Hall for two hours, behind teenagers and foreign couples and pregnant women clutching the hands of their nervous grooms. Zach and Abby made up life stories for all of them—political refugees, Mafia shotgun bride, escapees from Queens. She had not realized how nervous she'd been until she'd looked down and found herself holding a handful of broken stems, the violets floating to the dirty floor like purple confetti.

That night, at Umberto's Clam Bar in Little Italy, Zach had brought her two dozen bouquets and filled an entire table for two with violets. Later, in the glare of warehouse lighting that filled her loft on Grand Street, Zach had whispered, "I'll probably be a lousy husband." "I know," she'd said.

But then, and even now, their time together made up for all of the crazy years, the times apart. She had even left him once for over a year, only to take him back when he'd finally started calling and sending her letters cluttered with pink and red hand-drawn hearts. The day he'd said he'd try living in Vermont with her and Hannah, Abby had felt like it had all been worth it. She and Hannah had spent an entire afternoon making him a sign that said "Welcome Home" in gold glitter. But after six months together full-time, she'd been almost relieved

4

when he'd gone to San Francisco for a "little while." Since then, it had been mostly just summers, with the three of them roaming the country in Zach's Plymouth Voyager looking for found objects for his America series collages.

Sometimes, Abby thought as Sean began to play the opening notes of "Both Sides Now" on his guitar, she fantasized about life without Zach, and then she'd feel a deadness at the very center of her. "Can't live with him, can't live without him," she laughingly explained to her mother whenever Deirdre pushed for her to free herself of Zach. In the meantime, Abby told herself as she leaned into the microphone to sing the chorus with Doug and Sean, she had Three-Legged Horse. It was a crazy system, but for now, it worked.

When she started to sing, Hannah finally looked at her, and gave her a wide, exaggerated yawn.

Abby and Sean hated doing the commercial jingle medley that Doug had written. Lately, though, he'd been insisting more and more that they sing it. "The crowds love it," he'd say. "They request it." "That doesn't mean we have to do it," Sean always argued. Sean's wife, Mallory, even walked out of the room whenever they played it. Still, they kept it in and crowds like this one at Groucho's especially loved it. They sang along and clapped their hands like they were at a hootenanny.

In the middle of the Big Mac jingle, which had taken Abby weeks to learn, to memorize all the ingredients right, she thought Sean looked over at her and said, "Zach." Abby frowned at him. It was almost time to say all those silly ingredients. The audience was standing on the tables, all excited from singing about the heartbeat of America. She managed to get through the Big Mac song, and Sean was staring at her, hard, when she finished.

She started to sing her solo of "I'd Like to Teach the World to Sing" when he said again, "Zach." This time he pointed into the crowd of faces in front of her.

Abby looked out. The words to the song vanished from her mind as soon as she saw Zach, standing there, smiling up at her.

"My God," she said softly.

She wanted to dive off that stage and into his arms. She wanted to grab his hand and run out of there with him. To run and run and not look back. He had come for her in the middle of January. He was mouthing words now, words she could make out clearly. "I love you." And then she did it. She put her violin down while all around her people were singing about Coca-Cola, and she ran to him. He was waiting for her, his arms outstretched.

"What are you doing here?" she whispered. His hair and face were cold, wet from the winter rain.

"I missed you," he told her.

"Some people," Abby said, "would have called. Or maybe written a letter."

Zach laughed. "Some people," he said, "are not me."

Abby thought for an instant of all the men she had been with, trying to work Zach out of her system, to forget him. She thought about how none of them made her feel the way she did at this moment, in Zach's arms. He made her feel the same way her music did.

"No one," she said, "is you."

Zach talked and Abby listened. That's how it had been from the start. He could weave fantastic tales, or even tell true stories better than anyone. When Abby was with him, she seemed to be on an incredible roller coaster—

6

the excitement, the way her stomach felt like there was another thrill just around the corner.

Like now. The way Zach was describing his decision to come East from San Francisco to her and Hannah. How he woke up three days ago needing her so bad that it hurt.

"So I just got on a plane and—zap!—here I am."

"It's been so long—" Abby started. But already Zach had turned his attention on something else.

"I need inspiration," he said. "I don't think another America series is right. It's been done."

"I'll say," Hannah muttered.

They sat together in Abby's Holiday Inn room, all on the bed. Behind them, *Mr. Mom* played noiselessly on the television. While Zach talked, Hannah watched, studying both his and Abby's faces, scowling as she stared at them. Abby reached out and played with Hannah's black corkscrew curls until Hannah pulled away from her.

"Do you know what I think?" Abby said. "I think you need to go from the general to the specific. Not a broad topic like America anymore. Something tighter."

Since they'd met, Abby had been able to inspire Zach's art. Even the months before they were married, when he was in Europe, he would call her, his voice crackling across the Atlantic to her, explaining what he'd seen and felt. Then Abby would help him make sense of it.

Zach thought about what she said now. Then he smiled again. "You're a genius!" he shouted. "Of course. From the general to the specific."

He held her face in his hands. "I married a genius," he said, his voice softer.

"Oh, please," Hannah moaned.

Zach turned his attention to her. "What? What, Hannah my manna?"

"Don't," she said sharply. "Don't call me that."

He looked at her, surprised. "I've always called you that," he said.

Abby hid a small smile. She often thought that Hannah was the only female who could resist Zach's charms.

"It's dumb," Hannah said.

"It isn't," Zach insisted. "It's nourishment. Nourishment from a divine bounty."

"That's beautiful, Hannah," Abby said.

"Manna's a laxative," Hannah told them. "I looked it up."

Zach looked at Abby. "A laxative?"

She shrugged.

"From the stem of the flowering ash," Hannah said. "So stop. S'il vous plaît."

Zach laughed. "Oui, oui."

Abby started to giggle then.

"Stop," Hannah told her.

The more she looked at Hannah, the more Abby giggled.

"Mom!"

"You know what I think?" Zach said. "I think we need pancakes. What do you say, Ab? Some manna."

Pancakes were the way they always finished late nights like this one. When they were together in New York, they ate apple pancakes at dawn at the Moondance Diner. In Vermont it was pancakes at Nellie's. They always managed to find the best pancakes.

Abby grabbed Zach by the hand. "Definitely pancake time," she said.

Hannah pretended to watch *Mr. Mom*.

"Not coming?" Zach asked her.

She didn't answer him.

"Okay," Abby said. "We'll eat an extra stack for you."

They were at the door, walking out hand in hand,

giggling together, when Hannah said, still focusing on the television, "Why did you come here?"

Zach and Abby hesitated.

Hannah still did not look at them. The TV flashed color across her face, made it look pale and wet. "We don't need you, you know," she said. "When you leave again, she'll be all upset."

"Hannah," Abby said. She wondered how she could explain to a twelve-year-old that these times together made the other times disappear. That she had agreed a long time ago to this arrangement. That on their wedding day Zach had told her he'd be a lousy husband.

But Abby didn't have to answer. Zach was talking.

"That's not true, Hannah. Your mother and I understand each other. We're not like other people, you know? We never had the Picket-Fence Syndrome, did we, Abby? Free spirits. That's what we are."

Abby felt her hand growing damp in his. She bit down on her lower lip as he spoke.

Hannah turned from the television and set her gaze right at Abby. She sat, waiting. But Abby just swallowed hard and took a deep breath.

"Pancakes," she said, trying to sound as if she still believed everything was the way she wanted it.

It was daylight now, but Zach and Abby had pulled the heavy green drapes as tightly shut as they could so the room would be as dark as if it were nighttime. Hannah had gone for lunch with Sean and Mallory and their kids. And finally Zach and Abby had made love. When they were together, she lost all track of time, so that when she woke this afternoon in the darkened room, for a minute Abby felt confused and frightened. The confusion passed once she looked around and got her bearings. But the fright stuck in the pit of her stomach.

9

Zach reached for her lazily.

"Hey," he said.

Although he didn't smoke, his voice was a smoker's, deep and slightly hoarse.

Abby climbed onto him and rested her head on his chest.

"I want to see you," he said, turning on the light.

She sat up and traced his face with her fingers, wondering how long he would stay this time. She tried to make herself think of something else. She had Three-Legged Horse. Three more months of steady gigs.

"How'd you like that commercial jingle medley?" she said.

Zach grimaced.

"They should let you do our song," he said.

"Are you kidding?" Abby laughed. "Jerome Kern? Doug's working on a television show theme song routine."

"Like *Mr. Ed*?" Zach said.

"And *The Brady Bunch*." Abby laughed. "And *Gilligan's Island* and—"

Zach covered his ears. "It's too painful. Stop."

Abby leaned down, pressed her mouth to his ear. "Someday," she sang softly, "when I'm awfully low—"

Zach put his hands in her hair, and sang too, softer than her, "When the world is cold—"

"I will get a glow," Abby sang, "just thinking of you, and the way you look tonight."

She placed her hand on his chest, and felt his heart beating quickly against it.

When they finally got out of bed and Hannah came back from lunch and a trip to the zoo at Roger Williams Park, Zach said, "I think I'll go to New York and see what's going on there. You know. Stay with Paco. Visit some galleries."

"Sure," Abby said. "Good idea." She tried to sound like she meant it.

"Maybe I can bounce this new idea off some people," Zach added. "Tell them my brilliant partner thought of it. I already have some ideas for some new collages. Prairies, maybe. Or shopping malls."

Abby nodded. Prairies, she thought.

Zach pulled a neatly folded train schedule from his pocket. "So," he said, "there's a train to Penn Station in about an hour."

Several departure times were circled in red.

Hannah said, "That's why you came, isn't it? Just a short detour from New York so why not say hi to the wife and kid."

Abby told her, angrily, "Be quiet." She was afraid she felt angry at Hannah because she'd spoken Abby's own thoughts. Thoughts she did not want to have.

Abby brought him to the train station in Providence. Hannah insisted on waiting outside. When Zach tried to give her a hug, she slipped past him quickly. "See ya," she said, and dropped a quarter into a newspaper machine for a *USA Today*.

There wasn't even a place to have a cup of coffee in the train station, so they went right down to the track. Abby had forgotten her gloves, and Zach held both of her hands in his and blew on them gently.

"Fight for Jerome Kern in your repertoire," he said.

She managed a smile.

There was silence, then she said it. "Just think," she said, "it could be like this all the time. If we wanted."

Zach frowned. "Like in Vermont a few years ago?" he said. "We tried that. We tried in New York before Hannah was born. It's not us, Abby."

She had to try harder. "But it could be," she said. "You hated being so isolated. You're a city guy, that's all.

We could try to live someplace else. Boston maybe. As long as I got to the gigs I could live anywhere. And we could be together—"

Zach pressed his finger to her lips to quiet her. "We've been through this before. I can't do it. I just can't."

"Now we're a couple of old fogies. That's what Hannah says. Maybe at this point—"

"Ssssh," he said. He glanced down the track. In the distance the train was approaching, chugging slowly toward them. "Maybe it's time to call it quits," Zach said softly.

The words pierced Abby's gut.

"For real this time," Zach said. "You want something else, maybe. You want—"

"No," she said. "I want you."

He held his arms out for her. "Come here," he said.

She did not hesitate. She let him engulf her in his grasp.

"I will get a glow," he half-sang, half-whispered, "just thinking of you . . . and the way you looked last night."

THE IMAGE
SHE HELD

Hannah was used to men looking at her mother. Personally, she didn't think Abby was all that pretty. A few years ago, when Hannah was just a kid, her mother had seemed like an angel, all smooth porcelain skin and fine blond hair. But now, when Hannah compared Abby to other mothers, she felt a little embarrassed. Brent Balboa's mother always brought the class homemade brownies and chocolate-chip cookies. She would drive up in her Volvo wagon and carry big colorful trays of sweets into the class, walking with great confidence in her high-heeled shoes. Chelsea Kent's mother jogged every day, and played tennis. Mrs. Kent had dozens of short pleated skirts and matching tops all in soft creamy colors, and jogging outfits with sneakers that matched perfectly in shades of raspberry and baby blue. She wore lipstick. And perfume that she spritzed on herself from an antique silver atomizer. That, Hannah thought, was someone pretty.

Abby didn't even try to look presentable. She was always wearing old faded dresses from years ago with too-long hems and missing buttons. If she ever replaced a button, it was never with one that matched the others. She kept an old mayonnaise jar full of odd buttons on her dresser and would just pull one out at random and sew it on a coat or blouse. She even did that to Hannah's clothes, which Hannah used to think was cute but now that she was in junior high found mortifying.

Hannah had tried to improve Abby's overall appearance. Sometimes she cut out pictures from *Mademoiselle* magazine of models with hairstyles that might look flattering on her mother. But Abby would just laugh. "My hair would never stay like that," she'd say. Her hair was fair and fine and hung in a fluff of rippling curls. During the summers when they drove around with Zach, Abby's hair grew almost white from the sun. "Maybe," Hannah always suggested in the winter, "you could highlight your hair so it's always real blond." But her mother thought that was ridiculous. "Who really cares?" Abby had laughed. I do, Hannah had thought, but she hadn't said it out loud.

Instead, she concentrated on giving her mother manicures and pedicures, French-braiding Abby's hair, and leaving those magazine pictures around the house. Still, Abby always looked unfinished somehow. She usually forgot to put on her glasses—an old-fashioned pair of wire-rimmed ones—and ended up having to squint at everything. To Hannah, she looked like a bag lady, or a crazy person, with her ragamuffin clothes and half-blind vision.

Men, however, didn't seem to notice. Even Chelsea Kent's father got all red in the face when he met Abby one day. Mr. Kent had this gorgeous wife and he had still stammered and blushed talking to Abby. Not that she had even noticed. She had just complained to him about the destruction of rain forests and how all the songbirds were disappearing. "Listen!" she had said, leaning close to him so she could see his face. "No birds singing." Hannah had wanted to die. She had tugged on her mother's hand, urging her out of the school gymnasium and away from Mr. Kent.

Even now, from her table at the front of Groucho's, Hannah could see a small group of men forming around her mother. Abby sat perched on a stool at the bar, smiling and squinting at them. She had on an old shirt, so faded that it was impossible to tell what color it was supposed to be. Her skirt's hem had come undone in the back, and it dangled to the floor in a dusty vee.

"Oh, brother," Hannah muttered as she watched.

By the look of things, it was going to be a long night. Three-Legged Horse had finished its last set almost an hour ago. Sean had gone back to the Holiday Inn with Mallory, but Doug and Abby were still ordering food and drinks, surrounded by groupies. Doug thought he was some kind of hot rock star or something, and he made Hannah sick. To hear him talk, he was practically famous. Hannah used to even believe him. She'd listen to his stories about how he could have played backup for Bruce Springsteen way back in the seventies. Or how he once wrote a song that Mick Jagger almost bought.

For a while, when her parents had really split up that time four years ago, Abby had started to date Doug. He used to stay overnight and make Hannah hot cocoa with real chocolate. Hannah had still liked him then. But Zach had come back, and it had seemed to Hannah that Doug just didn't try hard enough to keep him away. She had decided then that he gave up too easily. He had proved that by not going off with Bruce Springsteen when he had the chance. By not fighting for Abby.

Abby called over to her. "Fried mozzarella sticks!" She held one up for Hannah to see.

One of the men, a short guy with dark curly hair and

a build like a football player, covered Abby's hand with his and guided the cheese into her mouth.

Hannah bet to herself that he had a hairy back. And hairy knuckles too. Gross, she thought. She spelled her name across the table in peanut shells. Behind her, Abby's laugh rose, a soft melody. Everything about her mother seemed rhythmic and flowing—her laugh, her walk, even the way she moved her long delicate hands. For years, Abby had tried to teach Hannah to play a musical instrument. "Once you learn," she had said, "you'll never really be alone. You'll always have music with you." She had tried everything—piano, violin, even harmonica. But Hannah could not learn. The notes had looked like hieroglyphics to her, the keys and holes and strings had felt awkward under her clumsy fingers.

Hannah heard her mother say, "Oh, you box. Like in a ring. Like Muhammad Ali. I thought you said you boxed things, like shirts or something."

She could tell her mother had had too much to drink by the way Abby's voice sounded—shriller and higher than usual. When Zach had announced he was leaving this afternoon, Hannah had known that they would stay late at Groucho's, that Abby would drink too much and probably leave with some man she didn't even know.

Abby was calling to her now. "Come over here, Hannah, and have some—what is this?"

Hannah turned toward the bar again. Only the hairy man, the boxer, was beside Abby. The other men had gone. Doug was still at the bar, though, and a woman in tight jeans and suede high-heeled boots was sitting on his lap.

The boxer said, "Squid. Calamari."

"That's disgusting," Hannah said.

But she walked over to the bar anyway. She couldn't get the image of her father out of her mind, the way he'd casually announced he'd be going to New York. The way Abby had pretended to think that was a great idea.

Hannah used to think her father was someone magical. Someone who led them around the country on adventures, to places with exotic names like Taos and the Badlands. It used to seem like her parents were special and wonderful, like no other people in the world. When she was little, Hannah would sneak out of bed and watch them dance across the living room floor, their eyes closed and happy smiles on their faces. She used to like the way they had private jokes and stories, how one word could send them into a fit of giggles.

But lately, her mother seemed saddened by Zach. When he left them, she moped around and drank. Abby used to say, "He's gone, but the magic isn't." She didn't say that anymore. And Zach seemed like a big phony. A liar. Like today, pretending he just got that idea to go to New York, like that hadn't been his plan all along.

More and more, Hannah asked her mother why they couldn't be a real family. The way the Kents were, having barbecues and trips to the shopping mall together on Saturday afternoons. "Chelsea's father gives her ten dollars to buy whatever she wants. Records or earrings. Anything. And Mrs. Kent goes to Sears and looks at the new model refrigerators and dishwashers. That's a family." Abby found this image funny. "Can you picture Zach and me looking at dishwashers?" "No," Hannah would say sadly, "I can't." "Besides," Abby liked to say, "you have an extra family. You have Three-Legged Horse too. I bet Chelsea would kill to spend weekends at Mount Snow or up in Portland." Hannah didn't tell her mother that Chelsea had said that sounded depressing.

Today, after Zach had left, Hannah had asked Abby, "Don't you wish he would stay gone? Or else stick around for good? Like before I was born and you guys lived in

New York? Or like when he came and stayed with us in Vermont for six months?"

What had bothered Hannah the most was that her mother hadn't answered her. She'd just bit down on her bottom lip and stared at the cement train station like Zach would be walking right back out.

Abby had taken her for dinner at an expensive Italian restaurant that they really couldn't afford. She'd had too much wine and no dinner and talked about how special Zach was. Stories about Zach always took on mythological proportions when he was gone. The story of the violets. The story about how he once painted a nude picture of Abby, then destroyed it so no one else would see her naked. The story about the time when Hannah was just an infant and Zach was out in San Francisco and Abby hopped a plane with Hannah and surprised him. They had stayed together for a month there, living above a Mexican restaurant. The apartment, Abby liked to say, always smelled like warm tortillas.

Lately, like at dinner tonight, Hannah liked to remind her mother of the other stories. The ones about all the times they waited for phone calls that never came, or plans to meet Zach in San Francisco that never materialized. But even Hannah found some kind of strange comfort in the love stories. Especially the one Abby told about the day she met Zach. Whenever Hannah heard it, she imagined her mother as young and full of possibility. She liked to watch Abby's eyes when she told that story. They grew soft and dreamy and she looked exactly the way she did when she played her violin.

Hannah especially liked that story on the nights when she and her mother stayed up late, cuddling together in bed. They'd eat potato chips and watch old movies on television, searching the small screen for Abby's father, Toby Nash. Toby had played kind judges and helpful neighbors and good pals in movies during the fifties.

"Is that him?" Hannah would ask, leaning close to the TV and pointing at a group of men.

"The one on the left!" Abby would say. "The one smiling."

Later, after the movie was over and Hannah was almost too sleepy to stay awake, she'd ask her mother for the story about how she'd met Zach that day in Washington Square Park.

"You had your violin," Hannah would start for her.

"I was only seventeen years old," Abby would say. "And I had a little fifth-floor walk-up apartment on West Fourth Street with two other girls."

"One was Melissa, right?"

"Right. And we all tried very hard to be flower children."

That part always made Hannah giggle.

"And I'd play my violin with the case open at my feet so people could drop in money for me."

"But first you'd put money in there yourself, right? So they'd get the idea." Hannah knew the story by heart and she never liked for Abby to forget any of it.

"Right," Abby would say. "And I always played something so beautiful that people had to stop and listen. It was a wonderful time to be so young and so adventurous. There were always people in the park performing. Singing, juggling. One woman, I remember, was a contortionist. She would twist herself in such a way that her head rested backwards on her knees. And then she'd smoke a cigarette."

"Like in *The Exorcist*?" Hannah always asked that question. "When Regan's head spins around and she spits out pea soup?" Her mother had told her that was pea soup.

"Sort of."

At this point, Abby got a real far-off look in her eyes, and Hannah knew she was remembering how Zach had come right up to her and stood so close she could feel his breath on her. After this part, her mother always needed a lot of prodding.

"Then?" Hannah had to say.

"Well, it was spring, but really cold and damp. And Zach had on a coat with brass buttons and he was so absolutely beautiful. That dark hair and—well, you look just like him. Except the eyes. On this gray day his eyes looked dazzling blue. They took my breath away. I was playing Vivaldi's 'Spring' from *The Four Seasons* and when I finished he grabbed my wrist and said, 'I want to marry you.' "

Hannah would smile. She loved the romance of that part, even though Zach hadn't been exactly true to his word. "And then you did, right?"

Abby sighed. "Well, three years later."

Hannah would be almost asleep by then, and she'd hear her mother still talking to her about the way the air had smelled of hot pretzels and rain and things about to bloom. She'd hear the *M*A*S*H* theme song and *The Mary Tyler Moore Show* and she'd feel her mother wrap her arms around her and then Abby would hum something softly and without really knowing, Hannah understood it was that song, "Spring," by Vivaldi.

Abby and the boxer hardly noticed how long she'd been standing there. So Hannah took her mother's drink and pretended she was going to taste it.

"Very funny," Abby said, taking the drink out of Hannah's hands. "Is this a great kid, or what? A comedian." She put her arms around Hannah's shoulders.

Hannah moved out of her mother's grasp.

"Last year she was still sitting on my lap," Abby told the boxer.

Hannah groaned. "I was not."

The boxer signaled to the bartender. "Another round."

"Hannah," Abby said, "Doug's going back to the hotel now with his new friend, Barbara. You can walk over with them, okay?"

"I guess so."

Abby smoothed Hannah's hair. "So curly," she said softly. "Like your father's." She sipped her fresh drink. "We're only going to have one more. Then I'll be back."

"Uh-huh."

"Maybe there's something good on cable."

Hannah shrugged.

Doug and the woman were standing and waiting for her. His hand rested lightly on the small of the woman's back and she was wobbling slightly on her spiked heels.

"Those aren't very sensible boots," Hannah told her.

"Do you have to have an opinion about everything?" Abby said. Then, "No kiss good night?"

Reluctantly she kissed her mother's cheek.

The boxer touched Hannah's arm. "Your mother," he said. "She plays that thing like an angel. She put a spell on me."

"Right," Hannah said.

At the door, she turned back to them. "She won't even wear lipstick," she said. "She even forgets to shave her legs sometimes."

She didn't wait for their reactions. Instead, she just followed Doug and the teetering woman out into the cold January rain.

CROSSING
LIFETIMES

Abby didn't remind Doug and Sean that it was her birthday. She didn't want a fuss, to sit in a restaurant and have a group of waiters sing to her over a candle stuck in a cupcake. What she wanted was to forget it. When she'd looked in the mirror that morning, she had seemed not just a year older, but old. Her mother had sent her a note that said: *Eye tucks? Liposuction? You decide and it'll be on me.* Thanks a lot, Abby had thought as she tossed the note in the garbage.

Three-Legged Horse had arrived in Portland, Maine, this afternoon after a trip full of arguing. Doug wanted them to do the television theme song medley tonight and Sean wanted to try some of the really old numbers. "Little Boxes" and "This Land Is Your Land." Neither of them gave in, so the arrangements were still not settled and they had to go on in an hour.

Abby stretched out on the twin bed. The motel room had a strange smell. Like a basement, she thought. She reached for the phone and called Hannah again.

"Any calls?" Abby asked, trying to sound casual.

"Who are you expecting?" Hannah snapped. "Prince Charming?"

Abby sighed. She wished Hannah had come with them instead of staying home with Mallory and her kids. This was Three-Legged Horse's last gig before the summer hiatus, and Hannah had refused to come. "Everyone gets all weepy," she'd said.

"What are you doing tonight?" Hannah was asking. "Going to a restaurant for a lobster dinner?"

"Probably," Abby lied.

"We're going to the Blue Benn."

"Well," Abby said, "if anybody calls—"

"I won't be here," Hannah said quickly. "I said—"

"I know," Abby said. "The Blue Benn."

The show went badly. Rather than decide, they did all of their numbers. None of them knew all of the words to the same songs, and by the end Doug and Sean were furious with each other.

"I need a drink," Doug muttered when it was finally over.

Abby looked at him. "I hate that TV thing," she said.

"Fine," Doug said. "Just fine." And he stormed off.

Abby saw Sean watching her, wanting to talk, but instead she went straight to the pay phone and dialed Zach's number. It was her birthday, after all, and she wanted to talk to him. The phone in his apartment in San Francisco just rang and rang. Abby dialed again, then sat, listening to the ringing, trying to imagine the apartment she had never seen.

She pulled the door of the phone booth shut, and a weak light flickered on, then died. The walls were wooden and carved with names and initials. Abby traced them, felt the shapes of lopsided hearts, the initials JD and SL. It

23

felt safe in there, like there was no world outside it, no birthdays or disappointments.

As a child, Abby used to lock herself in the huge walk-in closet in the hallway of her family's apartment for the same reason. She had felt safe there, away from her parents' bickering, her mother's opinions and her father's attempts at playing sober. She would squeeze herself into the far corner, keep the light off, and listen to the man next door practice singing opera.

The Nash apartment was long and dark and crooked, like a maze. All of the rooms were clustered at the end of a corridor that was carpeted with small Oriental rugs. The combination of all the patterns—bold geometric designs, crowded trees with scarlet and teal birds, thick pale flowers—made Abby dizzy. The walls along the hallway were crowded, too, with posters and reviews from shows her parents had been in. The names Deirdre Falls Church and Toby Nash were always highlighted in pink. "*Deirdre Falls Church Was the Only Bright Spot in an Otherwise Dreary Evening." "Falls Church Is a Triumph!" "Toby Nash Is the Real Thing!"* Abby knew them all by heart.

But alone in that darkened closet, Abby could forget about all that was going on out there. Instead, she would be serenaded by the man next door as he practiced scales and pitch, Italian and German. She would know that her father was in the kitchen, calling agents, looking for guest shots on *The FBI* or *The Patty Duke Show*. That her mother was surrounded by her entourage—personal secretary, designer, hairdresser—rehearsing lines or having a costume fitting or planning an extravagant party.

When she was very young, Abby used to serve canapés at those parties. By the time she sought refuge in the closet, she was hiding from them, or sneaking joints and sips of wine to help herself get through them. It seemed to Abby that everything changed when her mother landed the role of Dulcinea Day on the soap opera *Day's Destiny*. That was when Toby started skipping auditions and going instead to the Beacon Bar every afternoon. Abby used to peer in at him through the smoky glass on her way home from Juilliard. He would be wearing one of the fedoras that he had worn in some long-ago movie. Once, their eyes had met and he'd pretended not to see her. When he'd come home, he'd smell of peppermint and lie in a loud, slurred voice about his day and how it looked like he'd be getting a spot on a new cop show real soon.

At night, Abby used to listen to her parents fighting. She wished that they would scream at each other, or throw things, the way people did in the movies. Instead, they'd insult each another, exchange sarcasms. "So, the great Deirdre Falls Church," Toby would say, "a soap queen." "Are they really casting over at the Beacon Bar?" Deirdre would ask. At night, Abby would put a pillow over her head to block them out. She'd imagine running away from here, falling in love. She'd recreate the magical tenor of the man next door.

Sometimes now, Abby wondered if Zach had seemed like an operatic hero come to life. Her savior. He was five years older, and romantic. He'd smelled of paint and old clothes, of a wonderful closet that held treasures. That day, he'd told her that he was going to marry her. That someday he'd be a famous painter.

"Remember that," he'd said.

"Which part?" Abby asked him, her heart pounding from the closeness of him.

"Both parts."

"Well," she'd told him, "I don't usually marry boys I don't know."

"I'm Zach Plummer. Now you know me."

They'd gone to the White Horse Tavern for a drink.

"I feel like my heart is jumping out of my chest," he'd told her. He'd pressed her hand to him. "Right here. Feel it?"

She'd nodded at him, unable to speak. This was the way it happened in movies, she'd thought. Fireworks, lightning, star bursts. Just like this.

"I bet we've known each other for a thousand years," Zach had said. "That we've crossed lifetimes together. Isn't that amazing?"

They'd kept drinking Bass Ales and talking about their lives. It had seemed to Abby that they must have reconnected from other lifetimes. They were that much alike, that much in tune.

"I blew off art school," Zach had told her. "Rhode Island School of Design. What a joke."

"Yes!" she'd said. "I've been in music school forever. I mean, I can barely read anything except notes."

He'd told her about his idea for a collage series. "I know this guy," he'd said, "who studies Dylan's garbage. It's this huge sociological experiment, but he's going to give me some anyway."

"Some garbage."

"Not just garbage. Bob Dylan's garbage. I'm working on this idea for these huge collages."

"What's the theme?" Abby had asked him.

Zach had shrugged. "I don't know yet. There's the garbage, and old tokens, Brooklyn Dodgers baseball cards. I've got so much junk. You'll have to see it sometime."

"Oh," Abby had said, trembling at the thought of going with him to his apartment, of what she knew would happen there. "So, it's New York stuff."

"What?"

"All your collage stuff."

Zach's eyes brightened. "Yes!" he shouted. "We are going to make a great pair, you and me. Aren't we?"

Abby had smiled. "Yes," she'd told him.

But then he was suddenly getting ready to leave. "I'll call you, all right?"

"I don't have a phone where I'm staying," she'd said, standing too, not wanting to let him go.

He'd wrapped a soft cashmere scarf the color of eggshells around his neck. "I'll find you in the park, then."

"But when?" she'd insisted. "It's a big city, you know."

Zach had leaned down and kissed her very softly on the eyelids. "It doesn't feel so big today," he'd said.

She had tried to follow him out, but he had disappeared too quickly. And until he'd come for her two days later in the park, she had wondered if she'd created him herself, if he was just a figment of her imagination.

That was how she felt now, sitting in this dark phone booth in Portland, Maine, listening to his phone ring. How low can I sink? Abby thought as she slammed the receiver down.

Doug and Sean were still at the bar, their heads bent together, their voices serious. When she appeared beside them, they stopped talking.

"Do you know what I'd like?" Abby said to the bartender. "Champagne. The best you've got."

"Champagne?" The bartender laughed. "Are you kidding?"

"Yes." she sighed. "I am."

He put a draft beer in front of her.

"So what are you two whispering about?" Abby asked them.

Sean shrugged unconvincingly. "I don't know."

"You really fucked up *The Beverly Hillbillies* song," Doug said to her.

"You can't be serious."

"The fiddle is important in that one," Doug said.

Abby drained her beer. "I don't believe this."

"These long nights take their toll, don't they?" Sean asked her.

"After ten years, I'd say I'm pretty used to it," Abby said, frowning. "What's up, anyway?"

"Maybe you never get used to it," Sean said. "Maybe none of us do."

He looked at Doug, but Doug was staring down at the bar, running his fingers over the shiny brass railing.

"I'm going to bed," Abby said.

"Wouldn't it be nice to sleep in your own bed?" Sean asked her. He touched her arm lightly, to keep her there.

"Maybe if Zach was in it," Abby said. "I've been thinking about that, you know. Growing old with someone. Depending on someone. Settling in."

Doug laughed. "With Zach?"

Sean looked at him. "You're not helping this," he said.

Abby felt herself growing cold. "What's up?" she said again, wishing they wouldn't tell her.

Doug didn't say anything, just rubbed at a spot on the bar.

"Just talking, I guess," Sean said. It was not like him to avoid her eyes, but he did.

"Oh," Abby said. She forced a laugh. "Giving old Ab a scare, huh?"

"You know," Sean said. "Just talk."

Back in her room, Abby changed into the T-shirt Hannah had given her for her birthday. It was sea-green, and studded with shiny stones that formed a dragon across the front. Hannah always gave her the worst presents. But at least she had remembered.

Abby thought again about Zach, somewhere in San Francisco. She pictured him at a gallery opening, sipping white wine and nibbling on Brie. Tomorrow he would wake up and realize he'd forgotten her birthday. Then he'd do something wonderful to surprise her. Something extra special.

She took her violin from its case. Carefully, with her fingertips, she plucked out a song. "The Itsy Bitsy Spider." She felt almost immediately better. She rubbed her chin against the wood, closed her eyes and raised her bow. Her head moved with the music—Vivaldi. "Spring."

DISCONNECTIONS

It was June and already sticky hot. Every year around this time, Doug, Sean, and Abby always got together and made plans for Three-Legged Horse's upcoming gigs. Sean made his famous five-alarm chili and Doug brought icy-cold Dos Equis beer and they sat at Abby's kitchen table planning the routes they'd take, the places they'd stay, deciding which contracts to sign and which to refuse. Sometimes, it turned into a party that went into the night.

They'd call friends and invite them over too, asking everyone to bring a six-pack. By the end of the night, Three-Legged Horse would be playing an impromptu performance and Abby's old ramshackle house would be vibrating from the energy generated by dozens of people dancing in every room. Just last year, Hannah had called her friends too and a boy from her class had joined in on the harmonica. He'd done a great Bob Dylan imitation, getting the nasal vocals just right and the words all wrong. Doug had even wanted the kid to come and do a gig with them in Middlebury that fall.

But this afternoon, Doug and Sean showed up empty-handed. Except for the beer. "We'll probably need this," Doug said when he walked in.

Abby glanced toward the stove, where the giant pot Sean liked to use for the chili sat waiting.

"I didn't buy the stuff," she said, feeling confused. Sean always brought the chili ingredients—the jalapeños and cubed meat and tomatillos.

Sean looked over at the stove too. "I forgot," he said. Then he turned to Doug, as if he were waiting for something important to be said.

Doug opened three bottles of beer. Becks, Abby noticed. A few years before, when she'd split with Zach and she and Doug were just getting together, he'd told her how important ritual was to him. "Like I'll always remember the shade of blue you have on right now. And every time I buy you something—a sweater or scarf, whatever—it will be this exact color." So why the hell had he brought Becks when they always drank Dos Equis with their chili on the day they set their schedule for the coming season? For ten years, Three-Legged Horse had toasted themselves by clinking Dos Equis bottles together.

"Look," Doug said, "I'm not going to beat around the bush here. We want to split up. Dissolve the band. After this winter."

Abby almost laughed, would have laughed if Sean had only looked over at her and smiled. If only it was all a joke.

"There's so much happening musically in LA," Doug continued. "I'm going to head out there when we finish our gigs next winter."

"But you can't," Abby said. "You can't leave us."

She grabbed the edge of the table to steady herself. It felt like the floor actually moved, shifted slightly beneath her.

"If I don't quit this," Sean was saying, "my marriage will end. Mallory's had it."

"Mallory? She doesn't understand—" Abby started.

"Folk music is dead," Doug said. He said it so matter-of-factly that Abby almost believed him.

"So we could change," she said.

"Mallory is worried about Margot and Elijah. This isn't a life for kids," Sean said. His voice was so soft she could barely hear him.

Abby thought about Hannah. The way she looked sitting alone at a table in a bar somewhere. Sometimes she got so tired, she slept with her head on the hard wood. When Abby woke her to leave, Hannah's hair smelled of old beer and catsup.

"Are you saying Hannah's not as good as your kids? I mean, what the hell is this?"

But Sean just shook his head sadly and kept on talking. She supposed he had been rehearsing these lines. ". . . and I might be able to get a job teaching music back in New York."

Abby couldn't listen anymore. She told herself to try and imagine her life without Three-Legged Horse. All she could see was an empty winter ahead. All this time, they had been her family. Hers and Hannah's.

"Think how good this could be for you musically," Sean was saying. "You're too good for us anyway."

"Oh, please," Abby said.

Carefully, slowly, Sean peeled the label off his beer bottle. Hannah had told Abby once that if she could do that and remove the label in one piece, it meant someone loved her. Sean's label ripped, a jagged tear, right at the end.

Abby had joined Three-Legged Horse because she couldn't pay her rent or buy food for her and Hannah, and Zach had gone to San Francisco again, had told her he needed space, room to think and paint. Besides, Doug and Sean thought she played a mean fiddle. They told her that was just what the band needed.

The first time they'd heard her play was 1975, a year before she actually joined them. She was feeling disillusioned and angry—with Zach and with herself. The only thing she felt good about was her music. All year she'd been playing the violin at a Rumanian steak house on the Lower East Side, eerie gypsy music that made her sad. But she'd lost that job when she got pregnant and started to show too much. Her boss had told her it made the patrons feel uncomfortable. "Go home," he'd said, "put your feet up. Make your husband bring you cherries and sweets."

But Zach had gotten angry. They'd had a fight and he'd left her on Memorial Day weekend with a check to cover the summer's rent. The check had bounced and Abby had taken to playing the Astor Place subway station for money. In the heat of the summer, the cool tiles there, all green and yellow with beavers on them, made her feel cooler. She could imagine Canada, fur trappers, cold clear water.

That's where Doug and Sean had first seen her. Eight months pregnant, dressed in layers of salmon gauze, wearing an ankle bracelet of tiny silver bells, Abby stood on the platform and played Mozart and Bach as the No. 6 train roared into the station. Her teachers at Juilliard had told her once that she could make a violin weep. That summer, Abby let her violin do her crying for her.

She had noticed Doug and Sean standing there, letting train after train go by.

"Can we buy you a cup of coffee?" Sean had finally asked. "Maybe give you a business proposition?"

"Make it lunch and you've got a deal," she'd said as the baby tugged and rolled inside her.

Sean was already almost bald by then. He had a few wisps of bright red hair left and they hung down his back all loose and thin. Doug had a ponytail and permanent five o'clock shadow. Years later, when Abby and Doug became lovers for that short time, she would kid him and tell him he'd beaten Don Johnson to "the Don Johnson look." She'd make him watch *Miami Vice* to prove her point. But that first day she met him, she thought he looked sinister.

They'd taken her to Leshko in the East Village and told her that their violinist had quit to go to law school in Philadelphia. "He wasn't half as good as you," Sean had said.

She'd just eaten and listened. Around her, old men in stained T-shirts spoke in Russian and Polish. Their voices had sounded almost musical. The air had been heavy with the smells of cabbage and sweat. Leshko's air conditioner had broken from overuse and Abby had moved her chair closer to the one slowly whirring fan in the window. Sometimes during that summer she had gone to the supermarket three or four times a day, just to stand near the frozen-food section and cool off.

Sean had explained everything to her in his soft voice, how they had a standing gig every Thursday night at A Kettle of Fish. "One hundred bucks each," he'd said, and Abby had thought she must be dreaming this good fortune.

"Do you just play that classical crap?" Doug had scowled at her. "That's not what people want to hear. They want Dylan. Joni Mitchell. Things like that."

It had seemed that when he spoke to her, his eyes focused right on her swollen stomach. If she hadn't been so tired, so hot and dazed, Abby would have picked up her violin right then and played for them in Leshko with all the old men and the thick-legged waitresses with damp hair bringing cabbage to the tables listening She would have played Dylan and Joni Mitchell for them. "Chelsea Morning" and "Just Like a Woman." All of it. But she'd just rested one hand on her stomach as if to hide it from Doug's stare, and kept on shoveling food into her mouth with the other one. She'd eaten all the bread and two bowls of borscht and stuffed cabbage. Her last real meal had been when her mother had taken her to 21 for lunch a few weeks earlier.

"Well?" Doug had demanded.

"Do you think," Abby had asked, "I could have some more cabbage?"

"Jesus," he'd muttered.

But Sean had ordered it for her, and asked for more bread and a glass of milk, too.

When she'd finished eating, Abby had tried to clear her head. But it still felt fuzzy. What would she do with the baby? she'd wondered. What would she do when Zach came back?

She'd fixed her gray eyes on Doug. "I don't think it'll work," she'd said. "Besides, I don't like you. You think Mozart is crap."

"Fine," he'd said. "Keep playing the Lexington Avenue line then. I don't care how good you are, it'll only get you as far as Brooklyn."

While he'd paid the check, Sean had still tried to convince her to join them.

"Don't let Doug get to you," he'd said. "He wants to find a trend to ride. He's difficult, but he's talented. He's even trying to get us some gigs out of state."

Abby had shaken her head then. "I can't go out of state," she'd said. She'd thought of how many things four hundred dollars a month could buy. When she'd had lunch with her mother, they'd passed a shop on Madison Avenue with a mobile hanging in the window—a sleepy yellow half-moon and shiny stars in red and blue and green all hanging from a satin rainbow. She could buy that for the baby. And a cradle, too, like the one Zach had promised her when she'd told him she was pregnant. "We'll get an antique one," he had said. "White, with small flowers painted on it."

"Why don't you just play with us tonight?" Sean was saying. "A test run." He'd had a nice, chip-toothed smile that made her feel good somehow.

"Come on," Doug had called from the doorway. "Let's go." Behind him, the hot August air had risen in ripples above the cement.

Sean had hesitated. "You got a father around for that baby?" he'd asked her.

He had struck Abby as so sweet, she'd imagined that if she'd told him no, he might have offered to marry her himself.

"Yes," she'd said. "He's in San Francisco on business." It was only a half-lie, she'd decided.

"Do you know where A Kettle of Fish is? Over on Macdougal?"

She'd nodded and watched him walk away. He was slightly stooped, his back making a gentle curve beneath his thin dashiki.

Her mind had settled on that rainbow mobile in the store window. On how it would feel to have a job again, to walk with a purpose through the Village, clutching her violin case, going into A Kettle of Fish and saying, "I'm with Three-Legged Horse."

But all of this thinking had taken time. Her thoughts had been thick and slow and cloudy that summer. When she'd realized that she'd turned down four hundred dollars a month because Zach might be coming back soon, Abby had pulled herself up and run outside as fast as she could manage. She would find Doug and Sean, she'd thought, panicked. She'd join Three-Legged Horse and buy her baby a cradle and a mobile and stuffed animals. But when she got to the street, Doug and Sean were gone. It was as if they had disappeared. Three old men stood arguing in thick accents on the street corner. "I tell you," one of them was saying, "we grew wheat there. Wheat as tall as me. And as golden as my mother's hair."

Zach had not come home until after Hannah was born. On the day he'd arrived, he'd brought violets for Abby and a bag of toys for Hannah. "I'm a jerk," he'd told Abby. She had not forgiven him right away. But at night he'd insisted on bringing Hannah into bed with them, and they had slept holding hands with their daughter nestled between them. Every morning he'd bring Abby warm croissants from the bakery on Broadway and squeeze fresh orange juice for her to drink. And slowly, she'd forgiven him, and was finally happy he was back in their life.

Then a woman named Tracy Colt had called from San Francisco and Zach had said he had to go back. "This could be big," he'd told Abby. "She runs the 505 Gallery." He had been so excited that he'd taken her to dinner at Umberto's to celebrate.

The day he'd left them again, Abby took Hannah for a walk, all the way to Washington Square Park. Sitting there in the cold autumn air, almost tasting a frost about to come, Abby had her first suspicion that Tracy Colt might be more than a gallery owner to Zach. Tracys were beautiful, she'd thought. Like Grace Kelly in *High Society*. She'd thought of all the times she'd answered the phone and no one was there. Of Zach's whispered conversations that he'd told her were business calls.

She'd gotten so angry that she was halfway home before she'd realized that someone was following her. She stopped dead in her tracks, clutching Hannah's hand.

"What the fuck do you want?" Abby had said.

"A fiddler. I have a way of seeing you whenever we need one."

Abby had turned, her heart pounding, and saw Doug. He had cut off the ponytail, but she'd recognized him immediately, although she'd pretended not to.

He'd pointed to Hannah. "It was a boy, huh?"

"Hannah," Abby had said.

"Where's your violin?"

"What was your name again?" Abby had asked him. She had been too embarrassed to go to A Kettle of Fish that night a year earlier.

"Doug."

"Oh, that's right," Abby had said. "And you say you need a violinist again?"

"Actually, Sean's trying someone out right now," he'd said. "Sean's my partner, in case you forgot him, too."

"Him I remember." Abby had smiled to herself.

"He went back to Astor Place every day for a week, looking for you. He thought you were really great."

Abby had shrugged.

"We leave tomorrow," Doug had continued. "Four days in the Berkshires, then a month at Mount Snow with an option for one more month."

"I can play 'Moonlight in Vermont,' " Abby had said. "And Dylan and Joni Mitchell."

Doug had stared at her so hard that she'd looked away. The leaves were already turning, scarlet and gold.

"It would be beautiful in the Berkshires now," she'd said. "We used to spend summers up in Williamstown when I was young. My parents did summer stock there."

She'd turned back toward Doug. "I could really use a change of scenery."

"He might have already told this other guy okay," Doug had said.

Abby had smiled at him. For the first time that day, she'd felt good. "Just let me play for you," she'd said.

Abby had considered cleaning the apartment before they came. It had seemed another way to impress them, to show them she was organized and responsible. And if she was with Three-Legged Horse, she could show Zach that she was independent, that she did not need him in her life. She imagined him calling her and a mechanical voice telling him that the number had been disconnected. The thought had made her feel good. And determined to win this spot with this band.

When Doug and Sean had called up to her from the street, she'd thrown the key down to them, then studied the apartment before they got upstairs. There were toys and clothes everywhere, and a pan on the stove with a hard layer of vegetable soup on its bottom. This is not the image I want, she'd told herself. The deserted, disorganized housewife. She'd placed the pan in the sink, and as the elevator rumbled toward her she'd scooped up the toys and clothes and tossed them into the closet.

At the door, she'd taken a deep breath, then let them in, trying to seem casual and relaxed.

"Are you the only living thing in this building?" Sean had asked her.

"There's a Chinese take-out place downstairs, but they never seem to be open." Then she'd added, "And of course my husband. He's usually here."

"Ah, yes," Doug had said. "The husband." He had been studying one of Zach's collages on the wall. "Untitled New York City #17."

"That's his," she had said. It was a collage cluttered with subway tokens, *Playbills*, and *New York* magazine covers. "He's working on a California series now." Another white lie. She'd suggested that he do that, that the three of them drive around California and collect things for a series. But he hadn't exactly agreed.

Doug had nodded. "He kind of hired the other guy," he'd said, pretending to read the magazine covers.

"Oh. Well, that's fine," Abby had said, forcing lightness into her voice. But she'd had to lean against the red stepladder that Zach sometimes used to reach the tops of large canvases.

"I remember how good you were," Sean had said. "I even went back to look for you last summer."

"So I heard."

"It's like an omen," he had said. "The way we keep running into you just when we need someone."

She had not known then how important omens were to Sean. How he kept crystals and pyramids and threw the *I Ching* for guidance.

"Omens," she'd said, "are important."

"The kid," Doug had said. "Will this mysterious husband of yours take the kid?"

"If you've hired someone, it doesn't matter, does it?" she'd said.

"I told him I'd call at five," Sean had said.

"With the details," Doug had said. "You told him you'd call with the details."

Abby had known that they wanted her, not the other guy. She'd felt it.

"Is this husband of yours going to show up," Doug was asking her, "and drag you home?" He'd looked at Sean. "How are we going to find a replacement in Vermont?"

"Let's do this fair and square," she'd said. "I'll play

for you, and if I'm better than the other guy, I get the job. And if I get the job, I worry about Zach and Hannah."

They had all known that she was better than the other guy already. But still she'd played for them, to remind them of just how good she was. She'd played "Moonlight in Vermont." She'd played so beautifully it had almost hurt to listen.

When she'd finished, she'd kept her eyes closed, imagining snowy mountains, the thud of ski boots on wooden floors. She had not opened them until Doug had spoken.

"We leave tomorrow at eight. Lenox or bust."

Then she'd looked right at them. "I'll be there," she'd said. "No problem."

In the end, Abby had left a careful trail so Zach could find her. She'd called everyone Zach might get in touch with and left a complex series of phone numbers, dates, and motel names with them. Just in case, she'd told herself. In case she hated Three-Legged Horse, or grew tired of it. In case she and Zach still had even the slightest chance.

Doug and Sean had picked her up in a 1960 Chevy wagon. It was tan and had fake wood on the sides. All the suitcases and instruments were strapped to the top and Sean's wife, Mallory, drove.

"I feel like we're a TV family," Abby had said. "Danny Thomas's or Robert Young's."

Mallory headed north on the Merritt Parkway to Route 8, and Abby had felt the same sense of excitement she'd felt as a child traveling this road with her parents. Hannah had slept in a kind of sling that hung across Abby's stomach and chest, and as they drove, Three-Legged Horse discussed songs and arrangements. They taught Abby "Orange Blossom Special" and a song about a man named

Harry who gets lost on the MTA in Boston. "They love that one in Massachusetts," Doug had explained.

Mallory never turned around, just stared straight ahead, her jaw set hard. She wore large horn-rimmed glasses and her hair was the color of too-ripe strawberries. Under her breath she'd cursed the heater, which was broken and turned on and off by itself, sending blasts of hot, stale-smelling air throughout the car.

Despite it all, Abby had felt ecstatic, like she had taken charge of her life and done something wonderful. When she'd called her mother the night before, even Deirdre's disappointment could not discourage her. "A folk band in bars," Deirdre had said sadly. "Yes," Abby had said, "isn't it wonderful?"

In Torrington, Connecticut, Hannah woke up screaming.

"You have to stop," Abby had said, leaning toward Mallory. "I have to change her diaper."

"Can't she wait an hour?" Doug had snapped. "We're an hour away."

"Ninety miles," Mallory had said, her voice dry and even. Her breath had smelled like Listerine. Every morning and night, Abby would learn, Mallory gargled with Listerine, believing it had medicinal powers that would keep her free of colds, flus, and infections.

"She can't wait that long," Abby had said.

The leaves here had already all turned. A few trees were even bare.

"I could use some coffee," Sean had said.

"Fine," Mallory had muttered. Then she'd turned the car sharply into a Howard Johnson parking lot.

When Abby got out of the car, she'd felt a damp spot spreading across her chest.

"Coffee for everyone?" Sean had asked.

Abby had walked ahead of him. "Milk for Hannah," she'd called to him. "Okay?"

When she got back to the parking lot, they had all been standing around, drinking coffee, looking miserable. Abby had been struck then by the fact that these people were all strangers. She had committed herself to two months with them and they did not even like her.

"Now the whole car smells like piss," Mallory was saying.

"Wait until you hear her play that violin," Sean had said.

"I'm still worried that her husband's going to show up. Then we're left up shit's creek without a paddle," Doug had said.

Abby had neared the car. "Here we are," she'd announced. She'd wanted to reach out to each of them, to make them like her, trust her. She'd wanted to tell them about Zach, how she had to do this right now. But she'd just stood there, clutching Hannah's sticky hand as if it could save her.

"Let's disconnect this heater before we go," Mallory had said.

"We can't," Sean had said. "It's not that easy to break the connection. I tried before we left."

Abby had climbed into the car, pulled Hannah onto her lap. She'd thought of wires that connected things, imagined them snapping off, dangling free. It isn't easy at all, she'd thought as she'd watched the Connecticut landscape whiz by, a blur of maple and birch trees and brightly colored leaves clinging to their branches for another moment or two before they fell.

Doug and Sean did not stay longer than they had to.

"I know once you think about it, you'll see that it's time for us to split up," Doug told her.

"Just leave," Abby said.

At the door, Sean took her hand. She tried to break

out of his grasp, but he held on too tightly. "It's time to make a change," he said softly. "My chart says I'm about to enter a new phase of work. I have to leave myself open to it."

"All these months," she said, "you never even told me what you were thinking."

He didn't answer her. Instead, he just shrugged and looked sad.

"Remember that day you first heard me play?" Abby asked him. "At the Astor Place subway station?"

"It doesn't matter," Sean said. "It was too long ago."

"Right," Abby said.

Doug was already at the car, waiting. She watched Sean's stooped back as he walked away from her. It all looked so easy.

When Hannah came home that afternoon, Abby was stretched out on the couch, finishing off the Becks.

"Chelsea and Kate asked me to be the third Supreme," Hannah said proudly. "We have to go to Marshalls and get my dress." Then she added, "It's gold lamé."

"I don't feel like shopping right now."

Hannah stamped her foot. "Listen to me. I'm the third Supreme and I need this dress."

Abby frowned. "What does that even mean?"

"You're not listening!" Hannah shouted.

Abby sat up, a little dizzy from the beer and the heat. She had been on the couch all afternoon, and she still had no idea what she was going to do without Three-Legged Horse.

Hannah was explaining now, her voice shrill and excited. "It's for the school talent show. Nobody had asked me to do anything, as usual, and then finally, today at lunch, Chelsea Kent and Kate—"

"I know," Abby said, "the third Supreme."

"We're lip-synching 'Stop! In the Name of Love.'

They have all the movements down and everything and we're all going to wear those gold lamé dresses from Marshalls. The show is tomorrow, so I need to get it now and then go to Chelsea's house to rehearse. Her mother can take me home. That's the plan."

"I'm glad someone around here has a plan," Abby said.

"So can we go now?"

"I need to talk to your father," Abby said.

Hannah followed her into the kitchen. "Do you have to?"

On the third ring a woman answered.

Abby plopped onto a kitchen chair, exhausted. "Who is this?" she said wearily.

The chair wobbled slightly and Abby bent to replace the rolled-up matchbook under the short leg. On the stove, the chili pot still sat empty.

"This is Nina," the woman was saying. Her voice sounded cool. An ice princess.

Abby swallowed hard. "I'm looking for Zach," she said. "I'm looking for my husband."

"Yes," the woman said. "He should be there any day now."

He was on his way. She would tell him that everything was changing now, that Three-Legged Horse had broken up, that it was time to settle down after all.

Abby hung up and turned toward Hannah.

"Zach's on his way."

"Uh-huh," Hannah said.

"So let's go get you that dress."

He arrived three nights later. Abby and Hannah were watching television, sitting in their underwear in the dark to stay cool. Hannah had told her that Three-Legged Horse couldn't break up. "It's stupid," she'd said to Abby. "You'll see."

In the mail that day they'd received two tickets to *The Glass Menagerie* at Williamstown starring Deirdre Falls Church.

"Can we go?" Hannah had asked.

They got tickets every year and never used them.

"I don't think so," Abby had said. "I never did like *The Glass Menagerie*."

"Or Deirdre Falls Church," Hannah had said as she'd tucked the tickets back into the envelope.

Abby had not even bothered to read the note her mother had enclosed. It was written in lavender ink and sprayed with perfume. The sound of her mother's stage name always brought back a flood of memories to Abby. Her mother had been born in Virginia as Dee Foster. She'd left home to become a Rockette and had taken the name Deirdre because it sounded exotic and Falls Church because it seemed rich and important. Abby could still remember her shock when she was little and was in Washington, D.C., with her parents, who were performing at the National Theatre in *Ghosts*. They had taken a ride down Skyline Drive and passed a sign for Falls Church, Virginia. They had passed another sign for Roanoke, her mother's hometown, and Deirdre had waved her hands at it. "Drive past this road, goddamnit. Hurry past it."

Deirdre Falls Church spoke with a hint of a Southern accent, well rehearsed and insincere, and she tossed her mane of honey-blond hair with dramatic authority. But to Abby, she was a woman who had sprung from one road sign and hidden from another. During interviews, Abby used to listen in disgust at her mother's fabrications, stories of horse country in Virginia and old money. She'd toss that famous head and drawl, "Y'all ever heard of the Civil War? Y'all ever heard the name Falls Church?"

Reporters loved her. She enchanted them with her combination of bawdy and ladylike behavior. She was a

Southern belle who could drink whiskey like a man, hunt fox, and hostess glorious parties. To the world, she was someone important. To Abby, she was a fake.

As luck would have it, the night Zach arrived, the eight o'clock movie was *An Evening With Edie*. Toby Nash played one of the debutante Edie's admirers. He moved across the screen, a figure in black and white, beside two other men. They all chuckled good-naturedly at Edie's jokes, admiring her from afar as she flirted with the movie's leading man. Eventually, both Abby and Hannah knew, Edie would die of a fatal illness after hosting one final, fabulous party.

Hannah peered closely at the television, waiting for a glimpse of her grandfather. He had three lines in this movie. "Gee, you're really swell, Edie" and "That Edie. She's some kind of gal."

Abby and Hannah heard Zach's van drive up at the same time.

"I think we have a gentleman caller," Abby said.

"Well." Hannah sighed, "I guess summer has officially arrived."

Toby Nash delivered his first line. "Gee, you're really swell, Edie."

Abby ran upstairs. She wanted to look beautiful when she saw him. She put on an old peasant dress. It had a faded paisley print, all soft oranges and gold. She twisted her hair into a loose braid and put on her amethyst earrings. When she turned, Zach was standing in the doorway.

"Am I glad to see you," Abby said.

"Please," he said softly, "take it all back off."

His eyes were the same color as his faded jeans and he smelled familiar and comfortable. She lifted her arms and pulled the dress off. Together, she thought, we can work this out.

*   *   *

He had a plan for a new series called "Beaches," and they were going to spend the summer driving down the Atlantic coast.

"The hottest summer on record," Zach announced on the morning they left.

"Great," Hannah muttered. "Sweat City."

"A family that sweats together. . . ." Abby laughed.

"Chelsea's family is going to Disney World," Hannah said as she settled into the backseat.

Abby and Zach both groaned loudly.

"It's better than this," Hannah said.

"Nothing is better than this," Abby told her as their old green house disappeared from sight. Zach had told her she'd be better off without Three-Legged Horse. "You're better than that," he'd said. "Maybe it's time for a total change," she'd said. She had felt his body stiffen when she'd said that, but she felt confident that it would work out just right.

"Mexico," he was saying. "That's where we'll go next year. What do you think, Abby?"

"You could do some great collages there," she said. She imagined them going there, staying for a while in a white stucco house on the beach.

But first there was this summer, hot and humid, even on all the beaches they visited, from Maine to Florida. They collected shells and driftwood, starfish and sand dollars. In a town called Silverfish, Florida, they slept on the beach. With the sound of the waves licking at the sand and a full moon above them, they planned the trip to Mexico.

"We could come back with you," Abby whispered. "To San Francisco. Then head down to Mexico."

"Sure," Zach said. "That's a definite possibility."

She moved closer to him, licked the salt from his skin.

"I knew we'd work something out," she said.

Zach was quiet for a minute. Then he said, "Looks like rain finally."

She looked up too, into the starless sky. There were streaks of thin clouds, like cotton candy. And that moon staring down at them. A few hours later, she woke with raindrops splashing her face. Zach was gone, but Hannah was running toward her, hair whipping in the sudden wind.

"It's a real storm," Hannah said. "A bad one."

Abby grabbed her arm and together they ran to the van. Inside, the rain pounded on the roof, and Hannah and Abby huddled together under an old blanket. The blanket smelled like gasoline, and Hannah held her nose.

Zach did not come back until almost dawn. He was wet and tired-looking.

"Where were you?" Abby asked sleepily.

He didn't answer her. And when she studied his face, his jaw was set and rigid.

"Where've you been?" she asked him.

"I had to call the West Coast," he snapped. "Okay?"

Abby remembered that chilly voice on the telephone. A house sitter, she told herself. Nobody important. The three of them were here, in Silverfish, Florida. They were making plans together. But still, she could not fall back to sleep.

In a bar in Duck, North Carolina, Abby found Zach on the pay phone. He had said he wanted to buy a T-shirt at the surf shop, but she'd followed him and saw him go into the bar. It was filled with college students in fraternity shirts, all drinking beer and singing songs. The jukebox blasted U2, and Abby had to squeeze past all the people to make her way to the phones in the back.

He was saying, "I thought I could do it, but I can't."

Then he said her name. Nina.

Abby's heart seemed to stop beating. Her flesh grew cold and she could not move. Zach saw her then and across all of these happy, singing people, their eyes locked. Abby gulped for air. She turned from him and pushed her way back out through the crowd and onto the hot street. From somewhere behind her, she heard Zach calling to her, but she did not stop. She just kept going until she reached the beach.

There she could breathe again. She swallowed the salty air and tried to think. The light from Cape Hatteras spilled onto the water in front of her like a path. She could hear Zach coming up behind her, his breath quick and loud.

"Abby," he said, and gripped her shoulders.

The waves were breaking at her knees, and she almost fell backwards, but Zach was holding on too tight.

"You bastard," she said.

"Yes."

"Do you love her?"

He sighed. "I don't know."

She freed herself from his grasp, scooped at the water, and threw small handfuls at him. "You don't know?" she said. "Well, you'd better know."

She felt everything slipping from her. She was losing it all. "You'd better find out," she cried. Her knees were too weak to stand, and she fell onto the sand, with the water around her. Zach knelt, too, his face lit by the light from Cape Hatteras.

"I am so sorry," he said. "Give me a few months to sort things out. Please."

She studied his face for signs of untruth, for falsehoods and lies. Then the light shifted, and they were in darkness again.

MOUNT SNOW

From the late August day that Zach left her and Hannah back in Vermont, through the whole miserable winter that followed, Abby tried to focus on thoughts of Mexico and new beginnings. Even after the night in Duck when she'd learned about Nina, Abby and Zach had walked along beaches together, heads bent in search of unusual objects, and talked about this new plan. "At night," Zach would say, "we'll drink salty margaritas and dance to salsa music." "We'll make love on the beach," Abby would say. But it had been the first time in their long history together that she'd not really believed in their dreams.

And Three-Legged Horse was playing its last gigs without any enthusiasm. They traveled old familiar roads, to Maine and Rhode Island and western Connecticut, bored and distant, Abby clutching her violin for comfort. She sat, her face pressed against the cold car window, and watched the landscape as if she needed to memorize all of it, every inch of back road, each frozen stream and small town. Now and then, Doug and Sean would mention something, talk of LA or a job possibility in Brooklyn. Sean would ask her, "How about you, Abby?" And she'd say, "Zach and I have big plans. Moving to Mexico so he can really paint. Hannah and I will take Spanish lessons. We'll visit ruins." She wondered if they believed it any more than she did.

When they drove into Mount Snow in January for a weekend gig, Doug announced with relief, "The big countdown. Five more weekends before blast-off." A job had come through for him at a recording studio in LA and he had already found an apartment in Los Feliz. April in California, he'd said on the ride up here. Better than April in Paris or autumn in New York.

There was not much snow here, just lots of chunks of hard ice glazing everything.

"Remember our first winter here?" Abby asked them. "There was so much snow we could hardly walk. Remember?"

"I don't care if I never see snow again," Doug said.

In her memory, that winter of 1976 was like a postcard of a Vermont town—everything snow-covered and twinkling with Christmas lights. But the Christmas decorations looked dusty and tired now. The skiers were bored and cranky waiting for snow.

Hannah said it was just like in the movie *White Christmas*. "Before everybody falls in love and saves the general," she said.

They were playing at the same resort they'd played that first winter. The Merry Widow Inn. Then, it had just been renovated and it had smelled of freshly cut wood and new paint. Now, as Abby stood on the stage looking across the room, everything about it seemed sad and old.

"They should take down the Christmas tree," she said. "I mean, it's January already."

"If they leave it up long enough, they'll be ready for next Christmas," Sean told her.

Abby shrugged and looked at Hannah. She sat right up front reading, her lips moving carefully as she practiced her conversational French. Zach had sent them books and pictures of Mexico, and a Berlitz Spanish guide, but Hannah had stacked all of it in the back of her closet.

Doug leaned into the microphone. "Maybe we should sing all snow songs. Tell the gods what we're waiting for."

"You said it!" a guy in the audience shouted, and everyone laughed.

"This reminds me of *White Christmas*," Doug said. "Before everybody fell in love and saved the general."

Hannah looked up from her book and frowned at him.

"Let's do 'Let It Snow,' " Doug said to Sean and Abby. "We can wing it."

Abby shook her head. "I can't," she said, one hand covering her mike.

"How does it go?" Sean asked.

Doug started to hum the song softly.

"Forget it," Abby said.

She picked up her violin and walked off the stage. Doug was moving to LA and Sean was talking about brownstones in Park Slope, Brooklyn, and she had absolutely nothing. Behind her she heard Doug say, "How about a little 'Two-Legged Horse,' then?"

When she stepped outside she could smell snow in the air. Tomorrow, she thought, all these people will be happy. They'll be able to ski on fresh powder, to get their money's worth of fun. When Three-Legged Horse had played the Merry Widow that first time, Abby had felt like she was taking charge of her life. Their gigs in Lenox had been a huge success, and their month up here had seemed like a vacation. Like a new start. The day they'd driven into town in that old Chevy wagon, it had been snowing, large lacy flakes that fell so slowly to the ground that she and Hannah had been able to catch them on their mittens and study the patterns.

It had been the Bicentennial year, and the town's children had painted all of the fire hydrants to look like Revolutionary War soldiers and Colonial women. Painted bonnets and muskets and wide eyes had peeked out from drifts on every corner, like a whole separate village living under the snow.

Sometimes, Abby would call Zach's friend, Paco, back in New York. "It's great here," she'd tell him. "Really beautiful and great." "He hasn't called yet," Paco would tell her. "Who?" she'd ask, pretending not to care.

Slowly, though, she had started to care less. In the afternoons, she had gone skiing and she'd stood on top of Deer Run and looked across the mountaintops, all the way to New Hampshire. Standing there, in the crisp air, she'd imagined she could see even farther. Beyond New Hampshire, past the clouds and the hard blue sky. Out there somewhere, she had thought, Zach was getting on with his life, not thinking about her or Hannah. And up here, on this mountain, she had believed she could get on with hers too.

That night, when Three-Legged Horse had performed at the Merry Widow, Abby had played better than ever. She was a person in charge of her life, she had thought. And she'd picked up her violin and played "Tennessee Stud," closing her eyes, feeling the music. Behind her, nestled between the speakers, Hannah slept, already used to the noises and smells of barrooms. New York and Zach had grown more distant with each note Abby played.

When Three-Legged Horse had finished its set, the audience had exploded with applause. A man sitting right up front with a group of skiers dressed in snowflake sweaters and bright turtlenecks had looked straight at Abby. He'd held his eyes on her face until the applause had stopped. Doug and Sean had to nudge her off the stage and to the bar. On her way through the crowd, she'd looked back at him, and he'd broken into a grin. His teeth had been dazzling white and straight, his hair blond, and Abby had thought he must be a Nordic god come to life.

When she'd reached the bar, Doug's head was already bent in conversation with a pixie-like woman dressed all in green. Sean had patted an empty bar stool beside him, motioning for her to sit. The bartender had opened a bottle of Michelob and placed it in front of her, and Abby had had the feeling that finally, she belonged somewhere. She belonged, she thought, right here, playing the fiddle with Three-Legged Horse.

Sean had whispered to her, "Remember Joy?" He'd indicated with his head toward one of the waitresses. Doug had slept with her during their first week here. "She's driving him nuts," Sean had said. "Calls him every day at dawn, demanding to know who's in his room with him."

Abby had smiled, loving the feeling of really belonging to this.

Joy had stood at the edge of the bar, tapping her thigh with her drink tray as she'd watched Doug and the pixie woman.

"They all love him." Sean had shrugged.

Abby had felt a large, warm hand on her shoulder. She'd turned and looked right into the pale blue eyes of the Nordic god. He was smiling again, showing off all those great teeth. He'd reached down and took both of her hands in his. "The hands of a musical genius," he'd said. His voice, surprisingly, had reeked of New Jersey rather than Scandinavia. Or heaven.

Abby had tried to tug her hands free of his grasp. But he'd held on tight.

"A Heineken," he'd said to the bartender. "And a—" He'd turned to Abby.

"Yes," she'd said, finishing her last swallow of Michelob. "A Heineken would be great." From beside Sean, she'd felt Mallory watching her, that hard jaw set, green eyes cool behind oversized frames.

"You've had lessons, right?" the blond man had asked as he examined Abby's hands, her fingers. "Music lessons."

Abby had nodded. "Juilliard," she'd said.

"I knew it."

Mallory had laughed. "Right. Juilliard via the Lexington Avenue line."

Abby had looked away from the man then, and at Mallory. "Excuse me," she'd said, "are you in this conversation? Do you have something you want to say?"

Mallory had given her a smug, self-satisfied smile. "No," she'd said.

"Good," Abby had told her. Then she'd turned back around, spinning on the stool, feeling the swish of denim as her long skirt wrapped around her leg, tangling. She'd had to straighten it, to stoop over and unravel it.

When she'd looked back up, trying to smile at her own clumsiness, the blond man's attention had turned from her to Joy, the waitress, who was demanding in a loud voice, "Who's Gloria?" Joy was very tall, over six feet in her flat white waitress shoes. Her hair was platinum blonde, long and stick straight, with bangs that fell in a straight line across her eyes.

The Nordic god from New Jersey had laughed, his eyes shining.

"Is it Peter Pan here?" Joy had screamed, moving toward Doug and the woman in green. "Is it?"

The woman had answered in a squeaky voice, "Who wants to know?"

It had seemed to Abby that Joy could have bent down and squashed the woman with her thumb.

"Get out of here," Joy had said, "or I'll call Captain Hook on you."

Doug had said, quietly, "Knock it off, Joy."

Joy's eyes had widened from under her bangs, and she'd grabbed Abby's half-finished beer and flung it. The drink sprayed Mallory, Sean, and Doug, then landed with a thunk right in the pixie's lap.

"Yeeeee-ha!" the New Jersey Nordic had hooted. "I love it!"

Abby had felt a thrill creep up her spine. A wave of excitement like she felt when Zach touched her arm, or she played her violin. She had stared up at this man from New Jersey and said, "Me too. I love it too."

She had hoped his name would be Lars or Leif. Something strong and exotic. But his name had matched his accent. Vinny. That night in bed she had asked him, "How can a Vinny look like you? You're so fair." "I dunno," he'd said. "Northern Italy maybe."

It had been the first time in five years that she'd made love with a man other than Zach. But something in the clean Vermont air, in the feel and taste of snow, in the way Vinny had looked watching Joy and touching the rough fingertips of Abby's hands, had made her want to do it. She had thought that thrill and passion were hers and Zach's alone. But with the sound of Sno-Cats preparing the slopes for the next day and Vinny's harsh New Jersey voice in her ears, Abby had felt that maybe she had been wrong.

But the next night, when she'd climbed on the stage with Sean and Doug, she'd scanned the crowd for Vinny, expecting her heart to swell when she saw him, her body to shiver. Her eyes had settled on him. He had looked as blond and gorgeous as the night before. But all she'd felt was a numbness, a nothingness. Abby had forced herself to remember his flat, muscled stomach, the way she'd touched him there lightly, her fingers strumming his coarse blond hairs. Still nothing. Even when she'd woken up beside him that morning and watched as he'd pulled on his jeans and bright ski sweater, she had thought this blank feeling had come from guilt or sleepiness. But staring down at him from the stage, she had realized that there was just no feeling in her. Vinny had caught her eye and winked at her, and she had just picked up her violin and started to play. Only then, with the sounds of her music surrounding her and the feel of her violin beneath her chin, had any feeling returned.

That time at Mount Snow, all those years ago, had ended too soon for Abby. On their last weekend there, Abby and Mallory had sat suspended high above the mountain, on a chair lift to the top, ready for a last run. Somewhere below them, Hannah struggled through her last day of Ski-Wee. She'd hated Ski-Wee, and snow, and the way she'd had to wear a bib with her name in big red letters under a picture of Big Bird.

Mallory had said, staring at the mountain ahead of them, "I'm beginning to think you don't even have a husband."

"Well, I do," Abby had said flatly. She had scanned the children's ski class right under them, searching for Hannah in the line of pole-less children making big wedge turns down the hill.

"From the string of men you've been entertaining. . . ." Mallory had let the sentence hang there.

After Vinny, Abby had searched for someone who

could keep that feeling alive in her, the way Zach did. Someone who didn't leave her numb and empty, dead in the heart. But she hadn't been able to find anyone. A ski instructor named Tommy had done it the longest, almost a week. But then it had stopped and Abby had started to wonder if something was wrong with her. Or, she'd thought, was there something just right between her and Zach?

Now, Three-Legged Horse was getting ready to play the final gig of the season here. She and Hannah would go back to New York and have to start over—find a new place, a new job. And all of this with a dead heart. A cold, empty center.

When the chair lift had reached the slope, Abby had skied fast, away from Mallory and these sad thoughts. She'd pointed her skis down the mountain as if she were trying to fly away. Behind her she'd heard skis scraping against the hard, packed snow, Mallory struggling to keep up.

At the bottom of the run, Abby had stopped, breathless, waiting for Mallory. When she'd finally reached her, she'd said to Abby between breaths, "You could have slowed down. You know I don't like going fast. You know that."

But all Abby had thought of was doing another run, of skiing even faster, as if perhaps this time she really would take off and fly. She'd turned and started to ski away from Mallory.

"Hey!" Mallory had called to her.

Abby had stopped. Suddenly. Not for Mallory, but because there, looking out of place in his blue pea coat and faded jeans, standing among the skiers in their color-coordinated ski suits, had stood Zach.

Mallory had come up beside Abby, panting. "Can't you just slow down?" she'd said.

But Abby hadn't moved or answered. Zach had spotted her, too, and was moving toward her, and her whole being was waking up, screaming with excitement, making her shiver and tremble. This, she'd thought, will never go away.

"Oh, brother," Mallory had groaned. "Which one is this?"

"This," Abby had said, "is my husband."

He'd reached her then, and wrapped her in his arms. She had been able to smell, faintly, paint and turpentine.

"You ski?" he'd asked. "I never knew you skied."

She hadn't answered. Instead, she'd stood there in his arms, feeling herself come alive, hearing the music of his heart pounding against her, the music of their love.

"This woman," Zach had told her, "said my aura is a brilliant blue. Electric, she said."

Abby had not let herself think of who that woman might be. She'd just stared up at the ceiling as Zach talked from beside her in bed.

"Yours," he had said, "is all warm and yellow. Soft."

When she'd opened her eyes, his face was close to hers.

He'd said, "I thought I'd die without you all winter."

"But you didn't," she'd said, not reminding him that it had been longer than just a winter.

He'd smiled. "Not on the outside. But whenever we're apart, I die a little here." He'd taken her hand and pressed it to his heart.

"Me too," she'd said.

He'd held her hand in his, and traced an invisible line from his heart to hers. "There's a thread here, though. It keeps us together. You know it's there too."

Abby had kneaded the air between them, searching for that thread.

61

"She told me I was a wild animal. But I think I was like an eagle or something," he'd said. He'd caught the look in Abby's eyes. "This was some kook at a party in Santa Cruz."

Abby had nodded.

"I bet you were a bird too," he'd said. "A lark. My tiny songbird even then."

"This time," Abby had said, "I was afraid you wouldn't come back."

"You know that I always come back. I have big plans for us, Abby."

She'd smiled then, moved closer to him. "What plans?"

"When I hit it big, we'll go away somewhere. A Greek island maybe. How's that sound? All whitewashed houses and black-lava beaches."

"That sounds wonderful."

Zach had laughed. "Now all I've got to do is hit it big."

"If you do that California series—"

"It means I'd have to go back there. Just for a while."

She'd reached between them, traced that thread that kept them connected. "I know," she'd said.

"We are a great pair," he'd whispered, pulling her close. "No rules. No bullshit." He'd traced that invisible thread too. "We know this is the real thing."

"Yes," she'd said, really knowing it. "We know."

Zach and Abby and Hannah had been all set to drive back to New York in Paco's Citroën. They would go back there and plan Zach's California series collages. He had brought things he'd collected to show Abby. She'd help him organize the collages. She'd play with Three-Legged Horse on Friday nights at A Kettle of Fish. Maybe she'd even be able to get a second job, in a hotel lounge.

Her old roommate Melissa used to play her harp at the Algonquin for a while.

Over breakfast, they'd talked about all of this. And finding a new apartment. Abby had said that eventually he could do enormous collages. "America," she'd said, stretching her arms out. "We'll drive cross-country looking for things. Arrowheads and seashells and grain from Kansas."

When the Citroën had been packed and they were ready to drive away, Doug had come running after them, sliding across the ice-covered parking lot, his arms waving as he shouted for them to wait, to stop.

Abby had rolled down her window, wanting not to, wanting to just keep going.

"Doug," Hannah had said seriously. " 'Bye."

He'd tweaked her nose. "Maybe not, Hannah," he'd said.

Abby had laughed. "You need a lift back to New York?"

"We're booked through Memorial Day weekend," he'd said. He'd pulled a paper from his pocket, held it out to her in gloved fingers.

"Where?" Abby had said. "Here?"

It had been Zach who had taken the paper from Doug, stretching across Hannah and Abby to get it.

"Back in Lenox," Doug had told Abby. He had not looked at Zach. "You know where we played last month? They've booked us all spring, Thursday through Sunday. Pay plus dinner."

"Lenox," Abby had repeated. She'd thought of the place they'd played there, an old stable that smelled vaguely horsey.

"If it works out," Doug had said, "we'll be able to get more gigs. I'm already looking into a place up in Bennington for Monday nights."

"This is great," Zach had said, studying the paper. He'd said to Hannah, "What do you say, Hannah manna? You want to be a country girl?"

"No," Hannah had said.

"What do you know about it?" Doug had asked Zach. "Where've you been all winter? We found her in the subway, man."

Zach had held up both hands. A traffic cop halting oncoming cars.

Doug had said, "It means we'd have to move here. I mean, to Vermont or western Massachusetts." He'd laughed and pointed back toward the inn. "Sean and Mallory are having one hell of a fight. She says it's like moving to Mars."

"It sounds pretty perfect," Zach had said.

"Almost perfect," Abby had told him. "What about New York?"

Zach had said, laughing, "We don't even have a place. I'll go get all the stuff for the collages and meet you wherever. I'll help you get settled."

She'd felt relieved at his words. "In Vermont."

"Wherever. And we'll work on the California series and then I'll try to show it."

Hannah had said, softly, in her little girl's voice, "Oh, no."

"I'll feel better knowing that while I'm away, you'll be taken care of," Zach had said. "That you're playing your music."

Abby had nodded. She'd placed her hand lightly over her heart, searching for that thread that kept them connected.

Funny, Abby thought now, the cold air outside the Merry Widow making her shiver, how after all this time, that connection seemed more fragile than ever. All of her connections did. Her mother called them dependencies. "It's about time," Deirdre had told her long distance at Christmas, "that you get rid of all this crap and start over."

Her cheeks were numb from the cold, and her fingers had grown stiff. They did that easily, from playing or cold. They cramped, too. Sometimes at night she woke in pain, her fingers bent and crooked. She rubbed her cheeks now, with her calloused fingertips.

"Mom," Hannah said from behind her, "they're looking everywhere for you."

"I know," Abby said.

"They did the whole show without you."

She didn't answer.

"You don't even have gloves on," Hannah said.

"I think we should go to California," Abby said.

"Well, it's warmer there, that's for sure."

"Let's go inside and call Zach."

Hannah rubbed her mother's hands in her own. "You're frozen."

"We'll go there and start over."

"With Zach?"

"I think it's time, don't you?"

Hannah shook her head. "I think we should wait. Not do anything rash."

The tip of her nose was bright red, and Abby pressed her daughter close to her. "You're a smart kid," she said. "We'll give him a month. Then we'll call."

Hannah pulled away. "You're all wet."

As they walked inside, Abby tried to make a plan. He'd said he'd leave Nina by springtime. She'd call him then, tell him they were coming. She took a deep breath. She could handle this, she thought. She could.

"Besides," Hannah was saying, "if we're starting over, I think we should go somewhere exciting. Like Paris."

"You'll see," Abby told her. "California will be exciting."

"Uh-huh," Hannah said.

The winter, Abby thought, was almost over.

FLIGHT

It was not just that Abby wanted a different life now. She did not want to be the kind of person she had been any longer, the kind of person who lived in a part-time marriage, who spent ten years in a band with two guys who did not even talk to her about splitting up until after they had already made the decision. She wanted to be someone in charge of her life. And that meant winning Zach back from this Nina person. Winning him back and making something of their life together.

When she finally called him, San Francisco seemed as far away as the moon. As Pluto.

"Zach," Abby said into the telephone, "I've given you time. Plenty of time. What's going on out there?"

She looked over at Hannah, who sat at the kitchen table picking the marshmallow pieces out of a box of Lucky Charms. It was past noon. They had overslept and Hannah had missed school again.

Zach said, "I'm working things out. In fact, there's going to be a show in LA and it looks good for me. I'm going to go down there for a while."

"We'll meet you there," Abby said. "It'll be good to get away after Three-Legged Horse finishes up."

"That's a definite possibility," Zach said.

Hannah said, "Almost time for 'Day's Destiny.' "

Abby rolled her eyes. She covered the receiver with her hand and spoke with great confidence. "Zach says we should meet him in LA next month."

"Uh-huh," Hannah said. She studied a star-shaped pink marshmallow.

"Is Hannah home?" Zach was saying. "Why isn't she in school?"

"Snow day," Abby lied.

He laughed. "It's seventy degrees here. I'm trying to picture snow."

Abby looked out at the snow-less yard. The bare trees. "It's white," she said. "And cold. You remember now?"

"Very funny. Let me say hi to her, okay?"

"Okay."

"Wait," he said. "Abby?"

"What?"

"This thing with . . . with Nina. It's no big deal."

Abby nodded, as if he could see her.

"I miss you like hell. All of these terrible conversations we've had this winter. I can feel how awful it's been for you. Another person wouldn't have given me the time, the space, to work this out."

That's for sure, Abby thought. She said, "I'm not the same old Abby. I want you to know that. This time—"

"I do know," he said.

She nodded again. "So next month, after the band splits up, we'll come to LA. We'll talk things out."

"Yeah," he said.

"Okay." She handed the phone to Hannah. "See," Abby told her. "It's settled."

Hannah took the phone from her. "Uh-huh," she said into it, "so I hear." She looked at her mother. "Snow?"

Abby shrugged and turned away.

"Oh," Hannah said. "I don't know. Five or six inches, I guess."

Abby looked out the window. Against the fence she saw the tip of a crocus pushing through the dirt. A splash of yellow. It was almost spring. They would go to LA, he would leave Nina. They would all live happily ever after. She smiled, the first real smile she'd felt in a long, long time.

Abby brought magnetic Scrabble for their flight to Los Angeles. And a bag full of books and magazines. Anything to make the six hours go faster. But it didn't. No matter what she did, the flight seemed to drag on. She even tried walking up and down the plane's long aisles, counting her steps and the number of empty seats.

"Will you sit down already?" Hannah asked her as Abby passed their row.

Abby sighed. "You know," she said, trying to put things in perspective, "if we were on a train, we'd only be as far as Washington."

"Well, we're not on a train. What do you think we are? Pioneers?"

"Hardly."

"What are we going to do if he doesn't pick us up at the airport?" Hannah asked.

"He will."

"But what if—"

"He will," Abby said again.

Hannah sighed and looked out the window. "I don't trust him as far as I can throw a piano."

"He sent us the tickets, didn't he?" Abby said. She wanted to somehow convince Hannah that Zach wanted this too. That they were headed for a whole new beginning, as a family. But she didn't believe it enough herself yet, so she said, instead, "You'll see."

Zach brought them presents. A map of the stars' homes, an inflatable pink plastic palm tree, and a small dome filled with water that had a plastic carrot and top hat floating in it.

"A California snowman," he explained.

"Uh-huh," Hannah said.

"That is so cute," Abby said, clutching the blowup palm tree to her. "Isn't that cute?"

"Well, I figured with all the snow you guys had back East," Zach said.

"Right," Hannah said.

They stepped outside, into the sunlight.

"Gee," Abby said, looking around. "The air is sort of yellow."

"Smog," Zach said. With his head, he pointed down a long line of cars. "The car's down here."

"Great," Abby said, still smiling. Her lips were already aching from the effort to keep smiling and seem cheerful. And her eyes stung. Smog, she thought as she followed Zach. She felt like she was playacting the role of a wife returning from a visit back home. Except that the husband seemed strange, like someone she just met or whom she knew a long time ago. She watched his bright turquoise shirt recede in the crowd. It was so bright that she wondered if that was what was making her eyes sting. Now they were even starting to tear.

Abby stopped walking and leaned against a stretch limo with the license plate SHO BIZ. She was crying hard now, holding that pink palm tree to her like a child. All around her there was noise—car horns and people calling to each other, a tape of a woman's voice repeating

over and over, "The white zone is for loading and unloading of passengers only. No parking." Abby stood
there, crying, watching the turquoise blur of Zach, Hannah's nylon knapsack bouncing against her shoulder, afraid
that everything had come down to this trip, these few
days, this moment.

She watched as Zach opened the trunk of a red
convertible and Hannah looked up at him, her face twisted
in boredom, or disgust. Abby wondered if perhaps she
should have left Hannah back home with Sean and Mallory
and worked this out herself. She and Zach could have
taken long walks on the beach, eaten candle-lit dinners,
done all the romantic things people in love were supposed to do. But she had felt that she and Hannah were in
this together.

Abby wiped her eyes.

Zach was talking to Hannah now. It still startled her
to see the two of them together. Strangers who happened
to look alike. Hannah shrugged and stuck out her tongue.

It was like watching a movie, Abby thought. She
wished she could just stand here and watch it unfold,
send someone else in to play the wife and see how it all
turned out. As she moved, slowly, toward her husband
and daughter, she reminded herself that most movies have
happy endings, complete with a joyous swell of music.
She quickened her pace. She put on her best smile. When
she reached them, she said, "Isn't this great, Hannah?
Look at those palm trees."

Abby's head ached, even when she blinked. So she
kept her eyes shut.

"Too much saki," Zach was saying.

"She's probably poisoned from eating raw fish," Hannah said.

"Hannah, she's not poisoned. She's hung over."

71

Abbey wished they would keep quiet. Or leave her altogether.

"The woman drinks like a fish," Hannah said. "She doesn't get hung over."

"She doesn't drink saki, though."

She felt them still standing there, like they were waiting for something. She opened her eyes a crack and moaned, to prove she was alive.

Zach held something out to her. Something blue and cold.

"This will do wonders," he said.

"What?" She squinted to see it better. It was an eye mask, filled with a wiggly blue gel. Next thing he'll suggest an isolation tank, Abby thought. Or est.

He placed the mask over her eyes. The filling felt like Jell-O, all slippery and shaky.

She frowned, but he couldn't see that she'd frowned because the mask covered her eyebrows and part of her forehead.

"I knew you'd like that," he said. "Hannah and I are going to the gallery. I need her help with something."

"Aspirin," Abby managed to groan.

"Not good for you. It eats away the lining of your stomach."

"Aspirin does that?" Hannah said.

"I left some zinc tablets beside the bed. Take a megadose."

"Zinc?" Abby whispered. The sound of her own voice sent reverberations throughout her head.

"Isn't zinc in pipes or something?" Hannah asked. "In metal?"

"We'll be back," Zach said. "Don't forget. Megadose."

"Right," Abby said. Her face, under the mask, was growing numb.

*   *   *

Floating between two large pieces of glass was a rusty beer can, a child's sneaker, a used condom, a watch, a starfish, a fluorescent mechanical fish, a wooden mermaid, and a bottle with a note in it. The water was the fake bright blue of swimming pools.

"It kind of reminds me of that snowman," Hannah said.

"What snowman?" Zach asked her.

"The one you gave us. The California snowman."

He shook his head. "That's a whole different concept," he said.

She looked at all the things floating around in the water. "Seems like the same concept to me."

They stood in the gallery where "Beaches" was opening the next night. When they'd arrived, the gallery owner, Thornton Cairo, had put both of his hands on Zach's shoulders, looked him in the eyes, and said, "Art as we know it has changed. Thanks to you." Zach had nodded very solemnly. "Let's hope," he'd said, and held up both hands with all his fingers crossed. "Your father," Thornton had said to Hannah before he went into his office, "is a genius." She had nodded solemnly too. His mustache looked like he had drawn it on, a thin wavy line hovering between his nose and mouth.

The show consisted of only five pieces. One looked vaguely familiar to Hannah. It was a huge canvas cluttered with the things they'd picked up on beaches last summer. She realized that it wasn't that she'd seen the piece before, or even the things on it, but rather that it looked like all of her father's other stuff. She turned away from it and watched as Zach adjusted something across the room.

Half of the gallery floor was covered with beach sand. "Remember all that sand we took from that beach on the Jersey Shore?" he'd asked her earlier. "That's the sand from New Jersey?" Hannah had said, wondering who would really know the difference. A child's pail and shovel stuck out from the sand. The pail was decorated with Sesame Street characters, Big Bird and Bert and Ernie. Beside it was a half-finished sand castle. The rest of the sand stretched across the gallery floor, empty.

"Okay," Zach said, "come over here. You're going to help me finish this piece."

"I'm not going to finish that sand castle," she said. "Or sit there all week like a living mannequin or something."

Zach laughed. "I just want you to take off your shoes and socks and walk from the sand castle to the wall."

Usually, Hannah wished that her father did something normal, like drive a bus or teach remedial reading. But, as she walked across the New Jersey sand, she found herself happy that he did exactly this.

"Stop!" he shouted.

She had reached the wall, and was starting to walk off the sand.

Zach rushed over to her, stopping at the sand's edge. "The footsteps have to end right there," he said.

"So I'm stuck here."

He reached across the sand and lifted her off. Hannah put her arms around her father's neck. For an instant, he hugged her tight to him. She thought of the day they'd found that pail and shovel, discarded in the parking lot at Nahant Beach, in northern Massachusetts. Zach had acted like he'd found buried treasure.

Hannah hugged him, hard and quick, then squirmed out of his grip. She knew that it was dangerous to love Zach.

The mask and the zinc worked. Abby felt a little shaky, and every now and then when she swallowed she got a metallic taste in her mouth. But otherwise, she felt fine.

Zach was subletting this apartment from an artist friend who designed furniture. He had left Venice, California, to go to Venice, Italy. Last night, Zach had pointed out a series of dirty muddy canals that ran through this Venice. He'd explained how whoever had planned the city had wanted to re-create the other Venice. Even now, there were plans for cleaning the canals and filling them with water. Maybe even putting in a few gondolas.

Most of the furniture in the apartment was made from marble, strange-shaped slabs in pink, green, gray, and black. The table was an upside-down triangle, balancing as if *en pointe*. Hannah had slept on the couch, which resembled a giant marshmallow, or a child's drawing of a cloud. The apartment gave Abby the creeps.

People on roller skates kept whizzing by the window, the sound of skates on cement giving Abby an uncomfortable buzz in her head. She sat on the couch. It rose up, shaping itself around her like a blob in a science fiction movie that ate a major city, Tokyo or Philadelphia. She wished she had brought that mask in here with her. It seemed too much of an effort to get out of the blob and into the bedroom where she'd left it.

Abby pressed her head back, and the couch quickly oozed around her, cradling it. She tried to re-create last night. They had gone for sushi, and she remembered how Zach had ordered with such authority while she and Hannah had stared in horror at the glossy close-ups of raw fish on the menu. The three of them had sat in awkward silence, like strangers on a train, with Abby grinning the whole time and Zach blurting out facts about Los Angeles to them. "Did you know," he'd said, "that eight thousand people are moving here a week? That's compared to two thousand moving up to San Francisco every week." Every time he'd

said something, she'd said, "Really? Isn't that interesting?"
and then grinned even more.

What an idiot, she thought. She lifted her hands to
her head and they were immediately encased in couch.

Had she really tried to get Hannah to do her Supremes lip-synching act? Had she really said, "I'll do it
with you if I can be Diana Ross"? "Mom," Hannah had
said through gritted teeth, "you can't lip-synch without
music." Zach's face had seemed to grow blurrier as the
night went on. At one point, Abby had leaned over and
traced it, trying to bring it back into focus. But it had
grown even more indistinct under her fingers. Her stomach rolled as she remembered the raw, slippery fish, the
seaweed cradling yellow eggs, the slices of ginger that
had reminded her of flesh. But she had eaten it all, with
that stupid grin on her face, washing it down with saki to
drown out the taste and texture.

I will not drink today, Abby said out loud. I will not
make believe I love everything we do or see. I will relax.

Her headache was back. She pulled herself out of
that couch and went into the kitchen. The room was a
dizzying swirl of black and white, with too-shiny silver
appliances that made her head spin. She opened the
refrigerator, expecting to find the things Zach used to keep
in their own apartment back in New York—beer and old
Chinese food, still in the containers.

But this refrigerator was so full that it made her headache worse trying to sort one item from the next. There
was fruit she couldn't even identify for certain. She picked
up a small hairy one and sniffed it. Kiwi, maybe? she
thought. Her mind raced with the names of things she
always pushed quickly past in the supermarket. Pome-
granates, prickly pears, jicama. It seemed that all of those
things were gathered here, in Zach's refrigerator, pushed
beside jars of chunky preserves, grainy mustards with

French names, vegetables floating in marinade. She pulled out the one truly recognizable thing she saw—a bottle of wine—and poured herself a water glass full. It was cold and tasted slightly woody. She read the label, then put the bottle back.

Maybe, she thought, all this food belongs to the furniture maker. She remembered again the ease with which Zach had ordered all that sushi last night. Who the hell is he? she thought, and went back into the bedroom, where the furniture, at least, was nonthreatening. She sat on the bed, sipping her wine and looking around her for something that was from the Zach she knew. Back in New York, she used to pick up his things and press them to her nose, to fill herself with him.

That would comfort her. Abby opened the dresser drawers. Everything was neatly folded, row after row of California colors, shirts the shades of the ocean and sunsets. One drawer was empty. Zach had shown it to her last night, told her it was for her things. It had made her sad, like she was just a visitor who needed one drawer to hold her things. She was, she reminded herself, just a visitor.

Abby lifted a handful of his shirts to her face and inhaled. But a small sachet filled with balsam had invaded everything and all Abby could smell was that, like a forest. She let the shirts fall back into the drawer and began with real purpose to look for signs of who Zach was now, without her.

When he'd come to live with them in Vermont a few years ago, his habits had seemed foreign to her. He would drive into Bennington for fresh coffee beans. He would read books Abby was unfamiliar with. He had brought strange things with him for the shower—lumpy sponges and coarse loofahs, fluorescent-blue sea salts from Spain and hard black soap. Then too she'd searched—his eyes, the lilt of his voice, his smile—for who he was. She'd searched for traces of the old Zach, her Zach. Sometimes, after he'd left that time, taking all of his soaps and sponges with him, Abby had found herself wondering if the reason his move to Vermont hadn't worked was that she had wanted things to be the way they used to be. She hadn't, she'd thought, let them grow.

She wouldn't let that happen this time, she thought now as her hands moved through his belongings. She stopped when she found a bundle of letters and a photograph tucked far into a corner of a drawer. The picture was framed in heavy antique silver, ornate and slightly tarnished. In it, Zach stood, shirtless, with his arms circling a woman's waist. That woman, Abby knew, must be Nina. And Zach must have hidden all of this before Abby had come to California.

She sat on the bed and studied Nina's face. Her hair was short and black. It stood up straight on top, stiff as porcupine quills. Her bathing suit was black, too, an old-fashioned two-piece. Abby moved closer to the light, and held the picture under it, searching for some sign that might explain why Zach had fallen for this particular woman. Why he had considered leaving Abby for her. But all she could see was a man and a woman on a beach, looking into the camera and right at her. The man's pants were baggy white cotton ones, with a drawstring waist. His eyes were narrowed against the breeze. The woman's toenails were painted coral and her face was round with a tiny pointed chin, like a perfect heart. To Abby, they were both strangers.

She sighed, ran her fingertips lightly over the picture's cold silver frame. The letters were all postmarked London. She imagined scenarios—long-distance phone calls and foggy meetings, Zach writing Nina about the smog here, the overpopulation. Perhaps he sent her things. A California snowman. A pink blowup palm tree.

Stop, Abby told herself.

Think.

But all she could think about was the man and woman in the picture. The way his arms circled her waist. The way she boldly looked at the camera.

Abby tucked everything back into Zach's drawer, and stood in front of the mirror. It was bordered with cut black figures of naked women swooping down on giant calla lilies. Abby pulled her hair up onto the top of her head, tried to imagine it in short stiff spikes. She tried to look bold, like Nina. She thrust her chin out and stared back at herself, hard. But already her hair was falling free from her grasp. She did not look at all bold. She looked frightened. She looked ridiculous.

The front door opened, then shut, and Zach called to her. "How are you feeling?"

Abby pulled on his turquoise shirt from last night. It smelled like cologne. It was as if all traces of the real Zach were erased, taken over by balsam and his new Polo after-shave and Nina.

"Abby?"

They met outside the bedroom door.

"I got rid of her for an hour," he said.

Abby looked at him, confused.

"I rented roller skates for her," he added.

"Oh," she said. "You mean Hannah."

Zach laughed. "Is there someone else living here with us?"

Abby took a step back, away from him. "You tell me," she said.

He held his hands out, palms up.

"Nina," she said. "I thought you'd worked things out."

"Who says I haven't?"

She could not tell him she had looked through his drawers. She just waited.

His eyes narrowed, the way they were in the picture to protect them from the ocean breeze. "She called," he said.

It was one of those moments that seem to last for hours. For days. And in it, Abby knew that she wanted Zach back. She wanted to win him back to her so she would not have to live for the rest of her life with a dead heart. She had to fight for him.

So she looked up, into his eyes, as boldly as she could.

"Dump her," she said.

The moment passed.

Zach blinked and nodded.

"I have never meant anything more in my life," Abby said.

The front door flew open and Hannah came in, angry.

"You're supposed to rent pads, Zach," she said. "Knee pads and ones for elbows." She held out the roller skates, their bright red wheels still spinning a little. "Forget this," she said. "It's too dangerous out there."

Zach bought them new dresses for the opening. He gave Hannah a white lace one with spaghetti straps and tiny pearl buttons in the back. For Abby, he bought a black moiré silk with pale purple and blue flowers and birds water-painted on the front. He also gave her two hairpins, slender silver ones capped with chunks of amethyst.

"He's trying to woo us," Hannah told her mother as they dressed.

Abby traced the delicate, watery flowers and birds that shimmered across her dress. "When we got married," she said softly, "I wore this Mexican cotton dress." She laughed. "It was the only thing I owned that was white. But it had these bright green and orange birds and flowers embroidered on it." Her hands rested lightly on the delicate pattern of this dress. "I used to have a picture. An old blurry thing of us on the steps at City Hall."

Once, Hannah had spent an hour describing Chelsea Kent's mother's wedding album. How it was made of satin and lace, how Mrs. Kent's train had descended the church steps like a waterfall, how she'd been flanked by six bridesmaids in soft pink lace.

Abby was afraid that Hannah would bring that up now and ruin this moment, this balmy California night of silk and hope.

But Hannah just touched Abby's arm and smiled at her. "You look great," she said.

"You too," Abby told her. "Very sophisticated."

"Sophisticated?" Hannah said, tugging on her spaghetti straps. "Really?"

"Really," Abby said.

On the way to the gallery, they made Zach keep the top up in the car so their hair wouldn't get mussed.

"Ladies," he said, "we're in California. We're supposed to ride in a convertible with the top down. Even if it does muss our hair."

But he kept the top up anyway.

Abby had the feeling, as they rode down Sunset Boulevard, the wind making their eyes tear and their hair blow, the radio playing something old and familiar, that she had indeed joined the movie she had seemed to be watching from afar all this time. They were a family. They were on their way to her husband's opening. She rolled these words around in her mouth, savoring them. In the morning, she thought, they would all go for pancakes. For the best pancakes in Los Angeles. And they would talk about everything that happened tonight.

Zach reached over and took her hand in his, squeezed it hard. In that moment, Abby believed that they were a family, that she and Hannah weren't really leaving tomorrow, that Vermont and Three-Legged Horse were not in her life at all.

Abby stood in front of the one called "Beaches: Duck, North Carolina." It was a completely black canvas, lit every thirty seconds by a flash of sweeping light. She would not let herself think of that night last summer when they were in Duck, and she'd learned about Nina in the flash of light from Cape Hatteras. She made herself as empty and black as that canvas.

Zach came up beside her with champagne in thin crystal fluted glasses.

"Here," he said, handing her one, "to our success. To Mexico. To Zach and Abby, the greatest love the world—no, the universe—has ever known."

She turned her back on Duck. "Are you a huge success?" she asked him.

Around them, people swarmed, humming like bees, studying the giant canvases, a swirl of expensive perfume and fine fabrics.

"They love it," he said.

They stood together and watched the crowd. The woman in a sari of silk and gold threads, the group of six dressed all in black, the four men who stood huddled together, their eyebrows thick and animated.

"The Marx Brothers," Abby said, pointing with her glass toward those men.

"Come on," Zach said, taking her arm, "I want you to meet Thornton Cairo. He owns the gallery."

Abby resisted the tug forward. "And those people—"

she laughed nervously—"the ones all in black. They haven't smiled or even said one word all night."

"They're big investors," Zach said. "They live in Malibu surrounded by modern art."

"I like the woman wearing feathers. Do you suppose there's anything under those feathers?"

Zach smiled. "Are you delaying?"

"Delaying?"

"Why won't you come and meet Thornton?"

Abby's eyes flitted across the room. "Look at Hannah," she said. "Pretending she's an heiress or something." Earlier, Abby had passed Hannah as she talked to two thin men—twins—in an exaggerated French accent.

"It's too late," Zach said. "He's coming to us."

"Oh, dear," Abby said softly as she watched Thornton Cairo approach them. He was wearing a beret and a loose smock for a coat. He looked, Abby thought, like a caricature of an artist. Someone's bad drawing come to life. A woman walked beside him, tall and straight and dressed completely in tissue-like silver. "I think I have to go powder my nose," Abby said.

But Zach was already making introductions. "Abby," he was saying, "this is Thornton Cairo and his assistant, Gladdie Moore."

Gladdie lifted one thin eyebrow dusted with silver, but did not respond right away.

"This man is a genius," Thornton said.

Abby nodded and grinned.

"A real genius," Thornton said. "The Whartons are mad for the show. And Reggio is too."

Abby focused on the thin line above his lips. She was sure it was not a real mustache, that he had used black Magic Marker and drawn it on for effect.

Then Gladdie Moore spoke. "Nina told me you were

good," she said, and Abby gazed up into Gladdie's face, watched the silver lips move, heard the name Nina.

She wanted to walk away, to hide so she would not have to hear more. Ahead of her was "Beaches: Miami, Florida," four old and worn beach umbrellas decorated in once-bright patterns of tropical fish and fruit, now all faded. She wanted to hide under one of those old umbrellas until this was over and she could leave. When they'd found those, in a dumpster behind an old folks' home in Miami, they had smelled of mildew and seaweed. They had been damp and seemed so neglected that Abby had wanted to cry.

Gladdie's eyes followed Abby's to the umbrellas. "Nina said you got those from a dumpster? Is that true? I mean, a dumpster? Anything for art, right?"

Abby said so softly that nobody heard her, "They were like old people themselves, those umbrellas." She had said that to Zach as they'd lugged them across the parking lot to the van in the hundred-degree heat, the tar soft under their feet.

Now Thornton Cairo was talking about Nina, about how she'd shown him some of Zach's New York City collages when he was up in San Francisco. "I know you did those in another lifetime," Thornton said, "but I like them. Maybe we could do a show of them this summer."

Another lifetime, Abby thought. Our lifetime. She said, "He had all of this junk—subway tokens and old food cartons that someone claimed were Bob Dylan's and Brooklyn Dodgers ticket stubs, and I said, 'There's your theme right in front of you.' "

Everyone in the whole gallery seemed to stop talking at once.

Gladdie frowned. Even her face was dusted with silver. Didn't a person suffocate if they wore so much silver? Abby wondered.

Zach said, "Abby has really been my guiding force for years."

"Forever," Abby said.

Zach shifted uncomfortably.

"Nina told me—" Gladdie started.

"Well, Nina doesn't know anything about it," Abby said. "I do. I know."

And then she walked away from them. Maybe, she thought, if she got some air she wouldn't hit Gladdie Moore right across her silver lips. But she couldn't find the door out. Everything seemed to be covered with sand.

Zach was coming up behind her and she wanted to get away—from him, from beaches, from here. She wanted to curl up over there beside Hannah's footprints, to really be on the beach in Cape May. Anywhere.

But it was too late. Zach had found her and he was gripping her arm.

"You hate small talk," he said.

Abby shook her head. "Small talk," she thought. She wondered how little he really knew about her.

"Gladdie's a bitch," Zach told her.

Abby watched as the fake Cape Hatteras light swept across Zach's face, illuminating it.

"I want to leave," she said.

He seemed relieved. "I'll find Hannah, okay?"

She nodded, and watched as the crowd swallowed him up. She did not know for sure why her words—"I want to leave"—left her feeling so frightened.

On the flight home, Hannah wrote postcards to Chelsea and Kate. The postcards said the same thing: "I rollerskated and ate fish eggs. Saw Tom Hanks in a restaurant. He looked cuter in person. Can't wait to come home. Hannah."

"Why are you writing those now?" Abby asked her.

"I'm going to give them as souvenirs."

That morning, over breakfast at The Rose Tattoo, Zach had taken out a map and drawn a line from Vermont, down the East Coast, through the south, into Texas, and finally across the border to Mexico. The line was steady and blue. It did not waver or veer off in the wrong direction. He had lifted his mimosa and said, "To the future."

Hannah reached into the Alpha Beta shopping bag she brought on board and pulled out the review of Zach's show that had run in that morning's *LA Times*.

" 'Zach Plummer is a genius,' " she read. " 'Bold and different, unafraid to take chances, he takes us from New England beaches, to the Outer Banks—' "

"I read it already," Abby said.

"Good." Hannah dropped her tray table and lined it with the contents of the shopping bag—the California snowman, the blowup pink palm tree. "Do you want any of this stuff?" she asked her mother.

"It's all yours," Abby said.

Hannah dropped it all back into the paper bag with the review, and threw it away.

DREAMING OF
KIRK CAMERON

Hannah asked her mother, "Do you think a person can be in love with two people at the same time?"

Abby was cooking, something she didn't do very well or very often. Usually, she and Hannah ate frozen pizzas or TV dinners. On special occasions, those times when Abby tried to be more organized or to be a better mother, she would brush Good Seasons Italian dressing on chicken legs, and serve it with a salad and canned corn. On those nights, she made Hannah drink milk instead of soda, and eat fruit for dessert.

This afternoon, Abby had *Joy of Cooking* open as she tried to follow the instructions and illustrations for making beef Wellington. Her hair and face and hands were covered with flour and her fingernails were layered with pâté.

When Hannah asked her that question, Abby looked up, her head swiveling toward her daughter, who sat at the kitchen table amid all the flour, calmly reading *Tiger Beat*. As Hannah got older, she looked even more like Zach. So much so that lately, when Abby saw Hannah, she felt she was glimpsing Zach too. Except for the eyes. Hannah had the same gray eyes that Abby had. Eyes that could look as soft as smoke or as hard and cold as rock.

Hannah's eyes were somewhere in between now, picking up a hint of blue from the clear early May sky outside the window.

"Do you?" Hannah said again. "Do you think a person can love two guys at the same time?"

"Why?" Abby asked, and looked away from Hannah's gaze to the old green-and-yellow speckled linoleum floor. It was dusted with flour too. "What a mess," she said.

"Because I think I do, that's why," Hannah said. Her voice had an edge to it. An edge that told Abby that Hannah thought she wasn't listening. Again.

Abby just shrugged, the wrong person to give advice about love.

Hannah watched as she tried to form a lattice crust over the beef and pâté. "Why is Gavin Berry coming for dinner?" she said.

I have no idea, Abby thought. But she said, "Because he's nice."

She heard Hannah sigh, and rustle the pages of the magazine, but Abby didn't look up at her again. Instead, she worked on the dough, on wrapping it around the slippery beef.

She had met Gavin Berry the night after they got back from seeing Zach in LA. They had come home to find bunches and bunches of violets waiting for them on the doorstep, all wrapped in flower-shop green tissue paper. He hadn't sent a card, just the violets, and Abby had wanted to throw them all away, like they'd done with the stuff on the plane. Instead, she'd filled old bowls and empty wine bottles with the flowers and she had felt that Zach was there, watching her like a ghost.

When Sean called and invited her and Hannah to a party in Bennington, Abby had accepted easily, eager to escape the house and her thoughts about her marriage. The party had been at Gavin Berry's and she and Hannah had worn their new dresses, the ones Zach had given them for the opening. They had looked out of place amid the other guests, and Abby had grown sad in her black silk dress, sipping sweet wine from a paper cup.

Then Gavin had appeared in front of her, a small Japanese man with glasses just like hers. A papermaker, Sean had told her on their way to the party. "You are the most beautiful flower here," Gavin had told her. "And the saddest." His voice was soft, as lilting as music. It had made Abby want to crawl into Gavin Berry's arms and sob. "Well," she'd told him, "I think I might be leaving my husband." The words surprised her. Once they were out, she did start to cry. "He's a bastard," she'd said. Gavin Berry had led her away from the party, into the shop where he made his paper. In that wonderful voice, he'd explained to her how he soaked the bark from trees and boiled it with plant roots to make paper. The shop smelled bad, a strong and pungent odor that clung to everything. Gavin had held up a piece of grainy paper the color of sand for her to see.

When Abby got home from the party that night, she'd called Zach. "I'm having all these terrible thoughts," she'd told him. "Look," he'd said, his voice weary, "I told you I'll take care of it when she gets back from London." After they'd hung up, she'd gone from room to room, inhaling each bouquet of violets as if it held a secret potion.

Every time Gavin Berry took her out for the next two weeks, she'd brought Hannah with them. To poetry readings and movies and a dinner in Williamstown. She had said, lightly, casually, "Why don't you come for dinner on Friday night? At our house." Later Hannah had said to her, "Just what we don't need. A man."

But here it was, Friday night, and Gavin Berry was on his way. Abby looked around her. On the windowsill, the last bunch of violets sat shriveling in an old cracked pottery pitcher. She could not quite throw them out. Not yet.

"My mother," Hannah said.

She sat with her neighbor, Dara, on the old stone wall that made a crooked border between their two houses. When Zach had spent those months with them here in Vermont, he had told Hannah wonderful stories about these walls that ran through the fields and along the roads throughout New England. Stories about Indians and settlers and legends. It wasn't until she used those stories as part of a history project in school that Hannah learned none of what he'd told her had been true.

"She's driving me crazy!" Hannah shouted to the sky.

Dara nodded.

Dara was her friend by necessity. Their houses were so isolated from any others that they almost had to be friends. But Dara was fifteen, all soft white skin with red blotches of eczema, and breasts that were so large and fat the boys loved to make fun of them. Despite their age difference, they were in the same grade at school. Dara took class after class in Home Economics—International Foods, Advanced Sewing, Bachelor Living.

For a while last year, Hannah had begged Abby to move to a house in a subdevelopment. A split-ranch, like the Kents had, with wall-to-wall carpeting and a doorbell that chimed a little melody. Everything in the Kents' house was a soft shade of orange, and Mrs. Kent had names for each one. Salmon, apricot, tangerine. Whenever Hannah went there, she felt like she was sitting smack in the middle of a sunset, all warm and orange.

Sometimes lately, Hannah considered not being Dara's friend at all. Instead, she'd concentrate on Chelsea and Kate, on calling them and having slumber parties. When Dara walked by, Hannah would pretend she didn't see her. She'd pretend she lived next door to the Kents, in a house with a circular driveway, with a mother who dressed normal and wore lipstick. But she couldn't bring herself to really drop Dara like that, even though Dara was slow-moving and slow-thinking and more and more lately those things drove Hannah crazy. Sometimes she shouted at her, "Think, will you!" or "Hurry up!" Silently she added "Fatso" under her breath. Hannah was afraid this would slip out one day soon and hurt Dara's feelings.

Dara loved Hannah. She used to love to comb her hair, to French-braid it for her. Once, she made dozens of braids all over Hannah's head, like Bo Derek had. It had taken an entire Saturday afternoon, but Dara never once complained. When Hannah got back from LA, one of the first things she'd done was to cut her hair short, except for one long skinny rattail in the back. Dara had cried when she'd seen it, until Hannah had let her peroxide it, then dye it pink.

"You're smarter than your mother," Dara told Hannah now.

Hannah rolled her eyes. "That's stupid," she said.

Dara had on a sweatshirt covered with lime-green frogs sitting on hot-pink lily pads. Across the back it said I'M HOPPY TODAY. Hannah looked away from Dara and the bright shirt, out toward the house. She pictured her mother inside, spilling flour everywhere, making a big mess.

"She's in there," Hannah said, "making a big fancy dinner for Gavin Berry."

"Is she going to kiss him?" Dara giggled.

Hannah stood up. "Oh, brother," she said, and started to walk away. "What a dope."

"He's a Chinaman, isn't he, Hannah?" Dara called after her. "Hannah?"

Hannah didn't turn around.

"Hey!" Dara shouted. "I got the new 16 magazine. It's got pictures of Kirk Cameron."

Hannah stopped and faced Dara. "You do not."

"No," Dara said, smiling, her spotted face all round and soft. "No. I don't really have it."

"Jesus," Hannah said, and headed home.

Up ahead, Gavin Berry's white VW Bug was pulling in, crunching gravel, its engine whirring like an eggbeater.

From her bedroom window upstairs, Abby watched as Gavin got out of his car and walked toward the house. He was short, and his mustache trickled down each side of his mouth like melting wax.

She looked around the cluttered bedroom, considered moving the magazines and discarded clothes from her bed. She thought of pulling the candy-cane-striped sheets taut, fluffing the pillows and folding the quilt. But she didn't. Instead, she filled her earlobes with earrings, a mass of dangling crystals and sterling-silver stars and moons. She sorted through the clutter on top of her bureau, searching for the bottle of perfume that Hannah had given her last Christmas. Abby's hand settled on the map, with Zach's straight line that led from here in Vermont to Mexico.

Downstairs, Gavin knocked twice.

Abby gently tucked the map into her drawer, beside her other useless things. She fumbled with the gift box that held the perfume, then fumbled with the bottle itself before the Jean Naté let loose and sprayed her right in the face and all over her hands.

Gavin's voice, soft as a lullaby, floated up to her. "Abby?"

She ran her wet hands across her sweater, an old thrift shop one with multicolored knit flowers that had rhinestones as their centers. The sweater sleeves were too short, so she'd lined one arm from her wrist to the sleeve's edge with thin silver bangle bracelets.

"Abby?" he called again.

"Coming," she said.

Then she sprayed her neck, lifted her skirt, and sprayed behind her knees, before running downstairs to let Gavin in.

But he was already in. When she got downstairs, Gavin was wiping the flour off the kitchen table with a damp paper towel.

"It was unlocked," he said.

Abby frowned. "Yes. Well, the lock's broken."

He nodded, his hands fluttering across the tabletop.

"Don't do that," Abby said. "I mean, you don't have to do that."

She was taller than him. A good three or four inches, she decided as she watched him. She thought of how her head perfectly fit on Zach's shoulder when they stood side by side, how she had to stand on tiptoe to reach his lips when they kissed.

"I brought you this," Gavin said. He held a manila envelope out to her. "A gift."

She took it from him, hesitating, then reached inside and pulled out a piece of paper. It was hand-marbled, the color and pattern of tortoiseshell. It reminded her of barrettes she'd owned as a child that hugged the sides of her head, clutched at her fine hair. Her mother had bought them in Antigua for her, and whenever Abby had looked at them, she'd imagined a tropical island, beach sand, and ocean.

"What else would a papermaker bring for a gift?" Gavin said.

The paper felt thick and heavy in her hand. "It's really lovely," Abby said.

She slid it back into the envelope, wondering what she'd ever do with it. She could frame it, she supposed. But most likely it would go in the same drawer she'd just put Zach's map in, beside all the other things she would probably never use. Bras and panty hose from her mother, self-help books and inspirational poems, bird-watching and hiking guides.

Gavin said, "It smells delicious in here."

Abby looked at him. Go home, she thought. She tried to will him back to his car, heading north on Route 7 to his own house.

"Today," he said, "I woke up and there were sixteen wild turkeys marching across my front yard."

Abby poured them each a glass of wine.

"I wish you could have seen them," Gavin said. "The way the littlest one kept getting confused and wandering off in the wrong direction."

She nodded. "Yes," she said. "Well."

"I was delighted when you invited me here."

"You've been so nice to us," Abby said. "The movies and everything."

He was standing very close to her. He smelled sweet, almost fruity, as he reached over and touched the rim of her glasses. "How do people with glasses kiss each other?" he asked carefully. "May we experiment?"

The kitchen door opened noisily and Hannah came in. Perfect timing, Abby thought. When she lifted her hand to adjust her glasses, she was surprised to feel it tremble.

*   *   *

The beef Wellington's crust fell off into a mushy puddle under each piece of meat. Still, Gavin said it was lovely. Hannah moaned. "Disgusting," she muttered.

He explained a project he was working on. A couple in Manhattan had commissioned him to make wallpaper for their daughter's dollhouse.

"Each room is different," he said. "Brocade paper for the living room. Tiny hand-painted flowers on the bedroom paper."

"Sick," Hannah said.

"Would you like such a dollhouse?" Gavin asked her.

Her eyes narrowed. "A dollhouse?"

"She's too old for that," Abby said quickly. Her tongue felt thick and lazy. Too much wine, she thought, but still she refilled her glass. Sometimes, she and Zach drank wine until they got dizzy-drunk. Just last summer, she thought, at Rehoboth Beach, they had done that. Hannah had been in the video arcade and she and Zach had gone to the beach with a bottle of wine and a few joints. He had dripped wine onto her belly and breasts and thighs, then carefully, slowly, licked it off. It had seemed to Abby like rubies falling onto her. Since she'd come back from LA, she sat up late and drank wine in bed, trying to sort out her feelings. Wine had seemed like a lonely thing here lately, and Abby was glad that tonight it was making her feel warm and slightly giddy. She felt cotton-headed. She felt happy.

"In fact," Hannah was saying, "I'm in love." She leaned toward Gavin. "Do you think it's possible to be in love with two people at the same time, Gavin?"

"Here we go again," Abby said.

"You never answered me," Hannah said, glaring at her.

"Yes," Gavin said. "I do. Because there are all kinds of love."

Hannah's eyes brightened. "That's exactly right," she said. "These are two different kinds of love that I'm talking about. One of them is this boy in my school—"

"Who?" Abby said, surprised at Hannah's openness.

"Brent Balboa."

Abby laughed. "The one who looks like a rooster?"

"He does not," Hannah said. "You're the only person who ever said that. Everyone else thinks he looks like Rod Stewart."

"Honestly, Hannah. Rod Stewart?"

"Who's the other boy?" Gavin asked.

"Kirk Cameron," Hannah said.

"From TV?" Abby asked her.

"Yes," Hannah said. "From TV. Just because he's famous doesn't mean he wouldn't like me."

Abby shook her head. "But he lives in California and you live in Vermont. That seems to be a problem."

Hannah leveled her hard gray eyes at Abby. "So?" she said. "You live in Vermont and Zach lives in California."

Abby cleared her throat, laughed uncomfortably. "Yes," she said, "that's true."

Gavin's voice floated toward her. "There are all kinds of love, Hannah. Old and new, for example. So you see, someone could love two people at the same time."

After Hannah went upstairs to bed, Abby and Gavin opened a new bottle of wine and went into the living room with it. She could not talk; her brain felt all muddled and cloudy. But he talked, on and on, about making paper, about how his grandmother taught him how to do it.

"In Japan," he said, "she used to stretch her paper across bamboo and bury it in snowbanks for the winter. Her grandmother taught her."

Abby lit candles as he spoke. She thought about how

right now, she felt alive deep down. And wondered how long it would last this time. Yesterday, Zach had called her, and even though she had not spoken very much, and his voice had sounded distant and flat, she had still had to hug herself tight to keep from shaking.

In the candlelight, Gavin's skin looked very white. Abby studied his face as he spoke about his grandmother, the ceremony with which she did everything, even the simplest things. His hands danced slowly in the air. Abby thought, here is a man who is gentle. A man who will teach his grandchildren how to stretch paper across bamboo and then bury it under the snow. She wondered if she could make that small feeling in her chest stay alive if she really worked on it.

Now he was talking about Japanese cedar, the way it smelled and felt. Something in her face made him stop talking. He said only her name. "Abby." She moved closer to him. She unbuttoned her sweater and slid it off, then stepped out of her skirt and stood beside him, in just her silver bangle bracelets and Jean Naté.

When Hannah came downstairs the next morning, she found Abby cleaning the kitchen windows.

"What's wrong?" Hannah said.

"Look at them. They're filthy."

"Uh-huh," Hannah said. She carefully unwrapped the foil from a Ring Ding.

"What's that supposed to mean?" Abby asked her. She unwrapped a Ring Ding too and took a bite.

"It means you never clean the windows." Hannah's eyes settled on the stack of dishes drying beside the sink. "Or the dishes either."

"Maybe I'm turning over a new leaf."

"Maybe."

Abby sat at the table beside her daughter. For a minute, neither of them spoke.

Then Hannah said, "Gavin Berry is short and skinny."

"He's not so skinny," Abby said. She thought of how last night, on the scratchy tweedish couch, he'd lifted her by the waist onto him. The muscles in his arms had been taut and hard. "He does Tae Kwon Do," she said. "He's stronger than he looks."

Hannah focused on her Ring Ding, on cracking the chocolate off it. "How do you know?"

"I'm a mother," Abby said. "I know everything."

Hannah sighed and licked the cream filling from the center with the tip of her tongue.

"Well," she said, "I had an interesting dream last night."

Abby froze. Had Hannah seen them? Had she heard something? Abby thought of Gavin's long, high-pitched moan when he came, the way the couch had knocked against the wall loudly the second time they'd made love.

Hannah said, "See, I dreamed I won this radio contest and the first prize was a date with Kirk Cameron."

Abby laughed with relief. "Oh," she said. "Great."

She pulled her daughter closer to her, softly twisting her finger around the long skinny braid that hung down Hannah's back.

"It was heaven," Hannah said.

"What about Brent the Rooster?"

Hannah pulled away from Abby's grasp. "That was the best part. When I flew back from California after my date, Brent picked me up at the airport on his dirt bike."

Abby smiled. "Good dream, Hannah," she said. "Good dream."

SIMPLE SYMPHONY #1

There were things that Hannah felt in her bones. Every summer, she felt Zach moving toward them, crossing the span of the country, across highways, through city traffic and down back roads. Some days she woke up knowing in her bones that her mother would be depressed, or cranky, or sad. Lately, it was change that Hannah felt. It was in the air, the way she could feel spring fading and Zach getting ready to leave California and come East.

Her mother had told her that as a little girl Hannah used to repeat everything she knew before she went to sleep. "I'm Hannah Plummer. You're my mommy and Zach is my daddy and he lives far, far away." Sometimes still, she woke up at night trying to remember something she had learned in school, afraid that it wouldn't come to her, unable to sleep again until she could rattle off whatever it was easily. The state capitals or the eight multiplication tables or which sister was which in *Little Women*.

Now, as summer was approaching, Hannah was waking up in the middle of the night, feeling change coming, but unable to say what exactly that change was going to be. So she'd lie in bed, and try to figure it out. There were so many things that she'd like to have change, and so many things that could change, that usually she ended up feeling more confused. Her mother was afraid of the dark and kept a light and the television on all night. Hannah listened to the familiar voices of Hawkeye and Trapper John while she wondered: What is happening here?

Her room was small, its walls covered with nosegays of violets. On the floor was an unfinished hooked rug of Snoopy and Woodstock. Her mother had started the rug as a project, an effort to get the house in shape, a long time ago, and had stopped working on it almost exactly in the middle. Snoopy's nose stuck out of a soft white head, as if pointing to the unfinished part, the black floor showing through the open mesh outline of Woodstock. Hannah had put up one bookshelf. It tilted downward slightly so that all of its contents bunched together on one end. She had two books on it—*Little Women* and her fifth-grade American History book that she'd forgotten to hand in—along with a picture of Zach as a little boy, looking as bald and fat and calm as a Buddha; a flowered, heart-shaped box with a braid made from Abby, Zach, and Hannah's hair tucked inside it; and one piece of rock that Dara swore was an authentic Indian arrowhead. On the wall above the shelves Hannah had hung black-and-white head shots of her grandparents. They were old pictures, from the fifties. Deirdre looked exotic and mysterious in hers, and Toby's eyes, in his photograph, were shaded by a tilted fedora.

Every night, when Hannah woke up, her first impulse was to look at all these things, to make sure they were still the way they had been when she'd fallen asleep and that they were in order. She'd panic, then look around at the violets on the wallpaper and the unfinished Snoopy rug, and the fake arrowhead, and the pictures of her grandparents. The light from her mother's room fell into the hallway, illuminated the scratchy, rust-colored, indoor-outdoor carpeting and the old desk that they'd bought for ten dollars, sure that underneath the coats of paint and wax there was a beautiful and valuable antique, but that they'd never got around to stripping. Something is coming, she thought. Something is changing. "Ten days in Tokyo," Hawkeye said from her mother's bedroom. "Can you beat that?"

One Saturday morning Hannah woke up to the sounds of her mother's violin. The tune was unfamiliar. Abby was playfully plucking the strings with her fingers rather than stroking them with her bow.

"What now?" Hannah said out loud.

She pulled on her jeans and one of her mother's T-shirts that said HANDEL WITH CARE and went downstairs.

Abby was sitting on a footstool in the center of the living room, her head tilted away from her violin. She looked at it almost lovingly, like she had forgotten she owned it and had just suddenly rediscovered it. Her cheeks were flushed, and Hannah could see the white of her mother's upper teeth as they pressed into her tongue.

Abby looked up quickly, her fingertips still holding the strings lightly, and giggled nervously.

"Britten," she said. " 'Playful Pizzicato.' "

Hannah frowned.

" 'Sentimental Sarabande.' 'Frolicksome Finale,' " Abby continued.

"Huh?"

She put her violin down, gently. "Yesterday I auditioned for Le Company. And I made it." She smiled triumphantly. "I'm a violinist again, not a damn fiddler. And believe me, I was rusty."

Le Company was an orchestra that performed throughout the Berkshires from September through May, giving concerts every month. Gavin Berry had taken Abby and Hannah to hear Le Company in concert once and Hannah had fallen asleep. When her mother had woken her up, she'd muttered, "Are they finished yet?" "Hardly," Abby had said. "Schubert never finished it. How can *they*?" Gavin and Abby had had a good laugh over that one.

"You can't believe this program," Abby was saying. "Barber's Adagio for Strings. Telemann. But that's all later. First I have to work on this Britten and some Tchaikovsky." She held some sheet music toward Hannah, like it meant something. "I haven't played Vivaldi's Concerto in Fa Maggiore since Juilliard."

Hannah took a step backward, away from her mother and Vivaldi. She thought of how Abby and Doug used to play dueling banjos with fiddle and guitar. Fiercely. The crowd would stomp their feet in time to the music. Abby's hair would come loose from its braid and she'd play with fine blond wisps circling her face.

Change, Hannah thought.

As if to confirm the thought, Gavin Berry walked in, without even knocking.

"I just heard," he said. "It's wonderful." His hands cupped Abby's face and he kissed her, right on the mouth. Hannah saw that he had to stand, slightly, on tiptoe.

Hannah stepped backward again.

"Hey," she said.

But they didn't answer her. Abby started talking again, excitedly, her words like those of a foreign language that Hannah had never heard before. " 'Boisterous Bounce,' " she was saying. "And look here. Pezzo in forma si Sonatina."

"Oh, yes." Gavin sighed, taking the sheet music

from her carefully. As he studied it his hands smoothed the pages.

Outside, Dara called Hannah's name, over and over, grating but familiar.

Hannah turned from Gavin and Abby. "Coming," she shouted, as loud as she could.

"And this," Abby was saying as she left, "in the spring, Corelli's 'Andante,' 'Sarabande,' and 'Giga.'"

Gavin traced the curve from Abby's hipbone to her stomach with the ball of his thumb. The walls of her bedroom were filling with his beautiful paper. He brought her sheets of it, and she taped it over the faded pink roses on the wallpaper. Lapis, malachite, and marble. Alabaster, jade, and one flecked with gold.

"Pretty soon," Abby said, "I'll have repapered the whole room." She closed her eyes and concentrated on the way his thumb felt as it moved along her body. "You know," she said, "I had forgotten how I loved the violin. The real violin. Once, in New York, I had a job playing at a Rumanian steak house."

"No," he said, his voice a whisper, his thumb now making a straight line from her belly button to her other hipbone.

"I dressed like a gypsy and played Rumanian folk songs. Then I moved from table to table and played for the customers while they ate these huge steaks. Like twenty-four-ounce sirloins. 'Oh,' I'd say, 'you're Italian.' Then I'd play 'That's Amore' for them. And 'Santa Lucia.' Then I'd play just a touch of Verdi. 'Va Pensia,' maybe. And they'd say, 'No. Play another Italian song for us. Play 'Arrivederci Roma.'"

"A gypsy," Gavin said. "A blond gypsy. Gold hoop earrings and a bandana in your hair."

She laughed. "I wore a skirt with bright stripes,

all different colors. And they stuffed my pockets with money."

His thumb circled her inner thigh. "It's so rare that I get to see you like this, in daylight. In your bed."

In the distance they could hear Dara's and Hannah's voices from outside drift in.

"I know," Abby said. "One baby and my body's ruined." Her breasts had never shrunk to their pre-Hannah size, and hung heavy, spilling against her ribs. Her stomach was still round and there were the lightest white lines across it. "I was so huge," she said.

Gavin was over her now, his face close to hers. "I would like it very much," he said, "if you had my baby. You would not be alone this time. Or ever again."

She smiled, remembered how Zach had promised her that too. Lately, his old promises had grown faint, like whispers. He had rubbed the swell of her stomach with oils that smelled like coconuts and honey. He had painted her picture, big-breasted and round-bellied. He had brought home baby books, and books filled with baby's names. He had liked to make love sitting up, so he could watch her belly between them. And then, when she was only halfway through the pregnancy, he'd left.

Gavin was whispering to her. Promises. Abby smiled again, sighed at the feeling of him inside her. She heard her daughter outside, heard the box spring's moans mix with her own, heard Gavin's words grow choppy, cut by his fast breaths. The wind chimes in the hall clanged together. In her head, with all these sounds, she heard Vivaldi, a tune from another long-ago spring day. She said, "Oh. Oh." Gavin's hands were on her and she tasted his skin, sweet. She said "Oh" again.

The day that Abby was leaving for New York with Gavin to deliver some paper to a store in SoHo, Hannah brought the mail in and tossed it on the table. Abby was dressed up for the occasion. She had bought a new dress, soft and pink, a little rosette on the collar.

"That," Hannah announced, "looks like a nightgown. An old lady's nightgown."

The day before, Abby had found her with Dara, in the woods, sharing a can of beer.

"Why aren't you in school?" Abby had said, startled to discover them there.

"Oh," Hannah had said, "all of a sudden you're worried that I'm missing school. For your information I've missed twenty-nine days already this year."

"If you miss forty," Dara had said, "you automatically stay back."

"You should not be cutting school and drinking beer," Abby had shouted, surprising Hannah and Dara and herself. "Now you get up and come home with me this instant."

That night, Abby had slept at Gavin's, creeping into her own bed at dawn. Just before she had fallen asleep, she'd heard Hannah's door click shut.

Abby smoothed the dress, touched the tiny rosette. "Really?" she said. "It looks bad?"

Hannah faced her, angry. "I don't care if you're fucking Gavin Berry," she said.

"Hannah," Abby said. "Don't."

"I don't care if you marry the little nerd. But what about Zach?"

Abby's fingers started to twist her hair into a French braid, but strands kept falling free. Hannah came up behind her, took Abby's hair from her hands, and began to braid it for her.

"Thanks," Abby said.

"If I were you," Hannah said, tugging a little too hard, "I would have dumped Zach a long time ago."

Abby thought about Hannah and Zach together. There were no special memories between them, no private jokes or secrets. She could picture them walking together in the woods, hunched over, all business, looking for pinecones or fossils, shells or broken glass, to go into collages that Hannah would never see.

"Not so hard," Abby said. She pulled away from her daughter slightly.

"What are you going to do? Be with Gavin and then take off for the summer with Zach? Marry Gavin? Divorce Zach? Neither? Both?"

Abby placed her hand over Hannah's, but Hannah drew hers away quickly.

"I'll never have a man ruin my life," Hannah said. "I'd rather live alone forever. I'd wear all white and let my hair grow like Rapunzel's and keep a hundred cats and walk on the beach, all alone, thinking lonely thoughts."

The closer they got to New York, the more nervous Abby felt. She hadn't been there in almost five years, when she and Hannah had gone home for Thanksgiving. Deirdre had set up three big tables, each with its own theme—one laden with fine china and heavily perfumed flowers, one with sleek black dishes and a single bird-of-paradise in an Erté vase, and one set with the pink speckled pottery that Abby had given as a Christmas gift one year and a mason jar stuffed with daisies. There had been two dozen guests, directors and actors and agents, and Deirdre had dominated them all. She had told the funniest jokes and the latest gossip while Toby got drunker and drunker. He dropped a plate of turkey—"Not the white meat," Deirdre had groaned—and sent the bird-of-paradise flying into another theme table while he did a bad imitation of Cary Grant.

The last time Abby had spoken to her mother, Deirdre had said Toby was drying out at a private place in Newport. That was over two months ago. As they made their way into the city, Abby wondered how long her father would stay sober this time. The memories of that Thanksgiving dinner, and the bird-of-paradise landing on the pink speckled plate, and her father saying, "Judy, Judy, Judy," combined with the jerking motion of Gavin's car, were making Abby feel sick. She rolled her window down and rested her head on the door, letting her face get sprinkled by a light rain.

Before Gavin brought his boxes of paper to the store, they agreed to meet in a few hours at Caffe Reggio. Then Abby was left alone on West Broadway in the drizzle. She started to head uptown, then stopped and inhaled deeply, trying to fill herself with as much of the smells of New York as she could. For a moment, she imagined that if she ran to Washington Square Park and stood under the Arch, Zach would actually appear.

He had told her when she'd left LA that he was leaving Nina, that this summer would be a new beginning for them. Standing here now, surrounded by art galleries and trendy boutiques, it seemed impossible. Abby knew that even if he came for them, even if they did drive to Mexico, September would still come. Zach would have excuses, stories, lies, to explain why he had to leave her and go back to San Francisco. This time, she would have left Gavin behind, and the winter would stretch before her, emptier than ever. No Three-Legged Horse, no Sean and Doug to keep her company. No Gavin.

It seemed to Abby, as she stood there fighting back memories and an impulse to run back to their old apartment just to see if the musical notes that Zach had painted across the tops of the walls for her were still there, that this time she had too much to lose. She couldn't leave Gavin for one more empty promise. She had made Le

Company. She could take Hannah and move to Bennington with Gavin. They'd go to the movies together, eat meals together, be a family. Abby imagined rehearsing her music in Gavin's sun-drenched living room while he made his beautiful paper.

She knew Gavin spoke the truth when he told her she would not be alone ever again. "We will get married," he'd said, "and have a dozen babies." Abby remembered the night Hannah was born, how she'd had to call Paco to take her to the hospital. She'd been frightened under the bright delivery lights, the white johnny decorated with faded teddy bears had slipped off her and exposed her swollen breasts and exaggerated stomach. The table beneath her had been cold and slippery and she had gripped its side with one hand while she'd tried to hide herself with the other, touching first her breasts, then her stomach, then finally covering her face.

It had been more than a week before Paco had located Zach to give him the news. She remembered how Zach had called her and shouted, "We did it!" We? she'd thought. But she had been so happy to hear his voice, she had let it pass. Instead she'd said, "We have to name her. The birth certificate says Baby Girl Plummer." For a while, Abby had thought this baby would have that name forever. "So," Abby had added, "you'd better get here fast." "Hell," Zach had said, "let's do it now." Abby had started to say that he had to see her, to know her, before he could choose her name. But already he was throwing names at her long distance, names like Violet and Spring, names, he'd said, that meant something to them. When they'd settled, finally, on Hannah, and they had hung up, Abby had turned to her tiny baby and said, "Well, you've got a real name now, Baby Girl Plummer."

Later, Deirdre had said, "Hannah? You named that sweet little thing Hannah? Hannah's an old lady's name.

Or a farmhand. 'Fetch the water, Hannah.' It's horrible.''
Then, just a year or two ago, hadn't Hannah herself had
the same complaints? She had told Abby that she was
surrounded by girls with beautiful names, Jennys and
Heathers and Lisas. "But you're our divine bounty. Our
nourishment from heaven," Abby had explained. "Our
manna." "Oh, please," Hannah had moaned. "Spare
me." Abby supposed it had been after that conversation
that Hannah had looked up manna in the dictionary.

Suddenly, Abby was filled with a sense of familiarity.
She looked around and was surprised to find herself in the
park after all. The Arch loomed in front of her, gray and
wet. She tried to conjure moments from the past, to
re-create them. If she could bring them forth now, she
could change them, like a time traveler.

But that was impossible. She stood and watched four
boys break-dancing, some old men playing chess. A couple in NYU sweatsuits, all purple and white, jogged past
her, their eyes closed, their faces damp with sweat. She
and Hannah could move back here, she thought for one
crazy instant. They would jog around the park, shop for
exotic food at Balducci's, read *The New York Times* every
day.

Abby shook her head. What a ridiculous thought. As
if she and Hannah could make it on their own. She
walked toward Sheridan Square, fighting back the idea.
Before Three-Legged Horse had saved them years ago,
she had been unhappy, unable to do anything right. But
still, the idea stuck in her gut. Abby hesitated. Here was
the subway that could take her uptown to her parents'
apartment. She could walk in there and tell them she was
at a crossroads. She could look at her mother and tell her
about Gavin, about Mexico. She could even say, perhaps,
"Or maybe Hannah and I will just try it alone." She'd

laugh at the idea, let her mother know she wasn't serious about it.

At the 72nd Street stop, Abby got off the train and stood gazing out at the apartment building where she'd grown up. The same architect who'd designed it had also designed the Arch in Washington Square. She'd learned that in elementary school. She headed toward the apartment, stopping only once, at the Beacon Bar. She pressed her face to the smoky glass, and peered in, expecting to see her father there, drinking away the afternoon. But the bar was empty except for the bartender, who stood cutting lemons and watching baseball on television.

The doorman stopped her in the lobby as she headed toward her parents' apartment. She recognized him. Manny. He had been there forever, scowling at everyone, forgetting to send up packages of Chinese food.

"Where you headed?" he said.

"It's me, Manny," she said, smiling at his grumpiness. "Abby Nash. Remember?"

He studied her, then waved her on.

Abby tried to plan her speech to her parents. "I'm playing in an orchestra," she'd say, and she could already hear her mother's cries of joy. "It's about time, kiddo," Deirdre would shout. Abby practically ran down the long hallway that led to the apartment. Everything smelled exactly like it used to—slightly musty, slightly like lemons and ammonia. A soprano practiced her scales in an apartment somewhere. In this hallway, Abby used to roller-skate and, later, play Frisbee.

She rang her parents' doorbell and banged on the door, still smiling.

"Come on," she said.

The door of the apartment beside theirs opened and a tall, thin man stuck his head out. He reminded Abby of a cartoon character made of rubber.

"They're gone," he said. "Miss Falls Church took him up to Newport."

"Newport?" Abby said. She remembered her mother's voice on the telephone. "He's drying out up in Newport," she'd said. "Costing me a fortune too."

The man clucked like a hen and shook his head. He knew what Newport meant, too, Abby thought.

The man slammed his door shut and Abby listened to the click of his locks and the slide of his chain across the door. She rang her parents' doorbell again, gave it a final, almost desperate push.

"I told you, they're gone," the man shouted from behind his door.

Abby sighed. She opened her pocketbook to find a piece of paper so she could leave them a note. All she had was a piece that Gavin had given her this morning. It still smelled woodsy and clean. There were delicate swirls of mauve in it, against vanilla, and there were tiny flecks of cranberry.

It seemed almost sinful to write on it. But it was just paper, Abby thought, and wrote: IN THE NEIGHBOR-HOOD. SORRY I MISSED YOU. *MUCH* NEWS! CALL AS SOON AS YOU GET BACK. ABBY. She slid the note as far as she could under the door, but its corner still poked out, a small pinkish edge.

Abby started to walk slowly down the hall, then stopped and went to the apartment next to her parents'. She knocked and knocked, but the man wouldn't answer.

She pressed her face to the door. "Excuse me," she said. "But what happened to the other man who lived here? The man who sang opera?"

She waited, but there was no reply.

"This came while you were in the Big Apple," Hannah said.

She held up two tickets to *'Night Mother* at Williamstown in July.

"Starring Deirdre Falls Church, of course," she added.

Abby took the tickets from Hannah and studied them, frowning.

She and Hannah were eating nacho cheese popcorn, and the strong smell hung in the air. Abby kept studying the purple-and-white tickets, as if they held more information than dates and times and seats, while Hannah was already talking about something else, the tickets forgotten, as they were every year.

"I'm telling you," Hannah was saying, "Sean and Mallory rent dirty movies. I saw them in the bag from the video store. They showed us *Ferris Bueller's Day Off* and *Pretty in Pink*, but after we were asleep they put on *Steamy Stewardesses*."

The last time Abby had seen her mother onstage was as Golde in *Fiddler on the Roof* at the Warwick Musical

Theatre in Warwick, Rhode Island. Abby and Hannah, who had been still a baby really, had gone to the show. Later, Abby had said to her mother, "See all the pain when parents won't understand their children?" Deirdre had just shaken her head as she'd smoothed off the thick pancake makeup with a fat, porous sponge. "That child," she'd said, "looks like something out of a Dickens novel. Don't you ever bathe her?" "I listen to her," Abby had said. "I try to understand her." Deirdre, her face white without the stage makeup, her eyes ringed in smudged black, had faced her daughter and said, "I hope what she says to you is never what I've had to listen to. I hope she never tells you that she's wasting her life, waiting for a man who's a charlatan, who doesn't even pretend to love her anymore. I hope Hannah talks sense when she grows up."

"And guess what else?" Hannah said. "Elijah still wets the bed. His whole room still smells like pee. I think he needs to be housebroken before it's too late. Or whatever you call it when kids need to be taught to use the toilet."

That night long ago, Abby had blushed when her mother, as Golde, had sung, "Sunrise, Sunset." She had felt that Deirdre was staring right at her, past the stage lights and crowded audience. Her mother, as always, had looked radiant that night, despite the peasant costume and pinned-up hair.

Abby said, "I think we'll go."

Hannah looked around. "To Sean's? Where?"

Abby held up the tickets.

"To the play?" Hannah said. "Next month?"

Abby nodded.

"But what about—"

They looked at each other.

"Did Zach call or something?" Hannah asked her.

"I haven't seen my mother onstage since 1978. *Fiddler on the Roof*. She was . . . extraordinary."

Hannah's mouth opened, as if she might speak, but Abby didn't give her a chance. "You know what?" she said to her daughter. "Let's go to Joe's for dinner. What do you say? I could kill for a Joe's hamburger."

Hannah had that feeling again, in her bones. That one that woke her up at night, that scared her. They weren't going to go with Zach this summer. Instead, her mother would practice that classical music on her violin all summer, and make fancy dinners for Gavin Berry. And nothing would be the same.

That night, when Hannah woke up, something was wrong. Different. It took her a minute to realize that instead of light and television voices coming from her mother's room, there was nothing. Just darkness, and quiet. Hannah looked around her own room, memorizing it. The violets on the wallpaper. The crooked shelf. She got out of bed and went into the hallway.

"Mom?" she said softly.

She pushed open her mother's bedroom door. The full moon seemed to hang right in the window, casting a soft white light over Abby and Gavin Berry. Hannah stood in the doorway for a very long time, looking at the tangle of her mother's hair and the paleness of Gavin's skin.

Back in her own bed, her heart pounded, and she recited, out loud, all of the state capitals, from Montgomery, Alabama, to Cheyenne, Wyoming.

Everyone was a little awkward the next morning. It was the first time that Gavin had slept at their house, and he stood, blushing and nervous, in the kitchen while Hannah and Abby tried to perform their usual morning routine.

Hannah sat at the table, eating Ring Dings and doing

her math homework, last minute, looking puzzled. Abby watched her daughter work and tried to think of something to do or say. Maybe, she thought, she should make breakfast. Or coffee, at least. Instead, she unwrapped a Ring Ding from its foil and slowly ate all of the chocolate off it.

"Today," Gavin said, "I'm driving to Boston to visit a new paper store there."

Neither of them answered him.

"To see," he continued, "if perhaps they will sell my paper."

Abby nodded. She picked up a frying pan, then sat with it on her lap. She thought, he does not belong here.

Hannah looked up from her math. "Are you cooking?" she said.

Gavin said, "They don't have any paper like mine there."

"I've got to run," Hannah said, leaving her homework on the table and grabbing instead two more Ring Dings.

"Okay," Abby said. She picked up the math paper. It was full of smudges and erasures, a jumble of numbers in no apparent order.

"I'm going to Chelsea's after school," Hannah said. "Can you pick me up there before dinnertime?"

"Okay," Abby said again. "Gotcha."

Gavin watched from the window as Hannah ran up the road toward Dara, her bright purple jacket flapping behind her, her one skinny braid pale pink against it.

"So," Gavin said when Hannah and Dara had disappeared from view, "perhaps you will come to Boston with me? We'll eat at Durgin Park. Yankee pot roast and baked beans."

Abby shook her head. Gavin was starting to bother her with his politeness, his gentility. "Britten awaits me," she said. "Rehearsals start in one month and I want to be ready."

"Ready?" Gavin said. "But rehearsals are to rehearse, right?"

She couldn't tell him that yesterday she had stared at the notes for hours, unable to decipher what exactly they meant. That she wanted, more than anything, to call Doug and Sean and play with them, to be, again, Three-Legged Horse. In the end, as the afternoon sky had begun to turn to mauve, Abby had walked away from the Britten score, lifted her violin, and played "Moonlight in Vermont."

"I really need the practice," she said.

Gavin said in his soft voice, "They have a strawberry shortcake there made from biscuits, fresh strawberries, and real whipped cream."

She could not focus on Gavin, or Boston, or strawberries. Instead, she found herself wondering if she could devise some ritual, a sunset serenade perhaps, that could bring Three-Legged Horse back together. She thought of how an old roommate of hers, Michelle Summersquash, used to burn candles to bring things to her. Love, work, money.

When the telephone rang, Abby thought, for an instant, that she had really made it happen. That, somehow, maybe by just wanting it badly enough, she had made Sean and Doug call her. She almost expected to hear one of their voices when she answered, almost expected one of them to be saying it had all been a mistake and Three-Legged Horse was booked through the winter, at Mount Snow and in Lenox and North Conway.

She did not expect to hear Zach.

"As proof of my good intentions," he said, "I am calling to give you my exact date of arrival so that you and Hannah will be packed and ready to go."

He sounded surprisingly close, and for an instant

Abby feared that he was already here, calling from the Citgo station in town.

"Three days," he said. "I'll drive straight through."

Abby turned away from Gavin, who stood frowning beside her, his palms pressed together as if in prayer.

"Three days?" she said. Yesterday, the Britten had seemed all wrong and she had longed for Willie Nelson's music, Woody Guthrie's songs, for Three-Legged Horse. Now, she found herself wishing that Gavin was gone, off to Boston or back to Bennington. She wished that she could climb into Zach's Plymouth Voyager and head south with him and Hannah. Hadn't she decided that she'd hold out for such a day? She made herself say in her mind, "I cannot do this to myself again." She made herself try to remember the way a symphony sounded.

Zach was saying "I know it's later than usual, but the gallery here still wants to do a show of my earlier stuff. I figured it was better to set everything up before we hit the road so we wouldn't have to rush back."

She listened to him as he weaved his story, his explanation. She did not even try to separate what might be true from what was fabrication. Hadn't there always been the promise of a show, a journey back together, a new start?

"We can find a little town on the ocean," he said, "and live like royalty. Tequila, tacos, and thou."

Gavin stood in front of her now, looking small and pale and not at all like a savior. He touched the tips of his fingers to his temples.

Abby said to herself, tell Zach not to come. Tell him that you are moving to Bennington, Vermont, with a man who makes paper. A man who keeps his word. When she had been a teenager, her mother had told her once as they waited in a winter rainstorm for her father to pick them up, "Someday you'll get married, Abby. Make sure he's a guy who keeps his word." Toby had never showed up that night. Deirdre had placed Abby's violin under her cloak to protect it, then the two of them had walked eighteen blocks. "Do you feel like Debbie Reynolds?" her mother had kidded. But Abby still remembered the way her jaw was set, hard and clenched like a fist.

Zach was still talking, and Gavin was still in front of her, pressing his head and frowning.

"It's only six o'clock here, but I couldn't wait to call you," Zach said. "Cairo took me to Spago last night. To celebrate. He actually bought a magnum of Dom Pérignon. Can you believe that?"

Once, Melissa had told her, "Abby, you're like a junkie, and Zach is your heroin."

"What about that other matter?" Abby asked him.

"She's still in London. But as soon as she gets back—"

"Right," Abby said.

"I've got this great idea for a new series. Remember Matisse's painting? 'The Waves'?"

"You took me to MOMA once just to see it," Abby said.

"Something big. To cover four walls."

The telephone cord had wrapped around her waist as she kept turning away from Gavin. She freed herself from it, twirling slowly, like a dancer.

"Ink me in," Zach said.

"Thursday," Abby said. "June 3."

Years ago, when Abby had first left New York, Deirdre used to send her clippings from newspapers and magazines, articles with titles like: "Yes! You Can Make Five Meals From One Chicken!" and "How to Be a Single Mother." "I'm not single," Abby had reminded her mother. "Remember Zach?" The next article Deirdre had sent her was: "Letting Go: Fantasy vs. Reality."

Abby had saved all of those clippings, most of them unread, in the drawer that now held notes from Hannah's teachers, ads for Three-Legged Horse, and countless other useless things. But now Abby pulled them out and read every one of them. They all had one thing in common when it came to advice. "Having trouble with that all-important decision?" they asked, in one way or another. "Make a list of pros and cons!"

After Gavin left for Boston, without mentioning the phone call from Zach, and Abby read the old, yellowed clippings, she took out a pad and pen and began her lists. GAVIN and ZACH. PROS and CONS.

Around the paper that said ZACH, she found herself drawing tiny rain showers of hearts, like the ones he used to draw for her long ago. She thought about how he was coming for them in three days, how the years of waiting were over. She said it out loud, to hear for herself if she could believe the words. "He's coming for us in three days," she said to the empty kitchen. "The waiting is over."

The telephone rang.

Gavin.

"I'm here," he said. "Safe and sound."

Abby's eyes drifted to the paper with GAVIN printed on top. It was blank except for his name. Under PROS she wrote: Reliable. Thoughtful.

"You made good time," she said.

He laughed nervously. "I drove eighty the whole way."

Drives fast, she wrote under CONS. Then she crossed it out.

"I'm worried," Gavin said.

His soft voice agitated her.

"What?" she said. "I can't hear you." Even though she could hear him just fine.

"I know that was Zach this morning. I know he's coming for you and I don't want you to go with him."

She didn't answer him. Instead, she added to the shower of hearts that filled the page that said ZACH on top.

"There," Gavin said. "I said it."

"Don't be silly." The lie caught in her throat.

"Really? I'm just being silly?" He laughed again. Again nervously.

"Yes," Abby said, irritated. "Now I've got to get back to practicing."

"Britten," he said.

"Goodbye," Abby said, and hung up.

She thought of practicing, but was afraid the notes would turn on her again. She thought of going into town and buying a jug of sweet wine, the kind you would never serve with dinner or for guests but that she liked just the same. When she stood, however, her knees wobbled and her hands shook, rattling her car keys.

"Damn it," she said.

It had happened. Zach was back under her skin. No matter how hard she had tried to make it be Gavin that did this for her, or how she had tried to replace thoughts of Mexico with the smell of fresh paper, still Zach overtook her.

Think of Gavin, she told herself. But all she got was a cold emptiness in her heart. And no matter what she tried to imagine, the coldness stayed. Even when she tried to picture an unknown, faceless man beside her, one who could give her a neat ranch house like the Kents had, with new flowered wallpaper and thick carpeting. All of it left her blank inside.

She reached for the phone and dialed a too-familiar number.

When Deirdre answered, Abby tried to sound strong.

"It's me," she said.

"Ah, the prodigal daughter."

Abby closed her eyes. Her voice broke. "I'm so mixed-up," she said.

"From that note you left me—"

The note. Just a delusion. Then the crazy notion hit her again—leaving them all behind, making a better life for her and Hannah without Zach or Gavin or a faceless suburban man.

"Hello," Deirdre sang. "Anybody there?"

"If I went away for a while," Abby said, "would you take Hannah? It wouldn't be for long." Just, she thought, until I found the strength to be on my own. To not depend on anyone.

"What about her father?" Deirdre was saying. "Why can't he take her?"

Abby didn't answer. Her mind was racing, her heart pounding with the thought of it.

"I see," Deirdre said coldly. "You want to take off with him and leave the kid with me."

Abby sighed. She could never do it. She could never make it on her own. "Forget it," she said. "It was a crazy idea."

Under the kitchen sink, beside the Comet and S.O.S pads, Abby kept a bottle of Jack Daniel's. She had bought it once for a man she'd been seeing but had never had to offer it, to even open it. He had faded that quickly from her life.

"From your note," Deirdre said, "I figured you'd done something good for yourself for a change."

Abby laughed, a hollow, harsh sound. "I'm joining an orchestra," she said. "Three-Legged Horse split up and I'm doing this now."

"For that," Deirdre shouted, "I'll take Hannah. Maybe

you are back on track. You could have been playing Carnegie Hall by now."

"I know," Abby said softly. "But I never really wanted to."

Her mother was talking over her, on and on about what should have been. Abby hung up, not wanting to hear.

She poured herself a cupful of Jack Daniel's and drank it down in two long gulps that left her shivering.

The radio was playing a waltz. Strauss, Abby thought, then changed the channel, stopping when she heard Joan Baez singing "Joe Hill." She started humming along, thinking that would be a good song for Three-Legged Horse. If there was a Three-Legged Horse.

Gavin called again, to tell her he was leaving Boston and heading home. Had she practiced? he asked. Should he stop by?

Under his name in the CONS column she wrote: PAIN IN THE ASS.

She finished off the Ring Dings, and most of the Jack Daniel's. She read her list out loud to see if it held any answers for her.

"Gavin," she read. "Pros: Reliable, thoughtful, makes paper, loves me. Cons: Pain in the ass, too nice, leaves me cold in the heart. Zach. Pros: Hannah, possible past life connection, I love him. Cons: Unreliable, untruthful, I love him."

Somehow, the lists made her feel better, clearer.

She dialed her mother's number again.

"Your clippings are right," Abby said. "Making lists helps make decisions."

"What on earth are you talking about?"

"I have it right here," Abby said. She searched for the articles that had guided her. But all she could find were recipes using hamburger meat, with Deirdre's advice written across them—"See, you can eat cheaply but still be creative." Abby sighed. "I see it all so clearly. What I was trying to do."

"Don't even tell me," Deirdre said, "that you've been drinking in the middle of the day."

"I would never do that," Abby said. "I am making lists. And a Moroccan hamburger casserole."

Deirdre's voice was tight and strained. "I cannot spend my life chasing after drunks. Do you hear me?"

When Doug and Sean showed up at her house the next day, Abby almost thought they had changed their minds. Three-Legged Horse had somehow won out. But then Doug set a box on the table and said, as he unpacked it, "Do you want this junk?"

It was all of their old sheet music.

The kitchen table seemed almost invisible under all of the paper that covered it. Looking down at it made Abby's eyes tear and her head ache. But looking away from it and at Doug and Sean was even worse. So she sat and stared at the pages, the orderly stanzas, the neat lines dotted with notes and G clefs.

"Maybe you could even sell it or something," Sean said. "At a flea market somewhere."

"Yeah," Doug said mechanically, like this too had been rehearsed and it was his turn to speak. "Make a few dollars if you can."

When she'd woken up this morning, she had known that she would go to Mexico with Zach. It was that simple. Over breakfast she had practiced Spanish phrases on Hannah. How much is this? she'd asked. Where is the bathroom? Hannah had refused to answer her, had sat and pretended to do her Social Studies homework, filling in a map of the United States, putting Kansas too far south, Oregon too far east. After she'd left for school,

Abby had sat, asking herself What is your name? Where do you live? Do you like tacos?

Her eyes darted from song to song, laid out before her like something special. Each time she settled on one, she could almost hear Three-Legged Horse singing it. Sean used to call the three of them troubadours. It had sounded old and exciting, medieval almost. Mallory used to say they were Peter, Paul and Mary rip-offs. "Except," she'd say, "no one has ever heard shit about Three-Legged Horse."

Abby smoothed down the rumpled corners of "Where Have All the Flowers Gone?"

"We haven't done this one in ages," she said.

Doug looked over her shoulder at it and groaned. "Thank God."

"I always liked that song," Abby said. "I mean, it's no 'F Troop,' but it has its merits."

She stood and swept all of the sheet music in her arms. Some of the pages floated to the floor, like sad confetti.

"I probably *will* sell these," she said. "I'll be selling a lot of the stuff here anyway."

"Well," Doug said, "if worse comes to worse you can start a fire with it."

"You have our number in Brooklyn?" Sean asked her, knowing that she had it. He had written it down for her himself.

He and Doug were moving toward the door, and Abby stood still and watched them as she clutched the music to her. Suddenly, she was overcome by nostalgia, for things she had not thought about for a long time—for the days when she and Doug had been lovers, his playfulness with her during that time, the way he had of touching her face gently with the back of his hand. For the dinners Sean and Mallory used to have for all of them—big pans of lasagna and bowls of fresh salad and Ben & Jerry's ice cream. The way, after a show, the three of them would sit at the bar and drink together, laughing and talking in the most familiar way. And the times that they would all take Hannah to pick apples, in the days when Hannah still felt she was young enough to go with them. Abby would feel at those times like she had a family. That there were people around who cared.

"You're okay," Doug said. "Right?"

Abby nodded.

Sean's eyes looked watery. "Abby?" he said.

"Yes," she said. "Yes. I'm fine." She was thinking that if they were really so worried, they wouldn't have split up the group. They would have stuck together. But she smiled at them and said, "Zach's coming tomorrow. We're going to Mexico for a while."

The words calmed her, just as they had the night before with Gavin. She had said them to him and felt better, despite the sad look that had come across his face and the way he'd stared at the pink linen tablecloth as if it held some mystery. They had been eating at a restaurant, an old mill, and after she'd told him that she really meant to go with Zach after all, Gavin had not eaten anything else. He had just said, quietly, "But you shouldn't. I would give you a better life. I would love you more." Then he had studied the pink tablecloth. He did not understand what she did—that Zach was the only one who could give her the kind of love she needed.

Doug shifted uncomfortably at the door. She heard him playing with the knob, clicking the lock, in and out.

"Well," Sean said, "if you need me—"

"I know," she said. "Brooklyn."

* * *

125

"Then," Hannah said, "you go like this, with your arm stretched out and your hand up like this."

She demonstrated for Abby.

Abby's eyes drifted to the clock on the stove. She had never switched it after daylight saving time. She added an hour. Four o'clock.

"And the song is going 'Stop! In the name of love . . .' " Hannah said.

"Hannah, can you show me this later?"

Abby had gotten up this morning filled with excitement. Zach is coming today, she'd thought as soon as she woke up. She had made a big pot of coffee in case he arrived early. She had kept Hannah home from school in case he wanted to leave right away. She had expected to hear the van drive up at any minute all day.

"Then you put your hand on your heart like this," Hannah was saying, "and the song is saying 'Before you break my heart . . .' "

Gavin had called at noon. "You haven't left yet?" he'd asked her. "You've changed your mind?" She had sighed, anxious to forget Gavin Berry, to have Zach arrive, to get on with their lives.

"Then," Hannah said, "it repeats. Got it?"

"Hannah—"

"Ready?"

"I don't really want to," Abby said. She would not look at the clock again so soon, she told herself. She looked. Four-oh-seven.

"You can be Diana Ross," Hannah said.

"Why can't you just sit here and wait with me?" Abby snapped at her.

"Because we've been doing it all day," Hannah said. "Because it's boring."

Abby said, "Was that someone driving up?"

"I'm going to Dara's."

126

When she left, Abby went back upstairs and changed her clothes again. She wanted to look beautiful. She wanted Zach to walk in and gasp when he saw her. She put on a long white skirt, a lavender-and-peach-striped blouse with tiny gold tassels hanging from threads at the neck and sleeves. Then she went back downstairs.

Sean called. "I know Zach's there," he said, "but I just want to be sure you have my new number."

She did not tell him that Zach wasn't there. Yet. "Yes," she said, "I have it."

When Hannah came home, Abby was still at the table, the room dark by then. She was sitting and remembering a long-ago night when she'd had a big recital at Juilliard. She had been playing a duet with Cecily van Buren. Flute and violin. Abby had worn a new dress, black velvet and antique ivory lace, with her first pair of high heels and her mother's pearls. Throughout the performance, Abby had kept peering into the audience, searching for her parents. They never showed up. Later, she would learn that her mother had spent hours in her emerald-green beaded dress, bought just for the occasion, searching for Toby in bars up and down Broadway. But that night, all Abby had known was that they were late, and then, finally, that they weren't coming. Even though Deirdre had shown her the new dress. "It was Elizabeth Taylor's, you know," she'd said. Even though they had promised they'd be there. Abby had stood afterwards, still scanning the crowd of students and parents hugging, clutching bouquets of roses, going off to the Ginger Man to celebrate. The Van Burens had invited her to join them at the Ginger Man. "Oh, no, thank you," Abby had said, forcing a smile. "My parents are having a party for me at home. A catered thing. You know." Then she'd walked home alone, wobbling up Broadway on her new high heels.

When Hannah walked in, she asked right away, "Is he upstairs?" Even though she knew he wasn't.

Abby said, "Maybe he had car trouble."

"It's eleven o'clock," Hannah said.

"Remember last summer how the radiator kept overheating? We had to keep stopping and putting water in it."

"He's not coming this time, is he?" Hannah said, her gray eyes wide.

"Technically," Abby said, "he has one more hour to get here today. Technically."

"I'm going to bed," Hannah said.

"I'll have Zach wake you when he gets in, okay?"

Hannah just walked away, her head bent, her feet shuffling across the unpolished floor like an old woman's.

Abby had read once that Picasso had treated women horribly, but they had still loved him, despite it all. One of his mistresses had said that all the pain was worth it for those times when all of his attention was hers. Abby had found that woman noble, understandable even, when she'd read that. But, of course, back then she'd had Three-Legged Horse, she'd had Zach, and the belief that it would all turn out happily somehow.

As the night wore on, the loss of all those things was the most real feeling she had. She began to pace around the rooms of the house. They looked shabby and run-down. She made herself say it out loud. "Zach is not coming." She said it again. "Zach is not coming." Hadn't she decided before they went to see him in LA that she was going to be a different person? A person who took control?

Goddamn it, she thought. Then do it. Take control. Her mother had said she'd take Hannah for a while. Deirdre was a person who knew how to fix things. Maybe she could help Abby fix her life. Abby walked through all the rooms again, turning on every light in every room. She saw the peeling wallpaper, the floors that needed polishing. In the kitchen, shining new among all the drab colors and mismatched furniture, was this ridiculous stool that Gavin had given her. A stool painted black and white like a cow, with wooden pink udders hanging under it. Abby sat on that stool and called her mother again.

When Deirdre answered all sleepy and soft, Abby did not hesitate. "Come and get us," she said. "I need to change my life."

Her mother's voice grew alert and confident right away. "I know a place that can help you," she said. "I'll call them tomorrow."

Abby hugged the phone close to her, as if it brought her mother and safety nearer. "Hannah can be a real handful," Abby said.

"She couldn't possibly be worse than you," Deirdre said. Then she laughed. "You weren't so easy yourself."

"Zach—" Abby started.

"From now on, we don't talk about him. Just hang up this phone and get your things together. We're on our way."

Abby didn't answer. A part of her was holding back, holding on.

"Did you hear me, Abby?"

Abby looked around at this sad, cluttered house with all the lights blazing. "I heard you," she said. "I'm ready."

Hannah woke to the sounds of her mother packing.

"He's here?" she said sleepily to her mother.

Abby did not reply, she just kept packing.

"He never came, did he?"

Abby sighed and sat on the bed beside her. "This isn't going to be easy," she said.

Hannah rested her head in Abby's lap. "What?"

129

"Leaving him. But it's time."

"How can we leave him if he never even came?" Hannah felt both frightened and excited at the thought. She rolled the phrase over in her mind. "Leaving him."

"Deirdre called it 'getting my act together,' " Abby said.

"She would," Hannah said.

Before Deirdre arrived for them, Zach called. They were sitting in the kitchen, waiting, their bags packed. His voice sounded faint and faraway.

"I had some complications," he told Abby. "I'll explain later."

Abby watched Hannah's face, her gray eyes waiting, looking sad.

"It'll be another month," Zach was saying. "I'll be there for July Fourth. Then we're on our way to Mexico."

Hannah bent her head. Not this time, Abby thought. This time I'm making all the decisions.

"I love you," he said, as if reaching across a vast distance.

But for once it did not matter. Already Abby was thinking ahead. She was imagining clean new spaces. Control. Order.

BLINI AND CAVIAR

Hannah sat in one corner of the walk-in closet of her grandparents' apartment. It was the only place where she could escape Deirdre's presence. Next door, a man practiced a dance routine. Over and over, a recorded voice shouted: "A One, Two, Three, Four!" Then music began and she heard the man start to dance, his feet shuffling across the floor, the click of tap shoes. Sometimes he stopped, muttered "Shit!" then started again. "A One, Two, Three, Four!" The music sounded vaguely familiar, like something Hannah had heard once a long time ago. She remembered trips to New York with her mother to visit Deirdre, who would dress her up in frilly dresses and soft velveteen shoes and take her to Broadway shows. As if from a dream, Hannah could remember a long-legged kick line, a baroque ceiling, crushed-velvet maroon chairs. She could remember her mother squirming uncomfortably beside her, dressed in an old dress with ivory lace. She could remember, perhaps, this song, and people wearing sparkling gold hats as they sang it.

Outside of the closet, Deirdre Falls Church rehearsed

her lines for 'Night Mother. "It's a two-woman tour de force," she had told Hannah. She had shown her the script, a crumpled red book filled with yellow Magic Marker lines and notes in Deirdre's cramped writing, like some Egyptian border along the pages. "What," Hannah had asked in a bored voice, "is a tour de force?" Her grandmother hadn't bothered to answer her.

Every day, for the five days that Hannah had been in New York, she had sat in the closet while Deirdre rehearsed, or talked on the telephone, or gave orders to her secretary, June, a thin woman with pale limp hair and large glasses that made her look like a bug. June answered all of Deirdre's fan mail from Day's Destiny, signing DEIRDRE FALLS CHURCH to the same glossy picture that hung in Hannah's room back in Vermont. Sometimes, even after June and Deirdre left to go to the television studio, Hannah stayed in the closet, listening to the man next door dance and to a steady whoosh that came from the hallway outside the apartment.

She was angry. At everyone. Zach and Deirdre and Gavin Berry and her mother. Especially her mother. Hannah had told her that she didn't want to go to New York; that Deirdre Falls Church smelled too floral, like a funeral parlor; that the smell was suffocating; that she would do anything if only the two of them could stay together. "They need teachers in Australia," Hannah had told Abby. "We can move to the outback and get a pet kangaroo. We can even make up new identities and no one will find us." Her mother hadn't even smiled. Instead, she had clutched the edge of the table so hard that her knuckles had turned white. "If we stay here," Abby had said, "we will take off with Zach again." Her mother's determination had frightened Hannah. "But I thought you loved him," she had said. "I am obsessed by him," Abby had told her. "Do you know that once I told him that I loved him more

than I loved myself? More than God. More than life."
"We could go to Paris," Hannah had pleaded. "We could
make up new identities." She had thought, Please don't
leave me.

But Abby had left her, that very day.

"If I stop and think about this," she'd said, "I won't
do it."

She'd packed Hannah's clothes into an old laundry
bag of Zach's, a rough burlap one stamped U.S. MAIL.
Hannah had kept her hands pressed against the faded
violets on the wallpaper of her room, as if they could
somehow give her strength, or keep her there. Abby had
told her, "This room is so gloomy. We should have painted
it. Yellow. Something bright, cheery." "No," Hannah had
said. "I like it this way." Her mother had looked up from
her packing. "It's so gloomy," she'd said again.

While they'd waited for Deirdre to come, Hannah
had kept asking her mother about Zach. Was he coming
for them? Would they be back in time? Abby had told her
about a play with a character named Godot, whom everyone was waiting for. "You know what, Hannah? He never
really comes."

"What's that supposed to mean?" Hannah had said.

But Abby had only shrugged and stared out the window, watching for the car.

"Aren't we even going to call Gavin Berry?" Hannah
had said, feeling panic filling her. "Or Sean and Mallory?"

Abby had laughed. "Right," she'd said, "Sean."

"I could maybe stay with them," she'd whispered.
"Until you feel better. Even if Elijah wets the bed it would
be better than going with Deirdre."

Her mother hadn't answered.

"What about Doug?" Hannah had asked, her voice
desperate.

Finally, her mother had looked away from the win-

133

dow and at her. "We have to start relying on *us*," Abby had said. "Three-Legged Horse is a thing of the past. Doug took off for LA today and he didn't even call to say goodbye."

"He's gone?" Hannah had said, not believing it. She was thinking that her whole life was crumbling, like the pictures of ancient buildings that she'd seen in geography class. The Acropolis, the Coliseum. She remembered all the nights she'd fallen asleep with her head on a table as Three-Legged Horse played in a corner nearby. She knew all of their songs by heart, and the order in which they performed them, and the jokes that they told the audience in between songs. She knew it all, the way she knew every inch of her room and every state's capital. The way she knew that every summer, no matter what, Zach would come and get them.

"Sean's got a job teaching music in Brooklyn," Abby had said.

"You could get new partners," Hannah had said. And then, as a last resort, she had said, "You could marry Gavin Berry."

"I don't want to marry him," Abby had said flatly.

"We could go with Zach like we're supposed to. Like we always do."

Abby had pointed out the window, to the gray Volvo that was pulling into the driveway.

"She used to fetch me in a limo," she'd said.

Hannah had scrunched her face up tight, so that she wouldn't cry when her grandmother walked in. Deirdre had been dressed in a red-and-white-checked cloak and a big red hat with a white flower stuck in it.

"*You* could teach music in Brooklyn," Hannah had whispered. "In France. Somewhere."

Her grandmother's boots were short and black, like Army boots.

"She looks so weird," Hannah had moaned as she watched her walk toward the house.

"She sure does," Abby had said, and for a minute she'd seemed to waver.

"Mom?" Hannah had said quickly, thinking of pictures she'd seen in school of the outback. The dust and aborigines, the animals and red sand, and the way it seemed to stretch out into forever. "In Australia, they have fish that walk. They have marsupials. They have opera in Sydney."

But Abby had already gone to the door to let Deirdre Falls Church in.

"All right, kiddo," her grandmother said into the closet. "Have I got a surprise for you."

The closet door opened and Deirdre worked her way through the clothes, toward Hannah, who was pressed into the farthest corner.

"Lunch," Deirdre said. "At the Russian Tea Room, no less."

She waited for a reaction. When she got none, she said, "We have got to find you something to wear. Your mother dresses you like a ragamuffin."

Hannah looked at her grandmother's plum suede boots and silk dress with extra large shoulder pads.

"You," Hannah said, "look like a football player."

Deirdre hooted. "That's a good one," she said. "Say what you think. I like that. But you know something? A person has got to have style, kiddo. It's style that gets a person through."

Hannah sighed and wondered what Deirdre Falls Church had ever had to get through. Next to her grandmother, Hannah felt very old.

"Style doesn't pay the rent," Hannah said, repeating

something she'd heard her mother say more than once to Deirdre over the telephone.

Again, her grandmother hooted. "Oh, yes, it does," she said. "Don't ever forget it."

"Forget what?" Hannah said sullenly, trying to make her grandmother leave her alone.

"Come on," Deirdre said. "Let's go into the study and find you something to wear."

Her grandparents had long ago turned Abby's old bedroom into a study. Since Hannah had arrived, she'd been sleeping on the couch in the living room. While Deirdre was out of the apartment, Hannah searched the study for signs that her mother had lived here once. She wanted to find anything to feel some connection with Abby, who was somewhere upstate, at a place that would help her, as Deirdre had put it, "get her act together at last." When they'd dropped Abby off there, she had told Hannah, "I hope they give me Swedish massages and baths with salt from the Dead Sea and anything else that it takes." "Can they give you Zach? Or me? Or our house?" Hannah had asked, refusing to look at her mother. "She'll be a new woman," Deirdre had said. She had sounded, to Hannah, victorious, as if she'd won a very important battle. Now, Hannah wished she had hugged her mother goodbye, had told her she understood, that she believed in her. So she searched the high-ceilinged apartment for some sign that her mother had been here, even if it had been a long time ago.

In the study, Deirdre held up three dresses for Hannah's inspection.

"I gave most of your mother's stuff to Goodwill," Deirdre said. "No use cluttering up the place, I say."

Hannah fingered the antique lace collar of one of the dresses, a black velvet one that still looked new.

"She wore that once," her grandmother said. "And

believe me, it cost a fortune. I couldn't bear to see it on some bag lady sitting on Amsterdam Avenue."

"Very charitable," Hannah muttered.

Deirdre was saying, "Your clothes are pitiful. Long skirts. Uneven hems. Broken zippers. We've got to get you some decent things."

"I'm not staying very long," Hannah said sharply. "Don't worry about it. In Vermont, where we live, they don't care so much about fashion."

"Well," her grandmother said, "I have to look at you while you're here."

Hannah began to unbutton the velvet dress.

"Fine," she said.

"You absolutely cannot wear velvet in June. You'll sweat to death." She surveyed the other two dresses. "This one is lovely."

It was pale yellow, covered with tiny pink roses.

"Disgusting," Hannah said.

"You're absolutely right. Too sweet. Goodwill gets it tomorrow."

Hannah took the last dress from her grandmother.

"This dress," Deirdre said, taking it back from her, "belonged to Twiggy. It really did. I bought it at this terrific shop on Seventh Avenue that sells clothes from movies and television. I've given them some of Dulcinea Day's clothes."

"Twiggy," Hannah said, wondering who Twiggy was and why she had worn something so short and so orange.

"It's perfect," Deirdre said. "Very 'now.' Everything comes back. It's true, if you only wait long enough. I still have my father's raccoon coat from the twenties, and that's come in and out more times than you can imagine. The thing smells like a giant mothball." She handed Hannah the dress again. "If you cut off that braid you have, your hair would look just like Twiggy's, too."

"I don't want to look like Twiggy."

Deirdre acted like she didn't hear her. "I have these wonderful rubber earrings. And these terrific boots. What a getup! We'll go to the Russian Tea Room and make quite a stir."

Hannah looked at the orange dress. "I bet we will," she said.

Hannah felt ridiculous sitting in a fancy restaurant in a dress this orange. She completely clashed with the decor. On the way here, she'd left the large black rubber earrings with the lime-green stripes in the cab. They were that awful. Before they'd walked into the restaurant, Deirdre had said, "Wouldn't it be fun if Twiggy was here? Not that she would be, but I mean, if she *were*, wouldn't it be a kick?" She hadn't seemed to notice that the earrings were missing.

Hannah had almost asked her grandmother then who exactly this Twiggy was.

Instead, she'd just muttered, "Who cares?"

It seemed to Hannah that Deirdre never really talked *to* people. She talked *at* them. On the ride to New York, the three of them had been completely silent except for Deirdre's occasional exclamations about the wonders of the place she was taking Abby. "It's an entire syndrome, what you have. They'll fix it up," she'd announced, not caring that neither of them responded. As soon as Hannah was in the car alone with her, Deirdre had said, "That father of yours should be put away." Before Hannah could decide whether to agree or to defend Zach or to ignore her grandmother altogether, Deirdre had put on a tape of a man reading *Moby Dick* in a slow, fake British accent. At one point, she'd announced, "Abby may just finally pull herself together. She may still turn around. The day that man walked into her life, he ruined her. With his talk of love and destiny. All crap. And she fell for it like a—"

"She got into Le Company," Hannah said angrily, rushing to her mother's defense.

The only other thing her grandmother had said was miles later, when she'd looked at Hannah and asked, "Why do I always feel so bad for the damn whale?"

It had been a long time before Hannah had figured out what her grandmother had meant.

Hannah finally realized, after just a few days with Deirdre, that she wasn't expected to respond. Her grandmother said things for the sake of saying them, or to command attention, or to take control. In the Russian Tea Room, Hannah sat quietly as her grandmother made her pronouncements and observations.

Deirdre ordered them tea. It came in tall glasses perched in silver holders.

Hannah frowned when she saw them.

Why, she wondered, didn't the glass break when the hot tea was poured into it? She and her mother had once bought tall glasses with faded green shamrocks on them at a flea market. "For Irish coffee," the vendor had told them.

Abby had thought they were wonderful. She'd explained to Hannah that Zach had taught her the way real Irish coffee should be made. "Like in San Francisco," she'd said. "At the Buena Vista."

By the way her mother had looked, with her eyes cloudy and faraway and a dreamy smile on her face, Hannah had known that Abby was all wrapped up in the past again. In Zach and memories of the good times. In the end, they'd spent over ten dollars between the glasses and all the special ingredients needed to make authentic Irish coffee. They'd had to buy confectioner's sugar, and heavy cream, and a good Irish whiskey. As Hannah had watched her mother assemble everything and brew the coffee, she'd felt herself growing angry at her. This, Hannah had thought, is a waste of time. Abby had held up the glasses, dripping wet and sudsy. "The shamrocks," she'd said sadly, "are all coming off." "Great buy," Hannah had grumbled. She'd imagined all the things that ten dollars could buy. Curtains for some of the bare windows. A meal at Pizza Hut. A million things.

"This is going to be so delicious," Abby had told her. "You spend a day in San Francisco in the cold, wet fog and you really appreciate one of these."

Hannah had glanced out at the Indian summer afternoon, at the sunlight pouring into the kitchen, dancing off the fake-stained-glass items her mother had hung on the window above the sink. More silly flea market purchases. A teapot, a clown's face, a sailboat, all dangling from suction hooks.

"Here goes," Abby had said proudly.

She'd poured the hot coffee into the prepared glasses. Each one of them had cracked, then shattered with a loud pop, while Abby and Hannah had sat and watched.

Hannah studied the glass full of tea. It was perfect and intact.

"I think," Deirdre said, "I'll just have the blini. And some caviar. What do you say?"

Hannah shrugged. The menu was filled with unfamiliar foods, long lists of them. Blini, she thought, searching for it on the menu, trying to picture in her mind what it might be.

Her grandmother ordered, then turned to Hannah.

"Did your mother raise you in any religion?" she asked.

Hannah thought for a minute.

"Zach's a Buddhist," she said finally.

"A Buddhist!" Deirdre laughed. "A fraud's more like

it. The day I met him I saw right through him. With all his talk about past lives and auras and all that nonsense. If only Abby had seen through him too we all wouldn't be in this predicament right now."

"He says that his Japanese ancestors—"

"Really, Hannah. He's as Japanese as I am. The man is a fraud." Deirdre shook her head. "He's like Rasputin."

The name sounded familiar to Hannah, but by the time she remembered the face of a big black dog named Rasputin that someone from school had had, Deirdre was on another topic altogether.

"Does anyone in that godforsaken town you live in watch *Day's Destiny?*"

Hannah tried to picture her school, or the road that led to her house, or even Dara. But they were as fuzzy as her memories of her early trips to New York and the Broadway shows she'd seen then.

She sighed. "Yes," she said, "they watch it. Everybody loves Kira and Austen."

"Those twerps?" Deirdre said. "What is it about those two?" Her voice dropped to a whisper. "Do you know I'm only on two or three times a week, thanks to them and their ridiculous adventures?"

"I hadn't noticed," Hannah said, although she had.

"Do you mean that your friends actually believe that Emily could have lived through an avalanche, a train wreck, and a terrorist attack?"

"Who's Emily?"

"Emily Smith-Martin. Aka Kira Day. She was also Kira's evil twin, Kelly. The woman's gobbling up every minute of airtime she can get. Do you know that they are actually bringing Kelly back from the dead? She's responsible for that train wreck. And she had Austen's baby."

"Wow," Hannah said.

The waiter brought their lunches.

Hannah studied her plate. Pancakes, she thought. With sour cream. Disgusting.

"I'll tell you what," Deirdre said as she piled caviar onto her blini. "I'll autograph some photos for your friends. I'll sign them myself. Dulcinea Day. What do you say?"

Hannah looked around her, at the heavy red ornamentation in the restaurant, and the wiggly red fish eggs on her grandmother's pancakes, and the amber tea in her glass.

"No," she said. "Thanks anyway."

Vermont, and her friends, and Abby all seemed very far away.

SEARCHING FOR
SAINTS AND GHOSTS

Three teenagers from Newark, New Jersey, claimed they were having visions in Washington Square Park. They said a woman appeared to them, near where the old men sat and played timed chess. The woman was see-through, they said. Like a ghost. She wore long-flowing pale blue and white robes. Her hands were as tiny as a child's.

When Deirdre came home from taping *Day's Destiny*, Hannah was waiting for her, clutching the *New York Post*.

"I want to see her," she said to her grandmother. She jabbed the paper. The headlines said: MADONNA TO SPEAK!!! "I want to see the Madonna."

"She's not the Madonna," Deirdre said. "She's some boy's crack hallucination."

Today, at work, Deirdre had had only two lines, both delivered in a hospital waiting room. She'd said, "Doctor, is Kira going to live?" The doctor was her ex-son-in-law and the real father of Kira, though Dulcinea Day didn't know that. She'd turned to all the waiting people. "That's what we all want to know, isn't it?" she'd said. Organ music. Close-up on everyone's horrified faces.

"One of the boys," Hannah was explaining, "brought his grandmother's rosary beads and the vision reached out, touched them lightly, and bowed her head. When he got back to New Jersey, he pulled the beads out of his pocket and they had turned to gold."

"Who is thinking up this stuff—the writers from *Day's Destiny*?"

"Well," Hannah said, "I believe it."

Then she went into the closet.

The man next door had left for a tour with the road show of *A Chorus Line*. Don't you remember when we went to see that? her grandmother had asked her. Then she'd described it to Hannah—the costumes, the characters' stories. She'd even sung one of the songs for her. But Hannah had pretended not to remember, even though she had a vague recollection of it, of that day. Now, when she went into the closet, the only thing she heard was that steady whoosh from the hallway.

Her grandmother knocked on the closet door.

"I'm ordering Chinese. Any requests?"

Hannah thought about the frozen egg rolls she and her mother sometimes ate for dinner, little squares that they dipped in French's mustard. Whenever they had them, Abby would sigh and say, "The best Chinese food in the world is in New York. Even better than China."

Hannah looked down at the newspaper, at the fuzzy-faced boys on the front page. She wondered why the vision had come to these three boys, what message it held for them, for her. Lately, at night, Hannah woke up screaming, calling for Zach. It was as if her mother was never coming back. As if she'd gone into one of those small shuttered cabins upstate forever. Yesterday, Hannah had tried to find Zach. She'd called Information in Los Angeles, but couldn't remember the name of the man who had gone to Venice, Italy, and let Zach use his apartment. She had called Information in San Francisco, but there was no Zachary Plummer listed there. When she'd hung up, she had felt like Zach was her last hope, the only person who could bring her mother back to her. Her future seemed long and empty, her time here in New York, in this closet, with her grandmother, endless.

"Do you like it spicy?" Deirdre was calling to her. "Fiery?"

"Go away," Hannah said.

"Kiddo," Deirdre muttered, "you are a pain in the ass." She leaned against the closet door and closed her eyes. She had never smoked in her life, but there were times when she craved a cigarette. Like now. She couldn't explain how she could crave something she'd never even tasted, but she sometimes did. She believed that as a teenager, she'd craved caviar without having had it. And good champagne. She believed that people didn't listen to these things their bodies told them. If they did, they could be guided by them. Deirdre tossed her head back and imagined herself taking a long drag on a cigarette. Menthol. It would, she knew, taste wonderful.

In the cab on her way home from the studio, she'd opened Monday's script, searching for the pink Hi-Liter that June used to indicate her lines. There were none. For fifteen years she'd played the dominant, conniving, two-timing Dulcinea Day. She'd played her beautifully. There were three Emmys on the mantel to prove it, and scrapbooks full of interviews and pictures. The last time a television show had called her to appear was when Regis Philbin had aging soap opera actresses on to discuss how their parts were deteriorating. "I'm not aging or just a soap opera actress," she'd shouted. She'd listed all of her stage roles, her shows in Williamstown. The production assistant who'd called her had thanked her and hung up before she could finish.

Last week, she'd had to fight to get rid of a line they'd wanted her to say. "How about some of my famous oatmeal cookies, Kira? They always make you feel better."

"This woman," Deirdre had screamed, "has never baked cookies in her life. She's screwed half the town, embezzled money from her own father, was suspected of killing off two of her husbands, and even poisoned her sister. Do you think she had time to bake goddamn cookies?"

"That was ages ago," the producer had moaned. "No one remembers that stuff."

"*I* remember," Deirdre had said.

In the end, they had cut the line. But they still hadn't let her say what she maintained Dulcinea would have said: "How about a good stiff drink, Kira?" They had settled for letting her make a pot of coffee.

What Deirdre wanted, besides a cigarette and some decent lines, was for her granddaughter to leave. She shuddered at the word. "Granddaughter." When Hannah was a baby, Deirdre used to find it almost funny when people thought Hannah was her daughter. She had enjoyed telling them that she was her *grand*daughter and then watching their mouths open in surprise and hearing them say that was impossible. "You're too young to be a grandmother," they'd tell her. And they'd mean it. But now, Deirdre was afraid people would believe her right off. Assume, even, that Hannah was her granddaughter, that she was, of course, old enough to be a grandmother. It made Deirdre uncomfortable having Hannah around all the time, reminding her constantly of the fact that she was already thirteen, with breasts, practically. Looking at her in that awful haircut made her feel old. And it made her think of Zach, who had the same high cheekbones, the same dark hair.

What was almost worse than all that was the way—like Zach, now that Deirdre thought of it—Hannah had scorned everything. Or questioned it. Or seemed to pretend to know more than she did about things. Even the way Hannah asked Deirdre about work every night seemed mocking. "How's life on *Day's Destiny*?" she'd asked, not even trying to sound really interested. Just smiling a little, the very outmost corners of her mouth turned up a bit, her eyes focused elsewhere—on the television or a tabloid. And then when Deirdre had tried to show her one of her scrapbooks—from 1970, too, one of her best years—Hannah had said, "Maybe tomorrow." She had even yawned. She was, Deirdre thought, more interested in that ridiculous vision downtown.

"The Madonna," Deirdre said out loud.

Hannah walked out of the closet.

"What did you say?"

Her grandmother shook her head.

"And what is that sound in the hallway?" Hannah said. "It's driving me nuts."

"If you didn't sit in there," Deirdre said, "you wouldn't hear it."

"But I do sit in there."

"It's a boy. On a skateboard."

"Oh."

They looked at each other. They had absolutely nothing to say to each other.

Finally, Hannah said, "She's going to speak tomorrow."

"Who?"

She rolled her eyes. "The vision. The transparent woman in flowing robes."

"If she hasn't spoken yet, how did she tell them she was going to speak tomorrow?"

"They just know," Hannah said.

Deirdre studied her granddaughter's face. There was something old about it. Old and tired. Once, Abby had told her that she believed Hannah had been her mother. "In another life," she'd added.

"Your mother," Deirdre said, "could have been a concert violinist. She could have studied in Vienna."

Hannah frowned. "This was before Three-Legged Horse," she said. "Right?"

"Darling, everything was before Three-Legged Horse."

"Nothing was," Hannah said. "Except Zach."

Deirdre laughed. "Believe me," she said, "your mother's life did not start with Zach."

"Yes, it did," Hannah said.

Hannah's face, Deirdre thought, was exactly like Zach's.

"Do you remember telling me once about a man chugging an entire pitcher of beer?" Deirdre said. It had been one Thanksgiving, and Hannah had announced it proudly, a real feat to have seen such a thing.

She shrugged. "I don't know," she said. "Lots of people can do that. They do it all the time."

"I guess you're right."

"Big deal."

Deirdre hesitated, then said, "All right, kiddo. Tomorrow we'll go and hear what the Madonna has to say for herself."

"We can go?" Hannah said, her eyes flashing.

It was the first sign of excitement she'd shown since she'd arrived in New York.

Washington Square Park was crowded with people hoping to see the vision that the teenaged boys had described. Over breakfast that morning at Sarabeth's Kitchen, Hannah had explained the possible identities for the ghostly woman dressed in robes.

"The Madonna is most likely," she'd said. "But she could also be the spirit of a woman. Maybe someone who died in that very spot."

Her grandmother had not looked up from *The New York Times.*

"Her message," Hannah had said, "could change the world."

When they arrived in the park, they saw the three boys from Newark standing on a podium under bright television lights.

"She kind of floats," one of them was saying, "right over there."

"So her feet don't touch the ground?" the Channel 7 newsman asked.

"No," the boy said. "Not at all."

Hannah looked toward the spot he was pointing to. It was roped off and guarded by police on horseback. She wondered if the vision would appear with such a big crowd here and the cameras rolling, broadcasting her live on TV. She wished everyone would leave so that the woman would come and speak to her.

". . . so we says, 'Should we come again?' and the lady nods. And we asks her why we should come. And she takes one finger and touches her throat, and then she touches her lips." The boy demonstrated as he spoke. The nod, the sweep of the lips.

Hannah turned to her grandmother. "See," she said. "That's how they knew she was going to talk."

"Maybe she had a fish bone stuck in her throat," Deirdre said.

Hannah focused on the three boys from New Jersey with such intensity that her grandmother began to doubt if it had been a good idea to bring her here.

"Those two are brothers," Hannah told her.

All three boys looked alike to Deirdre—black hair

that seemed to be oiled somehow, thick eyebrows, and all wearing unlaced sneakers and black leather jackets. The one who was doing all the talking had a boy's first mustache above his upper lip, a downy black line.

Now the boys were kneeling in front of the police rope.

The crowd grew silent.

After what seemed like a very long time, the boy with the mustache said, "Isn't she beautiful?"

His voice was so awestruck, so young, that Deirdre almost believed he was seeing something.

The crowd, in unison, sighed with relief. She had come. She would speak.

Hannah craned her neck to see. There were only the boys kneeling, the police on horseback, the empty spot of grass beside the chess tables. All around her, people were making the sign of the cross, dropping to their knees.

"Do you see anything?" Deirdre whispered.

Hannah did not move her gaze from the spot. "No," she said. "Do you?"

"No."

The boys were pleading.

"Do you have a message for us?"

"Is it about Russia?"

"Is it about AIDS?"

"Those are silly questions," Hannah said.

Some people were leaving, shaking their heads and laughing.

Someone shouted, "Fraud!"

Suddenly, the boy with the mustache jumped to his feet. He shouted, "We will! We will!"

The other boys jumped up too, reaching toward the empty space in front of them.

"Don't go," one of them begged.

The boy with the mustache turned toward the crowd.

"For youse guys who couldn't hear her, she said, 'Fight for peace.' She said it twice, real quiet-like. And real sad."

"I heard her," a woman said. "Clear as a bell."

Hannah looked at her grandmother.

"Fight for peace?" she said. "That doesn't even make sense. *Fight* for *peace*? It's a . . . a . . . contradiction."

She looked so defeated that Deirdre placed her hands on Hannah's arm. She was surprised it was so skinny, so small.

"Let's get out of here," Hannah said, pulling away from her.

As they headed out of the park, toward Fifth Avenue, Deirdre said, "I thought we could go to the Forbes Museum." She hadn't been thinking it at all. But her fingers still felt the tininess of Hannah. She wanted somehow to do something for her, to make her eyes shine that way again. The symphony used to do that for Abby. Deirdre could still remember the way Abby, as a young girl, had sat, eyes closed, body swaying, on a blanket in Central Park one summer night while the New York Philharmonic had played the *1812 Overture*. Later, the sky had exploded in a brilliant burst of fireworks, spreading over them like magic. Abby had tilted her head back, her eyes wide, and had reached upward with her arms, as if she could embrace it all—the night, the music, the bright sky.

"It's right up here," Deirdre said. "Wait until you see the Fabergé eggs."

Hannah said, "Of course, if it's just some ghost, she could be saying that to make trouble. She could be a Communist or something, working against us, telling us to fight."

"The museum's right on Fifth," Deirdre said.

Instead of following her, Hannah stood, frozen.

"That arch," she said.

She looked around her. Somehow, she had come to the very spot her mother had so often described. The spot where Abby had played Vivaldi on a cool spring day, and Zach had told her he was going to marry her. Hannah took a deep breath, as if she might be able to taste or feel the love that had been in the air that day. Maybe, she thought, there was a little bit left, floating around.

She walked to the very place where she imagined her mother had stood, playing. There was no juggler, no contortionist smoking a cigarette with her feet. The only music came from two oversized radios. George Michael sang "Faith" on one. George Harrison sang "Back Whan We Was Fab" on the other.

It meant something, she was sure, that she had ended up here today.

She closed her eyes, trying to bring to life her mother's story. But when she opened them, there was no trace of it, just her grandmother staring at her.

"Hannah," Deirdre said, "what were you expecting the vision to say?"

"Answers," Hannah said. She felt like she was going to cry. She wanted to sit down right here and sob.

"What answers? Answers to what?"

"To anything," Hannah said.

Sometimes, Abby and Zach talked about how ideas and emotions floated in the air, through time and space, bumping into each other, separating, reuniting. She had thought that if she ever came to this spot, their love and connection would still be here. That it would float to her, and attach itself to her. But now, standing here, Hannah felt alone. She felt that perhaps she floated free from them, while Abby and Zach kept finding each other, again and again, beyond time and space. Beyond everything.

"Let's get out of here," Hannah said again.

She turned once, hoping still to see a woman, floating above the ground, wrapped in transparent robes. Or a woman standing under this gray arch, playing the violin while a man in a blue pea coat moved, inevitably, toward her.

But she saw neither woman, heard no answers, no Vivaldi.

On the street corner, a man held a Polaroid snapshot out to a small group of people.

Hannah pushed her way through to see it.

There were the three boys from Newark, New Jersey, kneeling. There were the policemen, the horses, the ropes. Above the empty strip of grass, floating, was a metallic blue haze.

Hannah stared at the picture. She could almost see a woman's figure, arms outstretched, head bent, in the midst of the haze. But the harder she stared, the vaguer the figure seemed. She blinked, and it disappeared, became just a spot of blue in the middle of the picture.

Again, her grandmother rested her hand on Hannah's arm. This time, she didn't shrug it off. She let it rest there.

"Probably just the flash going off," Deirdre said.

Hannah nodded.

Behind them, as they walked away, up Fifth Avenue, the crowd on the corner continued to argue over the blue spot in the photograph. Even though she wanted to, Hannah didn't turn around.

TOUCHING STARS

"Hey," Hannah shouted. "You with the skate-board."

She hung, swinging slightly, on the edge of the door, and called to the boy on the skateboard at the far end of the long dingy hallway. Her grandmother had told her that this building had once been grand. Now, the brocade wallpaper that lined the halls was beginning to fray and fade, the once-dark maroon carpeting had turned a dull pink in spots, and the ornate molding along the ceilings had blended into chalky spots, smudged cherub faces, and chipped wings. "That must have been a real long time ago," Hannah had said.

The boy did not move closer to her. Rather, he stood at the end of the hall and rolled back and forth on the skateboard, slowly, making short jumps as he reached a corner.

"That noise is driving me nuts."

He didn't answer her. Instead, he took off his glasses and carefully wiped them on the edge of his shirt.

"I'm stuck in here all day and all I can hear is you and that stupid skateboard," she continued.

When he still didn't answer, she started to go back into the apartment.

"Nobody," he called to her as she was closing the door, "wears their hair like that anymore."

She slammed the door. Hard.

"Jerk," she muttered.

Then she took a deep breath. Oh, no, she thought. Her heart was pounding and she felt sick to her stomach. I must be losing my mind, Hannah said to herself. The boy wasn't even cute, and here she was with her heart beating fast and her stomach feeling like she might throw up.

This had happened before, never when she had expected it to. Last year, she had fallen in love with her French teacher, Mr. Field. Every time she sat down in that class, she thought she was going to faint. Her stomach jumped around for the entire hour, while all around her everyone was conjugating *avoir* and *être*. Then, as quickly as it had hit her, it left. Mr. Field still drove away from the school in his dark green Triumph, shouting *à bientôt* as he passed her and Dara waiting for the bus. He still wore the same cologne, Vanilia, that made him smell like the Häagen-Dazs store at the mall. He still held his head in his hands and moaned, "Imbeciles!" whenever the class did poorly on pop quizzes. But now, all those things left Hannah cold, whereas before, one sniff of Vanilia had sent her reeling.

Then it happened with Brent Balboa. And Kirk Cameron on TV.

"Whenever I go into science class," Hannah had told her mother, "and see Brent, I want to puke."

"Does he smell bad?" Abby had asked her.

She tried a different approach. "When you talk to Zach, do you feel sick?"

Her mother had nodded. "Sometimes. Like someone has torn my heart out and ripped it in two, leaving me only half."

Hannah had groaned. "Not like that." She tried again. "What does love feel like?"

Then Abby had smiled her sad smile, and thought for a long time. "It feels like you can touch the stars."

"I think," Hannah had said, giving up, "it feels like throwing up."

Her mother's romantic ideas, and the predicament that was their life, had made Hannah decide that if she ever really fell in love, she would go off to Africa to help starving children. Or to Antarctica to do penguin research. Anyplace where they could not rip out her heart and tear it in two.

But it seemed like love lurked in the most unlikely places. While she was watching television, or memorizing French vocabulary words—ZAP! It struck. Or the day she walked into Earth Science class, thinking about how she had not done her homework, trying to figure out an excuse to give the teacher, and Brent Balboa leaned over and said to her: "How many dinosaurs did it take to screw in a light bulb?" She'd shrugged. "None!" He'd laughed. "They didn't *have* light bulbs!" She had looked away from the homework questions at the end of the chapter on earthquakes and into eyes the color of grass. She felt, immediately, like she might be sick. Or have a heart attack. But instead, she laughed, even though the joke wasn't funny.

But since she'd been in New York, the thought of Brent Balboa hadn't affected her at all. In fact, his face had faded into the blur that was Vermont and home and everyone she'd known there. She'd asked her grandmother if she thought it was possible to get amnesia for just some things, and remember others.

"On *Day's Destiny*," Deirdre had said, "people are always getting amnesia. And they don't remember a damned thing."

Hannah had wanted to explain to her that although she knew who she was, and where she was from, and who her parents were, everything else was fading from memory.

"There's this boy," she'd said, "and I used to even dream about his face. I used to think his eyes looked like grass. But now I can hardly remember anything about him."

"His eyes looked like grass?"

"Well," Hannah said, "he wore green contact lenses."

Deirdre had said, "That's marvelous. Jot it down. Jot down things like that. Maybe someday you'll be a writer."

"That's not what I mean," Hannah had said. But her grandmother was already thrusting a pad and pen at her.

"Finally," Deirdre had said, "I see what it is you do. You're a writer. I worried. Even your mother had the violin. She used to love that violin. She should have gone to Vienna to study. You know, last spring I had to sit through someone's premier concert at Carnegie Hall—on the viola—and it just killed me. That, I said to myself, should be my Abby."

Somehow, it had all made Hannah want to call her mother. To ask her about amnesia and Vermont, to ask her why she'd never gone to Vienna. But there were no telephones at the sanatorium upstate where Abby was getting herself together. So Hannah had had to sit in the closet and try to figure it all out by herself, with her grandmother shouting in to her to write down her thoughts. "Eyes like grass!" Deirdre said. "Don't forget that one!" Hannah tried to remember if her mother had ever mentioned Vienna to her, even once. But she couldn't. Whenever they took off with Zach, though, Abby always left her

violin behind. Maybe that meant something. She'd tried
to place herself back in Earth Science class, with Brent
beside her making rumbling noises like an earthquake.
She used to write his initials over and over in her note-
book, in big letters, small letters, surrounded by hearts.
She used to believe that tides and rocks and glaciers were
inconsequential compared to Brent Balboa's fake green
eyes. And it was as if all of that had happened to some-
body else.

Now, here she was having palpitations over some
boy with glasses. A boy who had insulted her. Maybe,
Hannah thought, horrified, she was deviant! Just this morning on *The Phil Donahue Show* she'd listened to women
describe how they liked to be insulted by men. They had
said they enjoyed it. "It's a real turn-on," one of the
women had said.

"Oh, no," Hannah had said out loud. Her problems
were mounting each day.

When the doorbell rang, her stomach lurched again.
She stood on tiptoe and peered through the peephole. His
head and glasses looked huge, and she giggled.

"I've come to apologize," he said.

Hannah opened the door. "I'm not one of these
women who likes being insulted," she said. "I know there
are people like that and I'm not one of them."

Close up, his face—even with the glasses and short
hair—was nice. There was a very deep dimple in one
cheek. He was holding his skateboard under one arm. It
was a muddy purple with NOAH'S ARK written across it
in lime green and a yellow star burst at the tip.

"My name is Noah Meade," he said. Then he added,
"I go to Collegiate."

She supposed that going to Collegiate meant something around here. She said, "I go to Juilliard."

"Really? Wow! What do you play?"

"The violin."

"Well," he said. "I'm sorry about what I said. About your hair and all. I just haven't seen hair like that in a while."

She laughed. "Everyone in Paris is wearing their hair like this."

"Oh." He nodded. After a minute he said, "I've been riding out here every afternoon, kind of hoping you'd come out and talk. Usually I go to the park."

"I'm in here rehearsing," Hannah said, irritated, "and it ruins my concentration and all. This Britten is very difficult."

He was, she thought, *very* cute.

"I'm fourteen," he said. "Almost fifteen."

"So?"

"Do you want to maybe get something to eat later? I mean, with me?"

"Maybe."

"Great."

She closed the door, right in his smiling face.

He knocked again.

"Excuse me," he said through the door. "But what's your name?"

"Hannah," she said.

"Hannah. Great."

She waited to hear him walk away. Instead, he started to talk again.

"Could you please dress up for dinner? It's kind of a dressy place."

"Fine," she said. "I've got to go practice now."

He still didn't leave.

"I'll come for you at six. I live at the other end of the hall. Five-hundred-sixty-five."

She waited.

"I'd come later but I have homework. Latin."

She stood on tiptoe and looked at him through the peephole.

"Six will be fine. It's better for digestion to eat early and then to walk a lot."

Noah turned his face upward.

"I see you," he said.

He stood on tiptoe too, and pressed his eye right up against the peephole. His glasses had sort of a rust-colored wire frame, and his eyes were the same exact color. His eyes are like an old bike, she thought.

After he pressed his eye against the peephole like that, he wiggled it.

Hannah heard her heart beating, fast and loud. She tried not to throw up.

It wasn't until Hannah was all dressed in her gold lamé dress from her Supremes act that she wondered if her grandmother would even let her go with Noah to dinner. Once, she had asked Abby, "Hypothetically, if Brent Balboa asked me to go to the movies, would you let me go?" Abby had seemed puzzled by the question. Finally she'd said, "Would I have to pick him up or something?" "Forget it," Hannah had said.

She decided to write her grandmother a note.

"Gone to dinner with Noah from down the hall," she wrote. "His eyes are like an old bike."

Then she took out her can of spray-on hair color and sprayed a tuft in the front metallic blue. Her braid was hardly pink anymore. It had started to return to its natural color so that now it was reddish, like clay. At least, half of it was. Hannah considered cutting it off. She thought of the braid she had back home, made from strands of all of their hair—hers and Abby's and Zach's. Dara had told her that was creepy, keeping hair like that. But to Hannah it had seemed beautiful, permanent and strong, the only thing about the three of them that stayed together.

When Noah rang the doorbell, she yelled, "Just a minute."

She took the scissors and cut off her rat's tail. For an instant, she stared at it in her hands. Then she unbraided it, marveling at how easily it came apart.

"Your grandparents are famous, aren't they?" Noah asked her.

He was very polite. He had even buttered a piece of bread for her.

"Sort of. At least my grandmother is."

"Dulcinea Day," he said.

"I guess so."

They were at a restaurant called Ernie's, sitting at a table by the window. When they had gone to sit down, Noah had pulled out the chair that Hannah had wanted to sit in. So she moved around to the other chair. He appeared right behind her and pulled out *that* chair. She'd sat in it anyway. He kept doing things like that. He'd even ordered her Coke for her, as if she couldn't talk or something. It was like one of her grandfather's movies, the one where he lights this woman's cigarette for her, even though she has a lighter right in her hand.

Hannah studied the menu. Nothing looked at all familiar. She was beginning to wonder if people in New York ever ate anything normal, like hamburgers or tuna fish.

"The pizzas here are excellent," Noah said.

"Fine," she said, and put the menu down, relieved.

"Do you like goat cheese?" he asked her.

She thought a minute. It seemed possible that goats gave milk, that cheese could be made from that milk. "I adore it," she said.

He smiled at her. His dimple deepened.

During dinner, she told him that her dream was to someday play Carnegie Hall.

Since her mother had gone away, Hannah had felt that their life back home was pathetic. Sometimes, she used to feel that way, like when she'd sleep over at Chelsea's in her canopy bed, or when Brett's mother would bring the class cookies, or even when she ate at Dara's and her parents were there together, eating a real meal. But then she'd go home and see her own mother's face and she'd forget that she'd been wishing for someone different to be her mother.

But here, away from her mother and their run-down green house, Hannah felt mixed-up about what she wanted, about who she was. She couldn't tell Noah that no one could locate her father. Or that her mother was in a sanatorium. She couldn't tell him that she felt, suddenly, insignificant, surrounded by strange food, tall buildings, and her grandmother.

Instead, over goat cheese and basil pizza, Hannah wove fantastic stories. Stories that she almost believed, that seemed wonderful. She told him that her father was a famous artist and her mother, a once-renowned violinist, had thrown her career away for love.

"They're in Paris," she said, "getting ready for a tour of world capitals. His paintings are being exhibited this summer. Barcelona, Tokyo, Copenhagen."

Behind his glasses, Noah's eyes sparkled.

"My life is so boring," he moaned.

Hannah whispered, "I came to stay with my grandmother because I have amnesia."

"Amnesia?" he said. "But you seem to remember things."

"I have a touch of it. Like I can't recall my bedroom.

Hardly at all. Or my school. Or any of my friends. Nothing."

"Did you get hit in the head or something?"

She shook her head.

"Have you suffered some kind of trauma? I saw a man on the news once, a mailman, who saw his son horribly killed and he blocked out everything about his own life. He started a new one in Altoona, Pennsylvania. Then, one day, he saw another boy killed in a similar fashion, and his entire past life came flooding back to him."

Hannah said, "Yes. I've had a trauma."

That part was true. And she felt oddly relieved that perhaps she did have amnesia, that someday her life in Vermont would be restored to her.

"Well," she said, "at least I have my music."

"I'm like that with baseball," Noah said. "It's my whole life. I want to play for the Mets more than anything. Pitch. Except my father wants me to be an architect. Like him. He said when a baseball player's career is over, all he can do is open a restaurant. Even Mickey Mantle had to do that."

"My father's like that. He wishes I had pursued art. Because we're so close and all."

"Hey!" Noah said. "His stuff must be at MOMA. Right?"

"MOMA?"

"We'll go sometime and look at it. What do you say?"

"Great," she said, trying to sound like she meant it. She watched as Noah placed another piece of pizza on her plate. She hated goat cheese.

*   *   *

163

Noah held her hand the whole way home, even though it was slightly sweaty. She wondered how many other girls' hands he'd held, if theirs had been softer, smoother, drier. She wondered how many girls he'd taken to Ernie's. She tried to stop wondering and to concentrate on his hand. It was the only boy's hand she'd ever held. He had calluses.

"From pitching," he said when he caught her pressing one with her thumb.

Inside the building he led her into the elevator.

"Are you up for something really incredible?"

"I guess so," she said, trying to figure out how he kept his hand from sweating.

He pressed PH. "Good," he said.

When they got off, they climbed the fire stairs to the roof.

"If you're afraid of heights," he whispered, "don't look down."

Hannah stood there, with the city all around her, lit up and shining, and she gasped because it was so beautiful.

Noah pointed toward buildings. "The Empire State Building," he said, "is that one. It's lit in red, white, and blue for the Fourth of July. That Art Deco one is my favorite, the Chrysler Building."

They twirled slowly as he talked, facing first south, then east, then north.

"Over there is New Jersey," Noah said, as they turned again.

She felt dizzy from the height and the lights and the spinning.

"Wait here," he told her.

She watched him disappear into the building again. When he came back out, he had a red backpack.

"I left this up here before I picked you up."

He pulled a blanket from it and spread it in the center of the roof. Hannah went and sat beside him.

"It's not Paris," Noah said.

"It's better," she whispered.

In the starlight and city lights she could see him perfectly, his brown eyes, his dimpled cheek.

He opened a paper bag that had NOAH stamped all over it.

"My mother," he said, rolling his eyes. "She personalizes everything. I'm lucky I don't have my name stamped all over me."

Hannah giggled.

Noah took out a small gold box of chocolates and a tiny bottle of champagne.

"I pilfered these from my parents," he said.

When he opened the champagne, most of it spilled out in a bubbly explosion. The cork bounced and landed on the blanket beside Hannah. She hoped he wouldn't think she was stupid if she took it home.

In her thin lamé dress, she shivered, even though the breeze was warm. Noah put his navy-blue sport coat around her shoulders. They sat, eating the chocolate truffles and sipping the champagne that hadn't spilled, and tilting their heads back to stare at the sky.

"I wish I didn't have Latin," Noah whispered to her.

"I wish I didn't have to go away," she said.

Somehow, Hannah still believed that she and Zach and Abby would be going away together in Zach's Plymouth Voyager, to Mexico, to find pieces of pottery and threads from Aztec fabrics.

"Maybe you can pretend you forgot," he said. "And you can stay all summer."

"Maybe," she said.

They sat for a while more. Then, suddenly, so fast

that later she wasn't completely sure it had happened at all, Noah kissed her, right on the lips.

"Wow," he said. "I really like you."

"You do?" she said.

He reached his arm up, high.

"Here," he said, opening his fist, holding it out to her. "I picked a star for you, right out of the sky."

FASHION STATEMENTS

Hannah watched as her grandmother moved around the kitchen in a burst of energy not unlike Abby sometimes had. Whenever those moments had come, Abby would insist that Hannah drink milk with dinner, or say prayers before she went to sleep. "I don't know any," Hannah had complained. "Make one up, then," her mother had insisted. Hannah could rarely figure out what had made her mother so determined and energetic, although it usually had to do with Zach—a phone call, a note, a memory. Deirdre, however, immediately announced the source of her good mood.

"I'm going to try to kill Kira next week," she said gleefully as soon as Hannah walked into the kitchen that morning. "With poison, no less."

Usually, Hannah would not have answered her. But she was in good spirits herself. Noah liked her. She had become someone important, someone who mattered, a violinist, a student at Juilliard, the daughter of famous people. She had dreamed last night that she and Noah were astronauts, sent to Venus to build a city out of

Play-Doh. Her mother loved to hear what Hannah had dreamt the night before, and sometimes spent hours trying to analyze the dreams, looking in an old book of Zach's that listed, like a dictionary, the symbolism of dreams. Most of them, Hannah knew, were sexual—snakes, water, guns, roses, all meant desire and lust. She wondered what Play-Doh meant, and giggled to herself while her grandmother talked on about Kira and the poison. She would ask her mother this afternoon, Hannah thought, and hugged herself. While she had been on the roof with Noah, the sanatorium had called to tell Deirdre that Abby could have a visitor. It could not be, they'd said, Zach or Deirdre. So this afternoon, June would drive Hannah upstate where she could spend two hours with her mother, asking her about her dream, the meanings of Play-Doh and new cities. Where she could convince her mother she should come home.

Deirdre put a bowl of yogurt in front of Hannah.

"I noticed you don't eat right, " she said. "You start today, kiddo."

Hannah pushed the yogurt away. "Is Kira going to die from the poison?" she asked.

Deirdre laughed. "Are you kidding? Nothing could kill that little bitch. She gets too much fan mail. But I have to plot the murder, then attempt it, then try to cover it up. It could go on forever."

"Great."

"I'm putting it in paint," her grandmother said. She still had on the scarf she wore around her chin at night to keep it from sagging. It was tied on top of her head, the ends flopping like a rabbit's ears. "Isn't that clever?" she said.

"I guess so." Hannah peered into the refrigerator, but found nothing that interested her. She felt like she really was the fantasy girl she had created last night for Noah. She felt special.

"She'll probably lose the baby," Deirdre said.

Hannah leaned against the refrigerator, watched her grandmother as she added fruits and milk to the blender. "How long does it take to learn how to play the violin?" Hannah asked her, thinking suddenly that perhaps she was some kind of prodigy. Maybe she could take a lesson or two and really play.

"Forever," Deirdre said. The contents in the blender swirled, turned a chalky pink.

"What if you're a prodigy?"

"Who wants to know?"

"Nobody," Hannah said. She went back to the table and ate a spoonful of yogurt. "This is truly disgusting," she said. "Like sour milk. In Paris, people eat civilized breakfasts."

"I'm sure they do," Deirdre said. She put a glass of the concoction she'd made in the blender in front of Hannah. "Strawberries, raspberries, skim milk, brewer's yeast, one egg—"

"I don't want to know," Hannah said, sniffing it.

"By the way," Deirdre said. "June called this morning. She has actually tracked down your father. The woman should be a detective."

"He's coming for us?" Hannah asked, almost expecting a different father to appear at the door, a father who was world-famous, who lived in Paris, who loved her and her mother.

"Hardly," her grandmother said. "He's in England."

"England?" Hannah repeated. Since she and her mother had returned from LA, Hannah had heard her mother talking to Zach on the phone in angry tones about a woman in England.

"Oh, no," Hannah said. The father of her fantasy

vanished, and was replaced with an image of her real one. Zach with a woman in England. Zach talking to them about Mexico. Last time she'd spoken to him, he'd said, "Manna, *como esta usted?*" She had said, flatly, "I don't speak Spanish."

"Do you have any idea what he's doing in England?" her grandmother was asking.

Hannah shrugged.

"I know," Deirdre said, "maybe he's doing an England collage. Getting coal and tea bags."

Hannah had not done well in Social Studies. But she knew that Mexico was very far from England.

June opened the magazine, smoothed it out on the kitchen table. There, in black and white, Zach smiled out at them. His arms circled the tiny waist of a woman with short black hair. The woman looked like she was wearing armor, like knights wore in the Middle Ages.

"What is she wearing?" Hannah asked.

"ArtWear," June said. "Art that one wears. She designs it. That's a breastplate."

Hannah was sure she'd never heard a voice as flat, as toneless, as June's.

"Are those snakes on her breasts?" Deirdre said, leaning closer to the picture.

Hannah read, "Nina Marserelli, designer/artist, with American artist Zach Plummer at her London show."

"Coiled snakes," June said. She had obviously read the article, and now recited facts from it like a bored professor. "Papier-mâché. Painted bronze."

"And people probably pay a fortune for that stuff," Deirdre said.

Hannah walked out of the kitchen, away from Zach and the woman in armor, and into her grandmother's study. In her make-believe life that she'd conjured for

Noah, her mother looked like Abby, except less tired and better groomed—manicured hands and shorter, styled hair, like Cybill Shepherd's. Here, in her mother's old room, Hannah searched again for a remnant of who her mother had once been. Perhaps there had been a time when it had seemed possible for Abby to look like Cybill Shepherd, to go to Vienna, to be with a different man, in a different place. But all she found were Deirdre's scripts and photographs and awards, scrapbooks filled with programs and clippings from the career of Deirdre Falls Church.

Hannah tried to imagine what had hung on these walls when her mother had slept here, what movie stars she'd dreamed of, what books she'd read. But it was as if Abby had not existed before that day in the park when Zach walked into her life. Hannah ran her fingers along the walls, searching for marks from another time, when posters had hung here, or snapshots. But all she found was inch after inch of smooth wall, colored in a shade that Deirdre called dusty rose.

Her grandmother walked in, without knocking. She clapped her hands loudly, shouting, "Let's go, let's go, let's go!"

Hannah turned, her arms outstretched. "What was in this room when my mother lived here?"

Deirdre said, "Who knows? I lived in Virginia until I was eighteen years old, and do you know that I have never been back to that old house. What's the point?"

"Sometimes," Hannah said, "I like to pretend that my mother looks like Cybill Shepherd. I mean, she has her own face, but her hair and her clothes and everything are like Cybill Shepherd's. And she speaks with sort of a British accent."

Deirdre didn't answer right away. Then, her fingers lightly traced the wall. "The paper," she said softly, "was pink-and-white-striped and had tiny rosebuds on it. Right here, there used to be a gigantic print from a Mozart opera. *Don Giovanni,* I think. And the furniture was antique white wicker. We bought it all at a shop up in Sheffield, Massachusetts, while I was doing summer stock somewhere up there. Actually, Toby was doing it too, with me. *Barefoot in the Park.* I have the program in a scrapbook. The reviews," she added wistfully, "were wonderful."

Then her voice turned practical again. Theatrical. "Of course," she said, "that's when she was younger. Then she grew up, painted the walls some crazy color, and put up a special light that made certain posters glow. Down came Mozart, up went this psychedelic Adam and Eve standing in a neon Garden of Eden. Do you know that when I was a girl, I shared a bedroom with three sisters? Three? Little twin beds, pictures of Jesus everywhere. Except over my bed. I pinned up Clark Gable, Tyrone Power. Movie stars."

Hannah listened carefully.

"What I would have given for my own room," Deirdre said.

"You have three sisters?" Hannah said. "Where are they?"

Her grandmother laughed. "Who cares? Are you going to call them up?"

"No."

"Neither am I. They call at Christmas, tell me all the boring details of their lives, ask me when I'm going to get a real job."

"Where are all those things?" Hannah asked her.

Deirdre looked at her as if she hadn't realized she was there until just now. "What? The programs? The reviews from that summer?"

"No," Hannah said. "The Mozart poster. My mother's things."

"Do you know," her grandmother said, "that she sold that beautiful wicker bed for fifty dollars? Snuck in here and took it down to the street and sold it. It was worth a fortune too."

"Did she sell everything?"

"When I left Virginia," Deirdre said, "I left. But Abby used to run away, and come back, then run away again. She used to live downtown with a group of characters like you can't even imagine."

"Zach?"

"No. He was just the icing on the cake." She shook her head. "Here we are, rattling on while June is sitting out there, all set to go."

But Hannah didn't move. "Where are all those other things? The things she didn't sell?"

Deirdre opened her hands, palms up. "Gone," she said. "There's no use in being sentimental."

"Adirondack chairs!" June shrieked.

It was the only thing she had said in the two hours since she and Hannah had been driving north along the Hudson River toward Abby. They had finally reached the sanatorium, Goldens Point, and stood together inside the ornate wrought-iron gate, scanning the hilly grounds for some sign of Abby. The hills were dotted with these chairs, most of them empty, all of them painted a creamy white.

"I love Adirondack chairs," June said, then fell silent again.

"It looks like Bennington College," Hannah said.

Abby and Gavin Berry had taken her there once, to hear a famous poet read his poems. He had spoken, in a shrill voice, about trees and fruit, comparing them to death and sorrow and loneliness. Abby had fallen asleep early on, and Hannah had watched as her mother's head

173

jerked forward, then dropped down, down, until she caught herself and jumped awake. Later, Abby had told Gavin that the poems had been emotional. "That one," she'd said, "moved me to tears." "Which one?" Hannah had challenged. Abby had stared her right in the eye. "The one," she'd said, "about trees." "They were *all* about trees," Hannah had said. "Well, then," Abby said, "the last one." "For me," Gavin had said, "they were a little too sentimental." "Oh, yes," Abby had said quickly, "many of them were."

Hannah wondered if they brought poets here to read to all the people who were getting their lives together. Maybe they had people come and read about trees and flowers that compared with love, life, happiness.

"This sure doesn't look like a nuthouse," Hannah said, hoping to shock June.

But June was still fixated on those chairs. "There must be twenty of them," she said, her eyes moving as if she were counting them. "And they cost a pretty penny." Her eyes stopped on one of them. She pointed. "There she is," she said. "I'll go wait in the car."

"Hey," Hannah called after her, "you're talking a blue streak now. Don't go just when you've started to roll." She watched June's perfectly straight back until it was a tiny beige slash against the too-green hills.

She took a deep breath. Instead of walking to her mother, though, she stood and watched. Abby was sitting in one of those damn chairs, reading, with her legs tucked under her. She had on a pale blue cotton skirt that Hannah had never seen before. Maybe, she thought, it's like a uniform they all have to wear here. It had lots of buttons down the front and billowed around her so that it seemed she had no legs, no lower body at all. It was as if her mother was all light blue cotton and wild, loose blond hair.

Hannah surveyed the small white shuttered cottages, the hills that looked down on the Hudson, sparkling gray-blue below them. It was idyllic, like college or summer camp. She felt an urge to run after June, to demand to be taken back to New York. She felt dried up inside, like she had nothing to say to her mother. They should have been, by this time, bumping across the country with Zach, filling the van with roadside finds, sleeping cramped together in the back, lulled by the whooshing sounds of passing cars, distant sirens, each other's breathing.

"I want to go to Paris," Hannah said out loud. "I want to find my real family there."

Her mother's head remained bent over a magazine, unaware that Hannah was nearby.

Then Hannah said, softer, "I want to go home."

Abby studied the magazine, held it closer for better inspection.

Slowly, Hannah moved toward her.

The doctor Abby spoke to every day was a yellow-skinned, unhealthy-looking man named Dr. You-Can-Call-Me-Jeffrey Kornbluth. He wore poor-fitting mismatched suits, in varying shades of browns and rusts, with wide print ties. His hair was the same color as his worst suit, an orangy-brown, and it was thin on top. He combed the few sparse strands over to the side, as if no one would notice he was going to be bald soon.

Every day since she'd arrived, Abby had sat in his hot office and talked, while Dr. Kornbluth sucked on Halls mentho-lyptus cough drops and, periodically, nodded. In the evenings she talked in a group led by Dr. Kornbluth and a sexy, redheaded psychologist named Jamie. Jamie would plead with the group, "Feel, seek," dragging out the e's in a painful whine. Dr. Kornbluth would look down Jamie's low-cut blouses and nod. "Absolutely," he'd say. "Feel."

Yesterday, after Abby had talked for over an hour, telling Dr. Kornbluth about the summers, how the three of them were together then, and happy, he had said, "What besides Zach makes you happy?" It was the first question he'd asked her in the almost two weeks since she'd been there.

"Three-Legged Horse," she'd told him. "And Hannah."

The doctor crunched the last bit of his cough drop. "This Gavin Berry doesn't make you happy. Making Le Company doesn't make you happy." He said all of this matter-of-factly.

"Well," Abby said, "it does. Sort of."

He raised his pencil-thin eyebrows, like Joan Crawford. "Really?" he said.

"Look," Abby had said, "who wouldn't be happy doing the things they were trained to do? I was trained to play classical violin. I'm finally doing it."

"Van Gogh," the doctor said, "was trained to be a clergyman."

Abby stood up. "This is ridiculous," she'd said. "This place costs a fortune and all you're doing is telling me things I already know."

"Really? Do you know that you can live without Zach? Or Three-Legged Horse?"

"You horse's ass," Abby had said, "that's why I'm here. To learn to live without them. To make my life better." She'd headed for the door. Outside, a lawn mower whined. "Do you have a sore throat?" she'd asked. "Do you have a persistent, nagging sore throat or something?" Before he could answer she'd said, "And another thing. You look down Jamie's dress. All the time. It's disgusting."

Dr. Kornbluth said, "Abby, you can't always expect people to take care of you. You're a grown woman now."

"Oh, please. Who writes your lines?" She'd stormed out. In her fantasy, she would have a doctor who was dashing and handsome. A doctor who would save her, love her, show her what to do. Like Susan Hayward's and Bette Davis's doctors in the movies. She had wanted Dr. Kildare, Ben Casey. Not Jeffrey Kornbluth. She hadn't gone to him today. Instead, she'd gone into town and bought a stack of fashion magazines. Her roommate, Jocelyn, read them all the time. They seemed, somehow, to hold answers. "To get better," Jocelyn had told her, "you start from the outside and work inward. Nice hair. A solid wardrobe." Jocelyn's advice seemed every bit as good as Dr. Kornbluth's, or Jamie's, for that matter.

So Abby sat in the sunshine with her magazines, waiting for Hannah to show up, and planning her escape. She would buy new clothes, a wardrobe that made sense, that was interchangeable, color-coordinated, went from casual to dressy in just fifteen minutes. She would pretend that she was better, rested, unafraid of a life without Zach, without Three-Legged Horse. Then, away from here, she would start over somehow. Perhaps she would follow Hannah's advice and move to Australia, to the outback. She caught herself thinking of the wonderful things Zach could find there.

"June wouldn't even turn on the radio," Hannah said, first thing. "Noise gives her migraines."

Her mother seemed exactly the same as when she'd left her here. She looked up from her magazine. "Hi yourself," she said.

"It looks like you have no legs," Hannah said, pointing to the hem of the skirt.

Her mother extended her bare feet. "I do," she said. "See."

They were grass-stained, slightly dirty, and Hannah

177

smiled. Her mother, it appeared, was the same as always. Just to be sure, she asked, "Are they giving you electric shock treatments or anything?"

Abby laughed. "That at least would be interesting. All they do is listen to me talk. Yesterday, one doctor actually took a risk and asked me if I was happy. What a bore." She spoke with a Viennese accent, "Vat makes you happy? Vat can you live vithout? Men? Music?"

Hannah sat cross-legged at her mother's feet. "I brought nail polish," she said. "Can I do your toes?"

"Sure." She rested her feet in Hannah's lap. "I have a roommate who is totally gorgeous. Jocelyn. She sneaks in bourbon."

Hannah carefully began to paint her mother's toenails a bright pink. Bubble gum. They were quiet for a time; the only sound was of birds calling to each other and an occasional car door slamming.

"Jocelyn has these incredible clothes," Abby said finally. "By Japanese designers. Tunics and things."

"Uh-huh," Hannah said.

"I've been reading a lot. Magazines, mostly. I have no fashion sense at all."

"Deirdre *listens* to books," Hannah said. "Tapes."

Abby smiled absently. She was staring off, beyond the neat little cottages that lined the field where they sat. "Before you came I was imagining Australia. The things Zach would find there. Aborigine relics."

Hannah frowned. "They're probably sacred or something."

"I imagine that it would be hot there. Barren. Red. We could drive around in a Land-Rover."

"Is Zach coming for us?" Hannah asked.

"Damn it," her mother said. "I am not supposed to be doing this. I'm here to get over him. He just keeps invading me though. Butting in."

Hannah hesitated. She thought of the picture of Zach and that woman, smiling together. "He's not good for us," she said. "He doesn't come through."

Her mother looked at her, startled.

"Mom," Hannah said, concentrating on the small circles that were her mother's toenails, on painting them pink. "Why didn't you ever go to Vienna?"

"Vienna?"

"Deirdre says—"

"She can't get it through her head, can she? That was her dream, not mine. I wanted to dance in the streets, to make music that was fun, to fall in love. I didn't want to be locked up in that apartment and listen to them bicker. Or watch my father fall down drunk. I was just telling all this to Dr. Kornbluth. It was all such a disappointment." She shook her head sadly.

"Can't we just go back to Vermont?" Hannah said suddenly. "Can't we just go home?"

"I wonder," Abby said, her voice and eyes faraway, "if I could have done it. Made it as a classical violinist. Toured Europe. Maybe married an international banker." Then she laughed, her voice returned to its normal tone. "Can you imagine?"

Her toenails glowed a fresh pink. Hannah spit on her hand and rubbed at a smudge of dirt on her mother's ankle. "No," she said, "I can't imagine it."

Abby looked down at her feet. "Oooooh," she said, wiggling her toes. "They look good. You know, in group I was telling them how this boyfriend I had when I was sixteen painted my entire body paisley print. It took hours! I looked wild, like a bedspread or something."

Hannah leaned back, against her mother.

As if she had just realized it, Abby said, "Playing those songs, with Three-Legged Horse, made me the happiest."

"More than Zach?" Hannah asked.

Abby didn't answer her.

The air here, Hannah thought, almost smelled like home.

It wasn't until later, on the silent ride back to the city with June, that she realized she hadn't told her mother her dreams.

A FLOWER STOOD UP

Noah showed her a color-
ful map, bold lines criss-
crossing, halting at fat circles before moving off in other
directions. An underground world.

He said, "It's easy. But why do you want to go to
Brooklyn?"

There was a smudge on his left lens, a thumbprint.
Hannah could see, clearly, the wavy lines on the glass.
She could memorize them, his thumb's secret swirls and
loops, then identify him anywhere, just from a print left
on glass or paper. Like a code.

"I mean," Noah continued, "no one goes there.
Except to the Botanical Garden."

"Friends of ours live there," Hannah said.

"Oh. Are they musicians? Or artists?"

"Musicians," she said. "Classical guitar and flute."
The lies came easily to her now. More and more she
almost believed them herself.

"Why do they live in Brooklyn?" Noah asked her.

"You know what?" Hannah said. "You ask a lot of
questions."

Every day now, when Deirdre left for the studio, Noah came down to the apartment. He and Hannah sat, side by side, on the couch, clutching each other's hands as they watched a series of game shows. *The Price Is Right. Sale of the Century. Super Password.*

"My mother would kill me if she knew I was watching this junk," he'd told Hannah. "I only get to watch an hour a day. Unless it's a Mets game or a National Geographic special."

Hannah had a stash of goodies for them—Hostess Cupcakes, nacho cheese tortilla chips, Oreos. They ate and watched, shouting answers to the contestants. To Hannah it seemed like a perfectly normal way to spend a morning.

"Forget it," Noah had told her. "Baboons mating or the Great Barrier Reef. That's what I get to see."

In the afternoon, when he'd leave her to practice his pitching in Central Park, he'd always ask her the same questions. "When are you going to Paris? When are you leaving?"

Hannah would think of her mother up at Goldens Point, sitting in the white chair in the middle of the meadow reading fashion magazines, making a "Dress for Success" plan. She'd think of the pages Abby had shown her, pictures with captions that warned against wearing clear hose with miniskirts, advising the reader to buy an extra-wide belt, and explaining the importance of the little black dress. "When I leave here," Abby had told her, "everything will be in order." She'd held those pages to her as if they were valuable, as if they could solve everything. She'd said that she and her roommate, Jocelyn, were going to start the Liz Taylor diet, and read *Ulysses.*

Hannah would think of her mother there, with her bubble-gum-pink toenails, the way she'd looked off into the sky, expectantly, while Hannah had watched from atop one of those hills. When she'd turned to wave good-bye, Abby's head had been tilted up toward the clouds, the blue sky. Somewhere, Zach had his arms around another woman's waist. Somewhere, Hannah would think, he was smiling at a woman who wore papier-mâché clothes.

When Noah asked her when she was leaving, she'd try to picture Zach moving toward them, from London or California. He came every year, didn't he?

"Soon," Hannah would answer. "I'll be leaving soon."

But the summer wore on, slowly. June was coming to an end. The city smelled of hot tar, urine, people. Soon, Toby would be back from Newport and he and her grand-mother would be leaving for Williamstown. Hannah spent her afternoons after Noah left hidden in the hall closet, or, sometimes, reading her grandmother's scripts aloud, pretending she was Laura Wingfield, or Juliet. She did anything she could not to have to think about her mother sitting in that field, or the possibility that Zach wouldn't come for them, or what any of those things might mean.

Now Noah was asking her what orchestra this flute player performed with, if the classical guitarist had a record out, did they know about her amnesia? Hannah tried to imagine Mallory and Sean in the roles she had cast them in, but it was impossible. She could only see them in their Vermont farmhouse, Mallory acting bored and sarcastic, Sean trying to please everyone, picking at the strings on his old folk guitar.

"Stop with the questions," Hannah said to Noah. "I don't know the answers."

He left her with the subway map, her route inked out beside the bold printed lines. He gave her two subway tokens and advice: "Don't make eye contact with anyone. Avoid express trains, they'll just mix you up. Walk fast, like you know where you're going."

Mallory stood in the middle of the high-ceilinged kitchen, looking like she'd won an important prize, the way the winning contestants looked at the end of game shows when the emcee announced just how much they had won and let them wave to their families in TV land.

"A pantry," she told Hannah. "How about that?" Her eyes darted back and forth quickly, like a rabbit's. They were slightly pinkish. "Conjunctivitis," she'd explained when Hannah first arrived. "Elijah picked it up in school." Her voice had sounded triumphant then too. "It's a Montessori," she'd added. Her eyes, despite the conjunctivitis, had sparkled.

"The neighborhood is still a little iffy," Mallory said, "but it's an incredible find just the same."

"When are your eyes going to get better?" Hannah asked her, unsure of this new, animated, and almost joyful Mallory. Even her hair seemed to shine.

"There is so much happening," Mallory said.

She led Hannah down a long narrow corridor to the living room, where Sean sat. The chair he sat on, at least, looked familiar. It was from the farmhouse, a rattan rocker with a loud jungle print cushion—ominous green ferns and deep purple flowers. Everything else looked different, though. Even Sean himself.

Hannah stood in the doorway, peering in at him. The apartment was tall and skinny with lots of dark wood and ornate light fixtures. It smelled of pee. Probably from Elijah, Hannah thought. She wondered what they had done with their real furniture, why they had left their airy, light farmhouse in Vermont for this dark, cramped apartment. Back in Vermont, Sean had shown her the pegs in the floorboards. "Aren't they beautiful?" he'd said. "You don't see craftsmanship like this anymore."

She had an impulse to run over to Sean, to hug him hard and plant a kiss right on his bald spot. Sometimes, when she used to sleep at the farm, she and Margot would paint their lips dark red and then cover Sean's head with lipstick kisses. He wouldn't even wash them off.

But something in the way he was sitting there, in that one familiar chair, his face all droopy-looking, made her feel shy.

"Hi," she said, uncertainly, taking a small step into the room.

Deirdre had gotten a big bouquet of tulips for her to bring to Sean and Mallory. "Everyone loves tulips," she'd told Hannah. "You can't go wrong with them." It had felt silly to bring flowers with her, but she'd done it anyway. No one seemed to notice that she had them, though. So she stood there, clutching them against her bright orange Twiggy dress, waiting for one of them to do something. Shouldn't Mallory be complaining about the heat? Shouldn't Sean have a word puzzle for her to mull over? A cool Mexican dinner, he should say. And before she left she'd figure it out. A chilly chili. Or a naked grizzly. She'd tell him, a bare bear. She had spent the entire subway ride here thinking of one to give him, like a gift.

Finally Mallory said, "She has tulips! How about that?" Then she left the room, with Hannah still holding the splashy array of flowers.

"I thought we'd go to the Botanical Garden. It's only six blocks away. How does that sound?"

Hannah shrugged. "Where's Margot?" Even though Margot was only nine, they still had fun together. Hannah told her stories, or gave her a manicure.

"School," Sean said. Then he added, "Montessori." He didn't say it as happily as Mallory had.

Mallory came back in with a tray of bagels and lox. She held a fat pumpernickel bagel to Hannah's face. "Have you ever seen anything this gorgeous in Vermont?"

"Yeah," Hannah said. "Plenty."

Mallory laughed. "You can only look at so many cows, so many mountains. Then it's time to return to civilization."

For most of last year, Mallory had stopped going to hear Three-Legged Horse. "If I have to hear 'Moonlight in Vermont' one more time I'll puke," she'd said.

"I guess you really don't like Vermont," Hannah said.

Mallory laughed. "That's an understatement."

Sean cleared his throat. "I thought I'd take Hannah to the Botanical Garden," he said.

"That's a great way to spend an afternoon," Mallory said. She leaned closer to Hannah, and Hannah could smell the pumpernickel on her breath. "They have roses there as big as my fist. American Beauties."

The tulips were beginning to shrivel, to curl up at the edges. Their vivid colors—purple, pink, yellow—seemed dull and meager now.

"I brought these for you, you know," she said, handing them toward Mallory.

"I'll go dig up a vase," she said, finally taking them. "I wasn't sure. It didn't seem like something you'd do."

When Mallory left the room again, Hannah moved closer to Sean.

"Hi," she said again, wanting to start over.

He smiled at her sadly. "I don't know," he said. "I sort of miss those cows and mountains back in Vermont."

"Me too," Hannah said, resting her head on his knees.

"I don't want to teach kids 'The Battle Hymn of the Republic.' I really don't."

Hannah jumped up. "It's not too late," she said. "Three-Legged Horse can still get back together. My mom will do it in a minute. She's not even going to play with Le Company, I bet."

She was smiling, imagining it. The crowd clapping, stomping their feet in time to the music. Outside there would be snow, and country roads. But inside she'd be warm, surrounded by applause and the smell of beer. She imagined them singing "Orange Blossom Special," the way Sean leaned in real close to the microphone and whistled into it, long and shrill as a passing train.

"We can all just go home," Hannah said.

At first, Sean didn't answer. He stared down at the floor. It was almost black, with a big light circle by his feet, like something had spilled there a long time ago.

Finally he looked up and said, "It took me forever to convince Abby to join us."

"But who played the violin before her?" Hannah said.

Sean seemed to perk up slightly. "That would be Long John Silverman," he said, almost smiling. "Now he's a lawyer in Philadelphia. Sends us Christmas cards with his whole family wearing Santa hats. Even the dog."

"Let's call Doug," Hannah said quickly. "He'll come back."

"Doug?" Sean said. "Didn't your mom tell you?"

"I know. He's in LA. But he can come back. People come back, you know."

Sean shook his head. "Not Doug. He got a terrific job as a sound engineer. He's even got a girlfriend already. Some big model with one name. Thea or something."

Hannah looked down at the fat bagels, bursting with rye and sesame and poppy.

"Mallory wouldn't go back," Sean said.

"I want to go home," Hannah said.

Sean misunderstood. He thought she meant back to her grandmother's. But she meant back to Vermont.

He stood up, looking small and bald in the high, dark room. "Okay," he said, sounding relieved. "We'll go to the Botanical Garden next time. When Margot and Elijah are home."

She didn't correct him. She just said, "Sure."

All the way here, she had followed Noah's advice. She had kept her head bent and stared at people's shoes. She'd looked up only when the train slowed to a stop, and even then just for an instant, to be sure it was not time for her to get off. She had counted the cigarette butts that lay at her feet, made mental notes of how many people were wearing Reeboks, how many Keds, how many nonsneakers.

She supposed now that she was hoping that whole time that she would get here to Brooklyn and discover that Sean wanted Three-Legged Horse back together again. She supposed that deep down, she had wanted that more than anything. Then they would go and get her mother and meet Doug at the Crow's Nest on Route 20, where they would play again, "The City of New Orleans," "Amnesia," and "Orange Blossom Special." She would rest her head on a rickety wooden table, trace the name some stranger had carved into it, close her eyes and fall asleep to the sounds of her mother's violin.

Sean walked her to the door, his legs seeming skinny and white beneath ridiculous safari shorts.

Mallory said, "What? No Botanical Garden?"

The tulips, bursting from a mason jar, looked fresh again.

"I want to leave," Hannah said again.

Mallory's pinkish eyes narrowed. "Well, excuse me," she said, her old sarcasm finally surfacing.

At that moment, Hannah felt that she didn't care if she ever saw Mallory again.

Sean hugged her then, and Hannah wrapped her arms around him tight, hoping he would at least feel familiar. But he didn't. He felt, instead, like an old man, brittle bones and sagging skin. "Call us again," he said. "Soon."

Then she remembered.

"A flower stood up," she said, giving him her word puzzle.

He cocked his head and smiled. But then he shrugged. "Sorry," he said.

No one, Hannah decided, could help her get things back to normal. More and more it was looking like Zach was her last hope for bringing her mother back to Vermont. But the thought of having to rely on Zach frightened her so much that she ran off the subway train and up the station stairs, pushing past the crowd of people there clutching newspapers and briefcases. She ran across the street to her grandparents' apartment building, into the lobby, across the vast marble floors that shone like icing.

Upstairs, there were two things waiting for her.

Sean had called and left her a message. "A flower stood up," the message said. "A rose arose." She studied the message, written in Deirdre's large curlicued penmanship, searching it for a sign of hope. And then, she walked into the living room, where, having tea with Deirdre, sat Gavin Berry.

STORYBOOK
ENDINGS

Gavin told Abby that he would build them a new house. One with no memories. A fresh start.

"I will cover the dining room floor with a special rice paper that is decorated with fine maple leaves. Then, I'll polyurethane over it so that the paper will become transparent and it will look like our floor is a treetop with sunlight streaming through."

If Abby looked at him, she would see that his small graceful hands moved as he spoke. But she didn't. Instead, she stared off, into the sky.

"It will be like walking through a meadow in autumn," he said. "Like scattered fallen leaves on our floor."

When she still didn't respond, he turned to Hannah for help. She sat, frowning, a short distance away, concentrating on the blades of grass she split into thin green strands.

"I thought we could have a baby together," Gavin said softly. "And you could play your sweet music."

Despite herself, Hannah felt bad for Gavin Berry. She

hadn't wanted to accompany him up here to Goldens Point today. But after his visit, Deirdre was keen on him. "He's a wonderful man," she had announced after he'd left the apartment. "A gentle man." "He's a nerd," Hannah had muttered. "Nerds," Deirdre had said, "make wonderful husbands. Terrific fathers."

Sitting here, listening to Gavin try to win Abby's heart, she remembered how her mother had left Doug to go away with Zach. Doug's voice had had the same catch in it, the same notes of desperation as Gavin's. This time, however, she hadn't once mentioned Zach. Instead she had talked about how sorry she was, how the timing was so totally wrong. "I have to think for myself," Abby had told Gavin. "I have to think and decide and understand things, all on my own." Then she'd gazed off, away from Gavin Berry. "Maybe," she'd added, "in another lifetime." But she didn't sound like she even believed that.

"I would build you a music room," Gavin was saying.

Hannah almost called out for him to stop. To gather his soft green duffel bag, his presents of fine crackly white paper and Le Company's program with ABBY NASH listed as a violinist, and to leave.

"I would fill it with wildflowers," he said.

Abby turned to him then and smiled. "That's nice," she said.

Eager now, he said, "Some people are like roses. Bold and colorful. A little showy. Or like anemones. Exotic, warm, rare. But you, I think, are most like wildflowers. Growing free. They seem tangled and pale, but sturdy, and not at all plain. Like those." He was delighted to, at last, have her attention, and his voice and hands grew more animated. He pointed to the flowers that dotted the surrounding hills. "Aren't they lovely?" he asked her. He ran off to gather some for her.

"Some people," Hannah announced, "are pansies." She giggled.

"Don't," Abby said, but her mouth twisted to keep from laughing at the joke.

"Another one bites the dust," Hannah said, happy, too, that she finally had her mother's attention.

"That's not fair," Abby said.

"All's fair in love and war," Hannah said.

Abby groaned. "What did you do? Read a book of collected clichés?"

They watched as Gavin bent over picking the flowers in the hot sun.

When he had shown up a few days earlier at Deirdre's apartment, he had explained how he'd gone to the house and found it empty.

"I called and called," he'd said, "afraid that maybe—"

"Maybe what?" Hannah had prodded.

He had stared into his teacup, a thin china one decorated with a band of yellow rosebuds.

Gavin had sighed. "That Zach had come and the three of you were away together."

"This time," Deirdre had said, "we're getting all this straightened out."

The three of them had sat then in silence, each imagining what it might mean to get "all this straightened out." Gavin had nervously stirred his tea, the sound of his spoon against the cup and the air conditioner clunking and dripping the only noises in the room for a time.

Until Gavin had said, "I was mostly worried because the last day I saw her—"

"You mean the last *morning*," Hannah had interrupted. "After the night."

"Well, yes."

Deirdre had given Hannah a dismissive wave. "Don't

be so juvenile, Hannah. Who really cares if the man spent the night or not? It has nothing to do with anything."

"I *am* a juvenile."

"What happened?" Deirdre asked Gavin.

"That *morning*," Hannah had said. "After I left for school."

"Yes," Gavin had said, "after you left, in fact, was when Zach called. He said he would arrive in three days."

Hannah stood up, so quickly that she'd banged her knee against the ornate coffee table that stood on what appeared to be tree trunks.

"But he changed it," Hannah said. "He's coming on the Fourth of July."

She had wanted to run out of that apartment, out of that building, and not stop until she'd followed the Hudson to her mother and they had both reached home again.

"That man," Deirdre was saying, "is like Rasputin. She had to get away before she fell under his spell again."

Gavin had shaken his head sadly. "I'm afraid she may really love him."

Hannah had moved nervously around the room. "We've got to go," she'd said.

"Anyway," Deirdre had said, "I don't think he'll make it by next week. He's off in London, with another woman, of course. Abby's doctor advised me not to tell her. 'Let her come around to ending this relationship in her own way,' he said. 'For her own reasons.' She never had a good reason for getting into the damn thing, so I don't know if a bolt of lightning is going to zap her on the head and wake her up or what."

Hannah had stopped her pacing and stood in the center of the living room.

"Listen to me," she'd shouted. "I want to go and

wait for Zach." It had seemed the only possible way to pull it all back together.

"Don't be ridiculous—"

"Listen to me. I want to go home—"

"You're the one who won't listen," Deirdre had said, as if she were talking to a coma patient, each word loud and precise. "She doesn't want to see him. That's what this is all about."

Gavin and Deirdre had already started to talk about something else, as if there were no changes, or the changes didn't matter.

"When she plays Barber's 'Adagio for Strings,' " Gavin had said, "it makes me ache."

Deirdre had nodded. "When she was just this high, she played a simple Mozart piece, and you would have thought someone three times her age was playing."

Hannah placed herself between them.

"Has anyone bothered to tell Zach?" she'd demanded. "Does he know that she's hiding from him?" She had thought that if she stood on tiptoe, she'd easily be as tall as Gavin. What a shrimp, she'd thought.

"Not hiding, kiddo," Deirdre said.

Gavin had reached out to her, and Hannah had stepped back, away from him. She'd put her hands on her hips, pressed her feet hard into the floor.

"Hannah," Gavin had said, dropping his hand to his side, "he's unreachable." Then he'd added, embarrassed, "Even I tried to find him at first. I had this idea." He'd even blushed then. "You know, demanding Abby. That he turn her over to me." He had bent ever so slightly, so he was eye to eye with Hannah. "I could take better care of her."

Deirdre had said, "Come and see her little stool. When she was this big she would stand on it and play her violin."

She'd lifted the small, three-legged stool. It was painted a chalky blue, with red and white hearts stenciled on it. "I used to dress her in white dresses with smocked fronts and pinafores. She had so much potential. Everyone thought so."

Gavin had smiled sadly. "The conductor at Le Company told me she should have played all over the world."

"Stop it!" Hannah had shouted. "She's not dead, you know. You're both talking like she's dead or something."

"Hannah," Deirdre had said, "we're just reminiscing."

"How sentimental," Hannah had said as she'd pushed past the two of them. "How drippy and sentimental."

She'd waited in Deirdre's office until she'd heard them both leave. She'd heard Deirdre offering to walk Gavin to the elevator, offering to have Hannah go with him to see Abby at Goldens Point on Saturday, and Gavin saying, "You are too kind." Then Hannah had gone back to the living room. The tiny stool with the fading hearts stood, lonely, in the center of the room. On the coffee table, Gavin had left two pieces of his homemade paper—a thick, cream-colored piece and one that looked almost iridescent, like an opal. Hannah had picked them both up, flung open the window, and sent them sailing to the ground below, falling as slow and lazy as autumn leaves.

"He's so sappy," Hannah groaned as Gavin started to move toward them again, his arms laden with wildflowers.

Abby watched him too. "Dr. Kornbluth says that every time I hurt a man, it's a way of getting back at Zach."

Hannah said, "What do you think?"

Abby sighed. "I think that sounds like a bunch of baloney. I keep trying to stand on my own two feet, then I stumble. Sometimes it's when I hear Zach's voice, sometimes when I see him. Sometimes all it takes is a memory."

"Dr. Kornbluth should be in 'Peanuts.' PSYCHIA-TRIST FIVE CENTS. That's about all it's worth anyway."

"Gavin would build us a beautiful house," Abby said, "and cover the floor with scattered leaves."

Hannah bit down on her bottom lip, thinking about Chelsea's house and how Mrs. Kent had stripped the wood floor in their dining room, then bleached it, then rubbed white paint into it by hand. When she had finished, it looked, Hannah had thought, like snow. "They do this in Norway," Chelsea had explained as they stood with Mrs. Kent and peered into the room, waiting for the floor to dry.

"In Norway," Hannah said to her mother, "they bleach their floors and then rub white paint into them."

She didn't want to, but she found herself wondering, as she had done so many times while waiting for Abby to arrive at Chelsea's for her, what it would be like to live someplace beautiful. Someplace filled with wildflowers, with patterns of leaves on the floor.

"Don't the most wonderful things happen in story-books?" Abby said dreamily. "It's so sad to stop believing in those things."

"In storybooks," Hannah said, "children get cooked into soup, grandmothers get eaten by wolves, and women get poisoned by apples and spinning-wheel needles."

"But they always get rescued," Abby said. "Prince Charming always comes."

Gavin reached them, his hair damp with sweat.

"For you," he said, laying the flowers at Abby's feet and on her lap. There were small yellow ones, and long purple thistles, black-eyed Susans, and tight orange buttons. He picked up some Queen Anne's lace and slowly, carefully, wove it into her hair.

Hannah lay on her back, unable to watch, suddenly weary of all of this, the men—including Zach—who had cupped her mother's face in their strong hands, or kissed her fingertips, or brought her flowers. She remembered how once, Doug had taken them on a picnic and had picked buttercups. He'd had Abby tilt her head up, toward the sun, again and again, while he'd held a buttercup under her chin. "My," he'd said each time, "you really love butter, don't you?" He'd claimed there was a shadowy yellow reflection on Abby's neck, but Hannah had never seen it, not once, despite the dozens of buttercups he'd held there.

She focused on the sky, the clouds, high and thin like spun sugar. The grass and dirt smelled rich in the hot July air. Gavin's and Abby's voices became a distant hum, flies circling in the distance.

This morning, Hannah had told Noah that it looked like she wouldn't be joining her parents in Paris after all. "They're worried about this touch of amnesia I have," she'd said. "Plus, they're in a *très* romantic mood." Noah had smiled and clutched her clammy hand, while four game-show contestants tried to guess the price of a refrigerator-freezer. "Maybe you'll stay forever," he'd said, not daring to look at her. She'd focused on the TV screen, too, on the overweight woman dressed in a shiny purple dress who had guessed within two hundred dollars of the suggested retail price. "No," Hannah had said, "we can't stand to be apart for too long. We're like the Three Musketeers, the Three Stooges, the Three Blind Mice." "What about your violin?" he'd asked. "What about Juilliard? What about—" "You know," Hannah had said as the heavy woman in purple began to walk down a path lit with prizes, "I had no idea that kitchen appliances were so expensive. In Paris, we have just an icebox to keep things cold. And then only for forty-eight hours."

The clouds seemed to be lifting higher, almost disappearing. She tried to remember, again, her room, their house, Dara's face. But they remained still, as pale and elusive as the buttercup's reflection under her mother's chin.

Once, Abby had told her why she'd stuck it out with Zach. She'd told her how he'd tracked her down at Mount Snow and made her promise to never again give up on him, no matter what. "But after all this time," Hannah had said. Her mother had been drinking heavily that night, and her eyes sparkled from the wine and the moonlight that filtered into her bedroom. Mary and Rhoda were trying on bridesmaid's gowns on the television, and Abby had said, "All the waiting, all the crying—it's all worth it when we're together." Abby had still believed that when a person was in love, they touched the stars. That when a person was in love, nothing else mattered. Now she had stopped believing in those things.

A few years ago when Hannah was in kindergarten, she had sat huddled with Abby under the quilt Doug had bought them, and read a pop-up book of *Hansel and Gretel*. As they'd turned each page, a new three-dimensional illustration jumped out at them—Hansel and Gretel making their way hand in hand through the forest, the gingerbread house, and finally, their father, a woodsman with an ax, rescuing them from the witch. Hannah had studied that father, his forest-green clothes and shiny silver ax and pointy red beard. Zach, she'd known, would not rescue her from a wicked witch, or from a boiling pot of children stew. Not ever. But her mother had believed it. She'd said, "Enter the daddy! He'll rescue them and bring them home safely. Aren't daddies terrific?"

Hannah sat up, brushed the grass from her hair. She wanted to tell her mother that daddies—at least hers— were not so terrific, that she'd never believed in happily-ever-after, that she'd been afraid to tell Abby before because maybe then Abby would stop believing too.

But Gavin was talking, holding Abby's hands in his. "It could be," he said, "so wonderful."

Hannah stood up, almost shouted for Abby to come with her now. Life can be wonderful, she almost told her, not in a storybook way, not because daddies or Prince Charmings will come and make it wonderful, but because *we* make it wonderful. But she didn't shout. The words stuck in her mouth and Abby turned her head away from Gavin Berry, the Queen Anne's lace drooping, falling in a tangled heap.

"I can't count on you to make my life wonderful," Abby said, and her voice was clear and sure. "I can't count on you or storybook fantasies."

He reached over and brushed the fallen flowers from her hair.

"I cheated," he said. "Queen Anne's lace is really just a weed."

"That's okay," Abby said. "It's a beautiful weed anyway."

AMNESIA

The first morning that Noah didn't show up, Hannah sat and stared at the television until after two o'clock. She watched show after show, sure that at any moment there would be a knock on the door and that when she opened it, there would be Noah, wearing his Mets World Series '86 T-shirt, his eyes shiny behind his glasses. She imagined his excuses for not coming earlier. "I had to go shopping with my mother," he'd groan. Or, "There was no way I could miss practice this morning."

While she waited, her head cocked so she wouldn't miss the slightest stirring at the front door, her eyes glued to the screen, she didn't even yell at the contestants to buy the specially priced Warhol lithograph or to keep spinning. She just sat and waited. At two o'clock, when a spinning world and dramatic organ music announced the start of a soap opera, Hannah turned off the television, went into Deirdre's office, and read the entire script of 'Night Mother out loud twice. First as the mother, then as the fat, suicidal daughter, Jessie.

The next morning, Hannah showered and dressed in

the bright orange Twiggy dress. Her weeks in New York had proven to her that the dress was, indeed, terrific. Copies of it, in equally bright shades of yellow, pink, and green, were everywhere, on bone-thin bald mannequins, housewives at the Fairway market, and even models in magazines that Hannah had never read until she got here— *Details, New York Woman, The Face.* That morning she sat with a stack of magazines in front of her and a fan-shaped silver bowl full of sour cream-and-onion potato chips beside her, and waited. She didn't even turn on the television. The magazines remained unopened as she re-played again and again their last morning together, before she'd gone up to Goldens Point with Gavin Berry. Per-haps, she wondered, she had missed some clue or hint from Noah that he wouldn't be back.

Her mind raced. Maybe he had to go away. Maybe he was sick. Or in a terrible accident. Or worse. She went over that morning again, trying not to miss one detail of it. She had sat right here, with Noah beside her, her sweaty hand in his. A woman on *Sale of the Century* that day had won twin Mustangs, one blue and one pink. She was sure that before he'd left, Noah had told her that they could watch the fireworks together on the roof on the Fourth of July. He had said he could get ahold of some beer. "St. Pauli Girl," he'd said, and then he'd smiled and flashed his fantastically deep dimples at her. She was sure he had said that, sure he had smiled at the doorway as he'd left and headed for practice in Central Park. She could still remember the way his body had become a distant dot through the peephole as she'd watched him walk away.

Hannah thought she heard a sound at the door. But when she opened it, there was just a tall, leggy, redheaded woman going into the dancer's apartment next door. The woman looked startled when Hannah flung the door open.

"I'm just feeding the cats," she explained nervously.

Hannah could not hide her disappointment. She slumped against the door frame and watched as the woman tried to balance a few suitcases, a grocery bag, and the keys, which jangled from a miniature pink ballet slipper.

"All right," the woman said. Her face was very white, unnaturally white, and her hair seemed redder against that face, her eyes a strange translucent blue. "You caught me. I'm subletting. Please don't mention it to Alfredo. I've been evicted twice already this summer. You know?"

Hannah shrugged and went back inside. Who cares about this strange-looking woman, or Alfredo, or evictions? All she wanted was to find Noah.

At noon, she called his apartment. If he answered, she decided, she would just hang up. If his mother answered, she'd ask for someone else, Babette. She'd say, "Is Babette at home?" Then, when his mother said she had the wrong number, she'd say, "Oh, dear. I wanted Babette Moliere and by accident I dialed Noah Meade, whose name, you see, is right above Babette's. Well, is Noah at home?" She practiced twice, then called. The phone just rang and rang. Fifty-two times. As she counted the rings, she stared out the window at the marquee of the movie theater across the street. *THREE MEN AND A BABY.* Hadn't Noah said they would go to that movie? Tonight?

The doorbell sounded and Hannah dropped the phone.

"Coming," she shouted as she ran down the long hallway. She tried to seem calm when she opened the door.

It was the redhead from next door.

"Hi," she said. "Is your mother here?"

Hannah moaned. "I'm busy," she said.

The woman wore turquoise leg warmers and big flat suede shoes, like Minnie Mouse. "Look," she said. "I don't want to get kicked out. You know. It's illegal and all that. But it's only until Casper gets back from Toronto, you know?''

"I don't care," Hannah said. "Neither does my mother. And I'm very sick. I have amnesia. A head injury."

The woman looked baffled. She stretched herself like a cat, right in the doorway, her muscles and bones a map of odd lines and bumps.

Hannah closed the door and called downstairs on the intercom to the doorman.

"Excuse me," she said in a French accent, "but has anyone in this building . . . uh . . . died or anything?''

"Do you have anyone in particular in mind?" he said.

"Anyone on, say, the fifth floor?''

He was quiet a minute. "No," he said finally. "The fifth floor is all alive and well.''

"Oh.''

She hung up and went into the closet. From next door came loud music. "A One, Two, Three, Four!" Then the shuffling of dancing feet.

That night, Hannah stood in front of the movie theater, half expecting Noah to appear there. Maybe, she thought, they were just going to meet at the movies. He had told her in detail how the three men had diapered the baby and how the special-effects person had made it seem like the baby wet right on Tom Selleck. "I read it in *Premiere*," Noah had told her. Then he'd added, "Want to go and see it Wednesday night?''

When he didn't show up, she walked across the street to Gray's Papaya and ate three sour-tasting hot dogs. She pressed herself against the counter and watched the movie theater. Maybe, she thought hopelessly, he meant the late show. But she was sure he hadn't, sure that something was very wrong.

She walked back to the apartment, where Deirdre and June were making lists and packing suitcases.

"Has anybody in the building been hurt really bad lately?" Hannah asked her grandmother. "Maybe a kid?" She imagined Noah in a hospital room, IV tubes in his arm and nose, the steady hum of a respirator.

"We have to get organized," Deirdre announced. "They're letting Toby out, and let me tell you, he'd better be as dry as a leaf."

"I heard something about a kid falling off the roof or something," Hannah said.

She watched as June methodically folded silk scarves into perfect squares.

"Not that one," Deirdre said, pulling one free from June's hands. "It's too grim-looking." She turned to Hannah, waving the gray-and-tan-speckled scarf like a flag. "Agenda," she said. "On the Fourth we drive up to Newport to fetch Toby. Then it's back here for the bags and onward to Williamstown. We open on the Twenty-seventh."

"I can't go to Newport on the Fourth," Hannah said. "I have plans on the Fourth." She thought of sitting high on the roof, under the stars with Noah, watching the biggest fireworks display ever. Maybe it had been a mistake to tell him that she liked beer. Maybe he thought girls shouldn't drink beer. She flopped down on the couch, miserable.

"Your posture stinks," Deirdre said, tugging at Hannah's shoulders. "I used to walk around the house with books on my head to practice perfect posture. A dancer needs perfect posture. You'd be surprised how that carries over."

"What about my mother? We always spend the Fourth of July together. With Zach."

June answered in a flat voice. "She's not ready to leave there. Maybe in a few weeks."

"What's going to happen when she's ready anyway?" Hannah said. "What big special thing is supposed to happen?"

Deirdre snapped her fingers. The scarf floated gently downward. "I know," she said, "we'll bring Toby his favorite hat. What do you say?"

"I say I want to get my mother and leave here altogether," Hannah said.

She felt tired and off balance.

"That gray one," Deirdre said. "From *Edie's Esca pades*. He loves that one."

On the third morning that Noah didn't show up at the apartment, Hannah walked over to Central Park to find him. She told herself she was just going there to make sure he was alive, unhurt, safe. Before she left, she taped a note to the apartment door: NOAH, BE RIGHT BACK. WAIT FOR ME!!! HANNAH. Just in case.

A man with blond Rastafarian curls bouncing across his forehead and neck stood at the park entrance selling T-shirts. The shirts had a line of fat green trees across the front with YOU'VE GOT TO HAVE PARK printed under them.

"Do you know where the baseball teams practice around here?" Hannah asked in her fake French accent.

The man shrugged, sending his thin sausage curls haywire.

"Some boys," she said. "You know. *Très* American."

"Wanna buy a shirt?" he asked her. His front tooth sparkled, gold. He spit through a space in his teeth, a steady straight stream that landed inches from Hannah's toes.

"No," she said, stepping back. "I just want to find this boy." She forgot to use her accent this time.

The man smiled and nodded, his head a frenzy of jumping curls. "Some kids play over there," he said, pointing.

She followed the curved yellowed nail of his forefinger. In the distance she heard shouting. She imagined she could make out Noah's voice.

"This boy I'm looking for is the pitcher," she said.

"Uh-huh," the man said. He picked up a newspaper and started to read. The headlines screamed: BESS IN MESS!

Who isn't? Hannah thought, and headed through the park.

She saw him right away, on the mound, winding up. Just last week, he had explained different pitches to her—screwballs, knuckleballs, fastballs, curves. She had pretended to understand. He was wearing a black-and-orange Princeton T-shirt, baggy khaki shorts, and a Mets cap pulled low on his forehead. He looked very much alive, unharmed, and Hannah stood, frozen, watching him as he stood chewing gum and throwing some stupid pitch in Central Park.

Slowly, Hannah inched toward the game. Two girls sat on the edge of the field, eating frozen Tofutti and watching the game. They both looked fresh and clean, not hot and miserable like Hannah. They wore perfectly color-coordinated outfits, intricate pastel layers of T-shirts and polo shirts over faded denim miniskirts. Their Keds sparkled white against the grass.

"Hi!" Hannah said, straining to sound calm, cheerful. She shifted uncomfortably in her old sandals, painfully aware that the straps on the left one were held together with a Flintstones Band-Aid, Fred and Wilma chasing each other with Dino on their heels.

The girls looked at each other and didn't answer her, as if by some unspoken agreement.

"Let's go, Kevin!" one of them shouted.

"Do you come here every day?" Hannah asked them.

"Sometimes," one of them said, her eyes focused on the game. Her hair was in a long dark ponytail, fastened with a perfect floppy bow.

"I know the pitcher," Hannah said. "Is he all better?"

The girls looked at each other again.

"Is he all *better*?" The other one giggled. She had long curly eyelashes that fluttered like a Southern belle's. Hannah wondered why these girls didn't sweat under all those shirts, how their hair remained dry and clean in this heat.

"I just flew in from Paris yesterday," Hannah said. "I thought I'd come by and say hello to Noah. See if he was better."

"*Paris*?" the ponytailed one said. Her almond-colored eyes ran up Hannah's body, from the broken sandals to her badly cut hair, and Hannah squirmed under her gaze.

"France," Hannah added weakly. She wished she had dressed more carefully, worn the bright orange minidress instead of Abby's old shirt that had somehow wound up in Hannah's things. The shirt had once been white, with thickly embroidered butterflies hovering over chubby flowers. But it had turned a faded pink from being washed, long ago, with something bright red, and the embroidery threads had frayed, leaving strange clumps of colors in no particular shapes—worn circles that had once been daisies, zigzag lines that had once been an intricate pattern on a butterfly's wings.

The teams were trading places now, a new boy headed toward the mound as Noah and the infielders walked off, right toward Hannah. Her mouth grew instantly dry, like a giant ball of cotton or dust had settled there, and when she tried to open it, to swallow and moisten it, her tongue clacked noisily. The girls looked at her, then away quickly.

She watched Noah as one of the infield boys talked to him, seriously, earnestly. He must have been busy, Hannah thought. Or away for a few days. Hadn't he told her that his family went to Quogue every summer? Hadn't he described their house there? The crooked, steep path that led to the beach, the way the sheets and furniture felt damp all the time? She created a scenario in which Noah and his family arrived back just this morning. She imagined them unloading their suitcases from the elevator, his father urging him to get right over to the park for a game of baseball, and Noah hesitating, wanting to run down the hall to see her but his father pushing him outside to practice his knuckleball, his curve.

She was afraid that Noah and the infielders and these two girls wrapped in pastel shirts could all hear her heart pounding as she stepped forward and said, "Hiya," in a too-loud voice.

Noah threw his glove down and started to walk away.

"Wait!" Hannah shouted. "Noah!"

Noah turned toward her, angrily, no sign of the dimple that resided deep in his cheek. "How's your amnesia?" he said. "How's *Paris*?"

She didn't answer. Her knees under the old purple shorts she wore knocked together and shook, no matter how hard she tried to hold them still. "I do have amnesia," she said, and as if to prove it she tried right then to remember the wallpaper in her room, the slanted shelf. "I can't even hardly remember my room at home. Or even the state capitals." Her mind struggled with Alabama, the very first one.

"Give me a break," Noah said. And walked away.

The two girls and the infielders stared at her as if she

had just walked off a spaceship, as if her skin was green and tiny antennas bobbed from her head.

"I have this amnesia," she said. "I don't know what to think anymore."

"Maybe you should have your head examined," the girl with the lush eyelashes said. The others giggled with her.

"Wait," Hannah said. "Montgomery. Montgomery, Alabama." Then she walked away from them, quickly, then quicker, until she was running through the park.

"*Au revoir!*" one of the girls yelled after her. "*A bientôt!*"

Hannah sat with her grandparents in the restaurant at the Sheraton on Goat Island in Newport. Her grandfather's breath smelled sweet, like mouthwash, Life Savers, and gum. There were small beads of sweat on his upper lip that seemed like they would roll off at any moment and splash onto the crisp white-linen tablecloth. He kept lighting cigarettes with shaky hands, then snuffing them out, grinding them fiercely into the ashtray, then smiling nervously as he looked around the restaurant, like he was expecting someone else to join them.

Deirdre had thought it would be wonderful to spend the night in Newport after they fetched Toby. But so far, Hannah had found the trip awful, not even a little bit wonderful.

On their ride up here, as they inched along with all the other cars that clogged Route 95 on their way to long weekends at seashores in Rhode Island, Cape Cod, and Maine, Deirdre had pointed out ordinary things as if they were quite extraordinary—sailboats jammed into Mystic Harbor, long bridges that hung over the ocean. "Isn't this terrific?" Deirdre had said, again and again. It was as if she had no idea that every summer Hannah and Zach and

Abby saw things just like these. Bridges, boats, beaches—
they were as common to Hannah as Deirdre's silly sky-
scrapers were to her. Big deal, Hannah had thought each
time Deirdre had gushed over some scenery or announced
the wonderful things to come—lobster for dinner, tours of
mansions, the ocean.

Hannah had concentrated instead on the passing cars,
searching for Zach's Plymouth Voyager with the fake sunset painted on its back window. He'd be heading north
toward Vermont, perhaps on this very road. The traffic
had moved so slowly that Hannah had been sure that if
she'd spotted him, she could roll down the window, stick
her head out of the chemical-smelling air conditioning
into the July heat, and shout at him to stop right there and
get her, like a Chinese fire drill. But she only saw one
van, a new Toyota that was sleek and bullet-shaped with
windows tinted a smoky gray and a New Mexico license
plate. "Land of Enchantment." An Afghan's head stuck
out from a sunroof, the dog's hair and ears flapping gently
in the still air. Otherwise, the road had been clogged with
Suzuki Samurais and Mitsubishi Monteros.

Even now, in the restaurant, as Toby lit cigarette after
cigarette, Deirdre went on exclaiming about those stupid
bridges. "So majestic," she said, sweeping her arms out
dramatically. "And the ocean! God, it's like . . . like
what, Miss Poet? Toby, we've got a poet on our hands
here."

Toby pushed another cigarette into the cluttered
ashtray. "A poet?" he said. "You don't say."

"The ocean sparkled like diamonds," Deirdre announced. "That's so unoriginal, isn't it, Emily Dickinson
Junior? How about sparkled like sugar?"

"That's just fine," Toby said. "Sugar is really a fine
simile for the ocean."

Hannah dropped her head onto the table. The table-cloth smelled faintly of bleach.

"Hannah," Deirdre hissed. "Pick up your head."

Toby laughed, awkwardly. "Teenagers," he said.

Deirdre grabbed Hannah by the top of her hair and gently yanked her head up. "Really," she said.

"When our daughter Abby was a teenager," Toby said to Hannah, as if she didn't know who his daughter was, "she was always doing the most peculiar things." He leaned very close to Hannah as he spoke, breathing his sweet breath on her. Tiny reddish veins decorated his nose, like the small road lines on a map.

Deirdre stood up and glanced around the room, to see if anyone here had recognized her. "Let's go," she said too loudly.

Hannah groaned.

"I am ready," Toby said, standing unsteadily. He wore a red polka-dotted ascot and the gray hat Deirdre had brought him. When she'd handed it to him, his face had lit up. "My favorite hat," he'd said, cradling it carefully in his hands. "From my first movie." "No," Deirdre had said. "It's from one of the Edie movies." But he'd insisted. "No, not at all. It's from *Meet John Doe*. I had one word in the entire movie. 'Fraud.' I yelled it right at Gary Cooper himself." "Honestly," Deirdre had muttered, "your brain is pickled. You can't remember a damn thing." Toby had just laughed. "I remember that," he'd said. "I yelled 'Fraud' right at Gary Cooper."

Deirdre weaved through the tables rather than around them, her head held high, her canary-yellow scarf floating behind her like a dancer's.

"As we say in the theater," she said loudly, "the show must go on."

Toby chuckled as he followed behind her.

At the door, Hannah turned to all the other diners in the restaurant.

"In case you still haven't noticed," she said loudly, "that was the great Deirdre Falls Church herself."

Toby and Deirdre dragged Hannah through vast mansions and across skinny paths that hovered above cliffs overlooking the ocean. Deirdre kept exclaiming loudly how very grand it was, while Toby popped Life Savers into his mouth and nervously tapped his feet across marble floors that had been imported from castles in France and Italy. When one tour guide showed them the bathtub, which had hot, cold, and saltwater faucets, all gold, Deirdre had shouted, "How decadent! I love it!" Someone in the group had whispered that here was the real Dulcinea Day, and as Hannah shrank back against the perfectly balanced two-ton doors, Deirdre signed her autograph on everyone's brochures.

At dinner, they insisted she order lobster. While Deirdre explained how to eat it properly and Toby eyed the bottles of wine on the other tables, Hannah imagined bursting through the huge glass window, running down the dock to a boat headed for France. She would bribe the captain with her thirty-five-dollar lobster dinner if he would take her with him. Then she'd really go to Paris, away from her grandparents and even Abby and Zach, all of whom had seemed to forget all about her, to not care that she was frightened of the future or that her heart had been broken into a million little pieces by a dimpled boy with glasses.

"She's a quiet thing," Toby said over dessert, a biscuit piled high with strawberries and whipped cream.

"She's a sulker," Deirdre said.

"Stop saying 'she,'" Hannah said. "I'm right here, you know."

"Just like Abby," Deirdre said. "Already all upset over some boy. Not a good start at all. You don't want to end up all mixed-up, do you?"

"Oh, she's got a good head on her shoulders, I bet," Toby said.

"The Meade boy," Deirdre said. "Do you know the Meade boy?"

Toby shook his head. "Doesn't ring a bell."

The couple at the next table were drinking liqueurs out of gracefully fluted small glasses, and Toby bent his head toward them, as if to get a whiff.

"How do you know?" Hannah asked her grandmother.

"He came by looking for you the other day."

"*What* day?" Hannah's heart was beating so fast that she rested her hand above it lightly, as if to slow it down somehow.

"I don't remember."

"You have to remember," Hannah said. "Please."

Deirdre sighed and rested her spoon, thick with chocolate mousse, on the table. "The day you went up to Goldens Point. He came by to see about a movie. That silly new one about the baby. I told him you were upstate visiting your mother."

Hannah's heart seemed to shatter all over again, to drop from her chest, tumbling, tumbling down. Her hand fell away, too, and lay heavily in her lap, to catch all the tiny pieces of her broken heart.

"I was up at Goldens Point," Toby was saying. "In '80, I think. Quite a lovely place, what with the river and those fields."

"You told him my mother was upstate?" Hannah said, her voice a mere whisper, drowned out in her own ears by Noah's challenging, angry one. "How's Paris?"

But Deirdre had already grown bored with the topic and was, instead, discussing Toby's hat. "I remember as clear as a bell how you wore that hat in a restaurant scene where Edie waves over to you while she sips champagne."

"Did you say anything else to Noah?" Hannah said, already knowing that Deirdre had said plenty.

"He asked me a million crazy questions. About Paris and Juilliard. He thought *you* played the violin. He's all mixed-up."

Hannah slumped down in her seat. In front of her, her ice cream sundae was a puddle of melted ice cream and hot fudge, with an off-red cherry half floating on top.

"Yeah," she said. "He's all mixed-up." Her hand stayed palm up, ready to catch the pieces.

One year, on the Fourth of July, Hannah and her parents had watched fireworks at Mile High Stadium in Denver. They didn't have a blanket with them, and had just lay back on the grass, getting green stains and dirt smudges all over their clothes and skin, as above them sprays of sparkling color filled the sky, then fell seemingly right at them. "Just like Rhododendron Dell," Abby had whispered. "In San Francisco."

Now, Hannah stood at a bank of pay phones in the Sheraton lobby and reminded Abby of that night. "And we just plopped right down," she said, "without a blanket or anything and watched. Remember?"

Abby's voice sounded very, very faraway. "Yes," she said.

"And you said it was like San Francisco."

This time Abby didn't answer.

Hannah said, "I know Zach's coming for us today."

"So he says." Abby laughed, but not like she thought it was funny.

"Deirdre says I have to go up to Williamstown with her and Toby until you're better."

"You'll meet stars there," Abby said. "Christopher

214

Reeve. And they have a deli there where all the sandwiches are named after stars. Maybe there's even a Deirdre Falls Church."

"Remember how last year Zach bought all those sparklers and Roman candles? We were in North Carolina. In Duck."

As if she hadn't heard her at all, Abby said, "A bunch of us here are going to town to see some fireworks at the high school. Real American, huh?"

Hannah started to cry. Her chin and the telephone mouthpiece grew wet from tears. "I don't want to go up there with them," she said.

"I'm sorry," Abby said. "I have to be selfish right now. I have to be here alone and work through some things—"

"You *are* selfish already," Hannah cried into the phone. "I want a different mother. Someone who speaks French and knows how to cook. Someone who acts like a real mother, not a big fake like you."

She waited for her mother to cry too. But all Abby did was to quietly hang up the phone.

"I hope I never see you again," Hannah shouted, even though she knew no one was on the other end. She slammed the receiver down so hard that it bounced against the phone itself and dropped, jerkily, on its tight silver cord.

As Hannah walked through the crowded lobby, she wondered how she could find a passport, buy a plane ticket, run away. Somewhere, maybe, there was someone who would listen to her, and care about what she said. When she passed the coffee shop, she spotted Toby, sitting alone. He saw her, too, and started to wave in an exaggerated fashion, motioning for her to come and join him.

"Someday," she said as she sat beside him, "I'll

write my memoirs and everyone will be shocked at what they read in them. 'If we'd only listened,' they'll say. 'If we'd only known.' "

He nodded and smiled a big goofy smile at her. It was a smile she'd seen him use in the movies, as a helpful neighbor or good pal. It was the fakest smile in the world.

In front of him was a tall Bloody Mary, with curly celery and a slice of cucumber perched on the rim. Two glasses stood empty beside that one, the celery and cucumber uneaten, the sides thick with pepper and streaks of tomato juice.

"Very wise, Hannah," he said. "Memoirs. Very useful."

Hannah eyed the drink, then studied her grandfather's face. His eyes were a watery gray, but otherwise he seemed more relaxed, his hands steadier, the ashtray clean.

"A Virgin Mary," he said before he sipped the drink.

"Sure," Hannah said.

"I've been sitting here," he said, "thinking. Trying to get things in order. Deirdre won't take kindly to my decision, but I think I should stay in New York rather than accompany you two to Williamstown. Let the old gal have her day without baby-sitting me."

"She won't like that decision," Hannah said.

Toby crooked his finger at the waitress and raised the almost-empty glass.

"I've been on the phone all morning," he said, "with agents and the like. *The Equalizer* is looking for some people. Making lots of New York shows again these days." He met her gaze with his watery gray eyes. They, too, were streaked with thin red lines, like his nose.

The waitress placed another Bloody Mary in front of Toby.

"Order something," he told Hannah. "Have some waffles."

She stood up. "Someday," she said, "they'll name a sandwich after me. I'll look back on this awful summer and hardly be able to recall it. It will seem dim, and faraway."

"Yes," Toby agreed as he sipped from his fresh drink. "That's just the way it happens."

SAYING GOODBYE

The last thing Zach expected was to find the house empty, and Abby gone. The entire way up the main road that led to the cutoff for Abby's, Zach had tapped his fingers against the steering wheel, keeping beat to a silent, happy tune. He'd imagined the way Abby's gray eyes would look in this light, slightly blue, and full of surprise that he had finally come. He had pictured her smiling, running into his arms, and the way she'd feel against him on this warm July day.

By the time his van was rocking up the gravelly driveway, Zach was smiling, too, and singing out loud. He was full of promises—about Mexico, and the white stucco house they'd rent on a beach there, and the warm tortillas and cold beer they would eat in a sandy outdoor cafe.

He practically leaped from the van, as he called, "Abby!" loudly.

He ran up the broken, tilted steps, had a vague thought of maybe fixing them before they left, then was pounding on the door, chips of faded green paint falling on his shoes as he called, again, her name.

As he stood there, Zach could not let himself believe that she was gone. Maybe, he'd thought finally, she's with Hannah, shopping, or grabbing a pizza somewhere. He smiled again, at the thought of her gobbling up slice after slice of what she called "junk pizza." He and Hannah were left to pick off the things that didn't really belong on a pizza—Canadian bacon, tomatoes, pineapple. Hannah would twist her face in disgust as she gingerly lifted off an anchovy. "Hairy," she'd mutter.

Zach walked back down the steps and studied the house. The screen door stayed, stuck, open, and he went up the steps again to close it. The chain was tangled. He couldn't imagine how that had happened. He felt a mosquito bite, and heard, in the distance, a lawn mower or motorbike. When the chain was untangled, the screen door slammed shut easily, with a firm bang. Zach stood, uncertainly, and looked around him. He fought back the feeling that the house, the yard, even the driveway, looked deserted. There was no sign of life, except an occasional mosquito. Even the lawn mower had stopped. From somewhere deep inside him, Zach felt dread building. He knew somehow that Abby had really left, that she was not coming back in a few minutes or an hour.

He wondered what day it was, if perhaps she was off somewhere playing one final gig with Three-Legged Horse. He knew that he was pretty much on schedule. All the way here, he'd run into Fourth of July traffic, parades and vacationers in packed station wagons. Just last night, he'd looked off into the night sky and been surprised by a burst of color, fireworks spraying the stars.

All the way here, he'd been driven by one thought—Abby. He had known that this time, he could not talk his way out of it, or make excuses, or send her violets. They had reached the end of all that. Sometimes, Abby seemed like a stranger to him, someone special and glorious, someone who seemed to be from a different world than this one. Just thinking of her that way made his heart lurch violently. There were other parts to her, parts he had not wanted to know—the mother in her, the good wife. He would get to know them now.

He pressed his face against the kitchen window. On the windowsill, in a cracked and speckled pottery vase, was a bunch of long-dead violets. She had left them there all this time, he thought, and the thought made him feel better. She loved him. He was here.

A few weeks earlier, it hadn't seemed as simple as that. He had gone to London to break it off with Nina and had not had the courage to do it. Just as he'd teeter on the words, she'd flash him one of her unbelievable smiles, or he'd watch her work, transforming a simple piece of papier-mâché into something magical. And he'd be unable to do it. Instead, he'd think, "Later," and he'd pick her tiny body up and have hard, rough sex with her. Afterwards, his lips bruised from her biting, he'd lie beside her, studying her, wondering if he'd ever find the courage to leave for good.

Then came the phone call to Abby, when he'd called to tell her he had been delayed, and her voice had been flat and dead. He had tried to make her laugh, to understand, but she had refused. And he had not spoken to her since. Instead, the phone just rang and rang. He'd even tried Doug and Sean. Both of their numbers disconnected. He'd tried Melissa, but only got an answering machine. Fear had started to grow in him, a fear of Abby walking out of his life. And that fear had been what he'd needed to leave Nina.

Her flat in London was tiny, crowded with too-large furniture. Lace doilies hung over the arms of chairs and sofas. There were needlepoint pillows and footstools everywhere and Zach was forever tripping over them, or knocking the doilies to the floor. He kidded her that if he stood still long enough, someone might needlepoint him too. Or cover him in lace. He could not breathe well in that apartment, and every night he had to jump up at least once and stick his head out the window, to gulp in the damp London air.

On the morning that he'd left Nina, he had tried again to call Abby. He'd let the phone ring for almost ten minutes, watching the tiny clock beside the couch count the minutes for him. Then he'd hung up and gone to the kitchen, where Nina, her face still full of sleep, was busy making tea. She had to do it the real way, she'd told him, and followed an intricate process that he hadn't understood.

He'd watched her in the cramped kitchen, had thought: Don't notice the way her silk robe falls open when she bends like that. Don't look at the inside of her thigh there, or the way her lipstick from last night is so sexy, faded and smudged like that.

She'd looked up from her tea making, frowning. "What is it?" she'd asked him.

"I'm going back to Abby. I want to go back."

She'd pushed past him, her silk robe opening, her tight body there for him to see. But when she'd seen him looking at her, she'd held it closed and said, "Don't."

They had met two years earlier, at a gallery opening in San Francisco. He went to them regularly, despite the same white wine and hors d'oeuvres, the cheese puffs, the small sticks of vegetables, the flat breads cut into shapes and smeared with pastes and spreads—despite the same conversations and debates, despite the same people eating and drinking and talking at each other. He always went, looking for that one new person who could help him.

That's how he'd found Nina. She'd been wearing a papier-mâché copper-and-green Statue of Liberty crown that she'd made in honor of its 100th birthday. Zach had overheard someone talking about her, and her ArtWear. "She's hot," the man had said. "Making a bundle on that crap." Zach had stood across the room, watching her. She did not leave her spot by the bar. She'd just stood there and let people come to her. And they did. A steady stream of them. Every now and then, as she'd talked, she had touched the spokes of her crown, explaining, Zach had supposed, how she'd made it. "The color is so authentic," he'd heard someone saying.

Finally, as the crowd had thinned and the hors d'oeuvres had stopped, as people had gathered their coats and briefcases, he'd approached her.

"Here I am," he'd said, arms outstretched.

"Excuse me?"

"I'm your tired, your hungry . . ."

He had liked her laugh immediately, deep and hearty. As if it were erupting from her gut. Later, he would learn that she swore like a sailor, ate like a truck driver, made love ferociously, leaving him, often, bruised and bitten and scratched. She was, he'd learn, as deceptive as her jewelry. It seemed like metal, hard and heavy and cold, but was instead fragile and light. Nina was the reverse, a delicate exterior masking something rough and wild beneath it.

Zach never intended to fall in love with the women he met when he was away from Abby. He, in fact, loved only Abby. Loved her in the only way he could—tentatively and, mostly, from far away. The other women he wanted for what they could give him—their bodies, some pleasure, and, mostly, a boost to his career. Every time he went home with an art critic, or gallery owner, or art dealer, he told himself it was a way to get ahead. Sometimes, he even thought he was helping Abby, and Hannah. But he also thought, as these women lay in his arms, that he was free, of PTA meetings and diapers and dinners in front of the six o'clock news.

When he got all he could from the new woman, he would ache for Abby—the safety of her arms, the brightness of her ideas, her constant, unrelenting love. He would leave the apartments decorated in country French or New Wave black, leave the already fading scents and touches of the other woman, and head east.

The night he'd met Nina, Zach had thought she would be just one more connection. He had long ago perfected his smile, learned to turn his gaze so that it penetrated and held.

He'd said, "So feed me. Take me in, Lady Liberty."

She'd laughed again. But still hadn't moved.

He had touched her hair, beneath the crown, lightly. "Isn't that heavy?" he'd asked her. "Doesn't your neck ache from the weight?"

"No," she'd said. "It's surprisingly light."

Her eyes, though dark brown, were flecked with gold and green, as if flecks of paint from the crown had been sprinkled there.

Zach had had a premonition as he'd looked into those eyes. He'd felt that he'd better walk away from her, that she was somehow different from all the others. He'd had, in a startlingly clear flash, an image of Abby there in front of him.

But already, Nina had been agreeing, saying that yes, they'd go and eat somewhere.

He'd lifted his hand, to wipe away that image of Abby, and Nina had caught it.

"Hunan," she'd said. "But not the new one. I hate the new one."

"Me too," he'd said, not letting go of her fingers.

As they'd sat at the counter at Hunan, he'd told her stories about his Chinese ancestry, about his great-grandfather, the samurai warrior.

"When the civil wars ripped through China," he'd said, "he ended up having to make umbrellas to support his family. The guy was practically starving, but he wouldn't sell his swords. He was a man of honor. My father still has them, hanging above the fireplace in the family room."

Nina had laughed her hearty laugh. "Sounds like you saw *Hari-Kiri* too many times. Okay. I'm the granddaughter of Norma Desmond. See, as strange as it may seem, she was pregnant when she killed William Holden."

"*Sunset Boulevard*," Zach had said. He'd known for certain that he was in deep trouble.

For the two years since he'd met Nina, Zach had led a double life. Back and forth between Nina's aggressiveness and Abby and their history. Standing in front of Nina last week in the stuffy London flat, finally choosing, Zach had wanted to crumble, to fall onto the busy carpet into a tired heap.

"Just get out then," Nina had said. "Go to her. Get out."

Weakly, he'd said, "Our lives are just so connected—"

"Spare me your new-age bullshit. She's the one who buys that crap. You're getting us confused."

"I mean," Zach had said, "we have a shared history. We have Hannah." At that moment, he had wanted both to leave and to take back his announcement and stay.

Nina had laughed. "What are you, up for 'Father of the Year' suddenly? You don't even know for sure how *old* she is. What grade she's in. Nothing."

He hadn't answered.

Then, like a line from an old black-and-white movie,

she'd said, "If you walk out that door, Zach, don't ever come back."

He'd wondered if he was supposed to name the movie, the actress who had first said that, the actor who had heard it. He'd wondered what that nameless actor had actually done—gone or stayed.

He'd felt exhausted, had leaned his head against the wall, between two thick and heavily framed oil paintings of horses.

"I hate saying goodbye," he'd said. He'd meant in general, but Nina had misunderstood. She'd moved closer to him.

"Then go to her and tell *her* goodbye. Let go of all that history."

That had not been what he'd meant. Nina's words had sounded almost right, and he'd opened his eyes and pushed away from her.

"Don't you see?" he'd said. "There's a reason why we've held on all these years."

"Because she's a doormat," Nina had said.

"No," he'd said, feeling his chest, his heart lighten. "It's because I really love her."

Nina stepped back.

"Fuck you," she'd said.

"I'm sorry," Zach had said.

But he hadn't felt sorry. He'd felt free.

From London, Zach had gone to Los Angeles, where he'd spent a day with Thornton Cairo at the gallery, watching as his New York series had been hung, catalogued, lighted. Gladdie Moore had shown up and refused to speak to him. He'd wondered briefly if she'd spoken to Nina, if Gladdie had the power to cancel the show. But Thornton had opened a bottle of champagne, had toasted the new show and Zach.

At a party that night, standing amid artists and writers dressed in black, a perfect complement to the apartment where the party was being held, which was all white—walls, floors, furniture draped and tied with white sheets—Zach had felt terror at the enormity of what he had done. He had cut his ties with Nina. He had decided to stay with Abby, to keep his promise of Mexico. He'd thought, with dread, of Hannah. Of the three of them. Of being a family. He'd gone to the bedroom, also all white, and dialed Abby's number. But all he'd gotten had been the ringing telephone. A young woman came in, and watched as he'd stood, desperately clutching the telephone as if it could help him.

The woman had said, "Looks like no one's home, huh?"

And Zach had thought, It's not over. I haven't reached Abby yet. I'm still on my own. The woman had said, "My name's Harmony."

At Harmony's apartment, she'd tossed him a condom, neon-blue and ribbed, as she'd casually lifted off her black turtleneck sweater and climbed out of her black stretch pants, then twirled, naked for him.

Zach had felt awkward, embarrassed. He'd held out the bright blue condom to her. "Never mind," he'd said. He'd felt it again, the need to go home.

Harmony had pouted, lifted her hands to his arms. Her fingers had been bedecked with silver rings, dozens of them climbing up her knuckles.

"Come on," she'd said. "I'm not an intravenous drug user or anything."

He had not even been sure if she was kidding or not. "Look, Harmony," he'd said, "what's your real name anyway?"

"Jennifer," she'd said. "Like everybody else's."

It had felt good to leave her, to think of Abby. He

had stepped outside and taken slow, even breaths of the warm California night. He could do it, he'd thought.

Zach pressed his face to the screen. They were definitely gone. He knew, not by the overgrown, dandelion-spotted grass, but by the sense of order he saw inside. Everything was too organized, clean. They had left.

As he walked one more time around the house, rattling windows and doors, he felt more and more sure that they were not coming back.

A voice from behind him said, "They hit the road." The girl slapped her hands together, loudly. "Vamoose." She was fat and sunburned and hot-looking, dressed in baggy shorts and a sweatshirt covered with hot-pink and lime-green smiling frogs.

Zach smiled at her. "Do you know when they'll be back?"

"Maybe tomorrow," she said. "Maybe never. A car came and whisked them away. A big car, with New York plates. You know the new ones? With the Statue of Liberty on them?"

He nodded. "New York, huh?"

"Hannah didn't even come and say goodbye. Ever since she's been friends with Chelsea, you know?"

Zach nodded again. A big car from New York? he thought.

He said, "They weren't sick or anything, were they?"

The girl laughed, scratched at a line of scabby mosquito bites on her leg. "I just went through this with Gavin Berry," she said.

"Gavin Berry?"

"Abby's boyfriend. You know. Lover. Whatever. Once, I peeked in the window and saw them doing it on the kitchen table. Hannah called me a liar but I swear I did."

Zach looked down the dirt road, as if maybe Abby might appear suddenly.

"Gavin Berry's ass is white as anything," the girl said.

He tried to think.

"You're Hannah's father," the girl said, just figuring it out. "Hannah says you're not such a great one. That you're—"

Zach waved her off. He needed to think.

"I got a postcard from Hannah," the girl said. "She said she was doing time with her grandmother while Abby got her act together somewheres else."

"What the hell is that supposed to mean?"

The girl giggled. "Beats me."

He peered through the screen again, into the orderly living room.

There was a quilt folded, neatly, over the back of the couch. Someone had arranged the throw pillows, two on each side. Zach felt his heart sinking. He knew what it meant. Abby had put things in order and then left him.

THE WAY IT
USED TO BE

Zach said, "Just like old times, huh?"

Paco and Melissa looked at each other.

"Well," Melissa said.

"Except that Abby's not here," Zach added quickly.

"Right," Paco said, pulling at the long neck of his bottle of Rolling Rock.

They sat in Paco's apartment, a fifth-floor walk-up on East Tenth Street and Avenue A, where salsa music blared from outside and the smell of urine filtered in from the apartment across the hall where a man lived with nine dogs. Zach sat right by the window, hoping to escape the smell, but finding, instead, the odors of garbage and garlic and smoke.

The three of them returned to an uncomfortable silence. It was Abby who linked them together. She was the only one who all three kept in touch with, and it seemed wrong for them to be here without her.

Today, Zach had shown up here. He had bought Paco breakfast at Odessa. He had said, "Let's call Melissa. I'd love to talk to her." Paco had searched through scraps of paper, old address books, until he'd found her number. "Upper East Side." Paco had laughed as Zach dialed. "Can you believe it?"

She had not wanted to come. But Zach kept insisting. "It'll be fun," he'd said. "Relive old times. You know." She did not want to relive any old times she'd had with Zach. She had known from the start that all Zach wanted was to find Abby. "He'll come looking for you," Abby had told her when Melissa had last visited her. "He knows you'll know where I am." "Like Mount Snow," Melissa had said. But Abby had shaken her head. "I wanted to be found then," she'd said.

But it was a beautiful Saturday morning, and Melissa had—as usual—no plans. The weekend was before her, long and lonely, a stack of movies to watch, a new account spread out on her antique Japanese coffee table. She would watch the movies, play old songs on the stereo, and end up watching *I Love Lucy* at three in the morning. Zach had said, "Have you got something better to do?" "Actually," she'd said, "yes." She had glanced again at the movies. "But maybe I can break away for a few minutes."

Zach sipped his beer. He tried to will them to tell him about Abby. He wanted to ask them if she'd come back to him, what he would have to do to make it happen. He said, "I've changed a lot." Hoping that they would believe him, lead him to Abby.

But they only looked at each other again.

"I used to think," Zach said, "that I'd do anything to make it."

"You did," Paco said. "Do anything to make it."

They all stared at their beers.

Melissa remembered all the times Zach had not called Abby, not shown up when he was supposed to. She thought of all the stories he'd told Abby, all the lies. Years later, Paco had told her that at first, Zach had been living with another woman. When Melissa told Abby, she'd laughed. "He wasn't," she'd said. "I would have known."

Zach went over to study Paco's sculptures.

"These are good," he said.

"Sure," Paco said. "That's why I'm still tending bar at a chic Mexican restaurant."

"I thought you quit that," Zach said.

"I quit Caramba!!!! and Bandito! Now I'm at Olé! It's this drive I have to make frozen margaritas."

Zach shook his head. "You shouldn't be wasting your time," he said.

Melissa laughed. "Try Zach's technique, Paco. Sleep with anybody who can help you. Tell them you love them until they get you a show or a review or sell a piece—"

"Melissa," Zach said. "Come on."

"Even Abby wasn't fooled anymore," she said. "She finally figured you out."

Zach stood in front of her. "Please," he said. "You've got to believe me. I love her."

Paco cleared his throat. "Zach," he said. "We know you."

"Where is she?" Zach asked Melissa. "I don't have to convince you that it's going to be different. It's her I've got to tell."

She didn't answer him.

He pulled out three airplane tickets, held them out to her. Proof. "We were going to Mexico."

"She doesn't want to see you," Melissa said. "She's had enough."

"Where's Hannah then?"

"You weren't even around when she was born, man," Paco said. "You didn't turn up for three goddamned months."

231

Zach held his hands out. "I fucked up. I'm trying to straighten myself out."

Paco said, "She can't see you, Zach."

Zach felt his chest tighten. They had to help him.

"Please," he said again.

"She's upstate," Paco said quietly.

"Paco!" Melissa said angrily.

"Where upstate?" Zach demanded. Already he was thinking of driving up there. If she saw him, talked to him, she would understand. He imagined them driving away together, imagined how close he had come to losing her.

"No," Melissa said.

Zach sat on the futon that Paco had folded into a couch, covered with an inky-blue, batik-print spread.

"What do I have to do?" he said, not even trying to hide his desperation. "Wear a hair shirt? Go to confession? What?"

Melissa felt herself wavering. "There's that other woman," she said.

"It's over," Zach said. "All of it's over."

"She'll be leaving there soon enough," Melissa said. "If she wants to see you then, she will."

"Hannah then," Zach said. "Where is she?"

"With Deirdre," Melissa said. "Uptown."

Zach stood. "If you see Abby—"

"No," Melissa said, looking right into those blue eyes that had so many times won Abby over.

"Tell her I came for her," Zach said. "Tell her I kept my word."

Abby looked at Jocelyn, reading a book beside her. *Women Who Love Too Much.* Jocelyn read one self-help book after another, searching for her own diagnosis. She had eliminated the Cinderella Complex, latent lesbianism, a need to control others. She kept reading.

"He's probably on his way by now," Abby said.

"Mmmmhmmm," Jocelyn said.

Abby laughed nervously. "He might even be in New York. If I left here and tried to find him, I might even be able to do it. He might be on six-eighty-four right now."

Jocelyn did not stop reading.

"I have a confession," Abby said. "I tried to call him at the LA apartment he had. I got the real tenant. The one who was in Italy?"

Jocelyn nodded.

"I even asked Hannah if she'd heard from him."

Then she added, "She hasn't."

Jocelyn sighed, closed her book. "Well," she said. "It looks like I'm not a woman who loves too much."

"If I could just hear his voice," Abby said.

"Then go out there," Jocelyn told her. "Stand on six-eighty-four until he comes by. Spend another summer with him and watch him go when September comes around."

"I told you. The scary part is he would probably stay this time."

Jocelyn picked up the next book on her pile, opened it.

Abby stared out, across the rolling hills. She reminded herself of all the things she had learned up here. She reminded herself why she had come. She thought of Hannah.

"You know," she said softly, "the way it used to be wasn't all that great."

"I know," Jocelyn said. "It sounds like he was a real shit."

Abby nodded. "He was. He is. I'm in love with a real shit."

"Hi, honey," Noah's mother said. "Can I help you with something?"

She had a dimple just like Noah's, and wire-rimmed glasses. But her hair was a mass of soft curls.

Hannah sighed. She looked like a wonderful mother to have.

"Is it Girl Scout cookie time already?" Mrs. Meade asked her.

"Oh," Hannah said. "No. It's nothing like that. I was looking for Noah."

Mrs. Meade looked amused. "Really? Well, I'll go and get him then."

"Tell him it's important. Okay?"

She watched as Mrs. Meade's pink sweatsuit disappeared into the apartment. Maybe, Hannah thought, if she told him why she'd lied he'd understand. Maybe things could go back to the way they used to be. She would send him postcards from Williamstown. She would sign them with a series of X's and O's.

She heard footsteps, practiced out loud, softly, "I'm sorry I made up all those stories. It was a special amnesia. I wanted to forget." She heard voices, said it out loud one more time.

Mrs. Meade was standing in front of her, looking sad. "I'm sorry, honey. He's not able to come right now."

Hannah gulped hard. "Did you tell him it was important?"

Noah's mother hesitated. "You should probably just go home now."

Hannah tried to peek around her, into the apartment. All she could see was a dark Oriental rug, something brass in a corner, a painting on one wall.

"Maybe I could come back in a little while?" Hannah said. She wanted to add, "Please." She wanted to explain to Noah's mother why she had lied like that. Mrs. Meade looked like she'd be a good mother, a mother who understood.

But Mrs. Meade was shaking her curly head, closing the door.

Hannah stood there, in front of the apartment, for a few more minutes, hoping that Noah would reconsider and rush out to her. After a while, she heard sounds from inside, but they were just normal apartment sounds. Music, something electrical humming. No one was coming out.

The thought of going back to her grandparents' apartment, where June was carefully packing for the trip to Williamstown, seemed awful. Instead, Hannah took the elevator to the top, and then climbed the stairs that led to the roof. She sat up there, looking out across the river to New Jersey. She knew that if she looked the other way, toward the city, she would be able to name all the buildings she saw there. For a while, she used to get the Empire State Building and the Chrysler Building mixed up, but Noah had shown her the delicate scallops on the Chrysler Building, and how much taller the Empire State Building was.

Soon, she would get in the car with Deirdre and June and drive north, leaving behind this whole terrible episode. The next time she liked a boy, she would tell him only the truth. She would not make up stories so he'd like her more. Hannah sighed, forced herself to turn and gaze east, at Manhattan. The Empire State Building spired upward. She followed its tip to the sky.

Zach was not going to take Hannah to Mexico. Instead, he would save those tickets and the three of them would go later. In the fall or winter. Whenever Abby realized that they had to be together.

He let himself wonder, for the first time, how his daughter felt each time he left them. He carried no memories of her watching him go. It seemed to him that each time he left, she barely noticed. She sometimes refused to answer him when he said goodbye to her. When she was younger, she had once asked him if he was a magician. If he traveled in space, if he went places to perform miracles. He had told her yes. When, he thought now, had she stopped believing that?

The day Hannah was born, Paco had called him, his voice sounding more like a new father's than Zach's own. "It was so incredible," Paco had kept repeating. Zach had just wanted to hang up, to know that Abby was fine and then to hang up. His bladder had felt as if it might explode as Paco refused to stop talking. Zach had thought that day that he might never go back to Abby. He did not want this child, this life that seemed to be unfolding.

Zach stood on the corner of 72nd and Broadway and stared up at the building where Hannah was staying. He studied the turrets, the rounded cupolas at the top. He could not go in. He could leave without anyone knowing he had almost come for her. He could fly back to London, go to Nina, make up a story about how he had changed his mind, how he did not want Abby after all.

But none of that would be true.

He wanted Abby. And he knew that if he could win Hannah over, Abby would be next. He did not have to be afraid. Nina had been right—he did not really know Hannah at all. He was not even completely sure what day her birthday was, or who her friends were, or what subjects she liked at school. He had never really wanted to know.

Zach wondered if Hannah thought that her life was better after he left them each September, or if she preferred the times he was with them. He might even ask her, if he got up the courage. He imagined them driving together somewhere, getting acquainted. It did not feel altogether bad to imagine it.

Zach went into the building, to the elevator, climbed

on with a woman walking two standard poodles. The dogs sniffed at him. The woman smiled and watched the numbers light up for each floor. One of the dogs, the bigger, darker one, lifted his leg and urinated in a corner of the elevator. A long and steady flow. The woman laughed. "Niagara Falls," she said.

Zach had to step over the puddle when he left the elevator.

Deirdre opened the door when he knocked. She was dressed in a brilliant red caftan, her hair wrapped in a white turban that was clasped in front with a big rhinestone pin.

"I've come for Hannah," he said right away, to get it said.

"Have you now?" Deirdre said. She sounded almost amused.

Down the long hallway lined with pictures of Deirdre Falls Church, at the far end, Zach saw Hannah. She had cut her hair short and it made her look younger. He remembered then. Her birthday was in September. September 21st. He remembered how his mother had said Hannah was a cusp baby. How for a few years he had sent her puppets and stuffed animals. How he had stopped a long time ago.

"Hannah," he said, his voice cracking, "I've been thinking. Maybe you and I can go somewhere together. I mean, it's summer, right?"

She started to move toward him, her eyes narrowing. "Go where?" she said.

"I don't know. Niagara Falls, maybe."

"What about Mom?"

He shrugged. "She needs to not see me for a while. I can understand that."

Deirdre laughed. "Well, bravo for you."

Toby came out of the kitchen, grasping a coffee cup. It was pale blue with white fish on it and said PISCES.

"Hey," he said. "Zach. Right?" His voice was loud and exaggerated. "Of course it's Zach. Well, well."

Hannah moved closer to her father. "What's the catch?" she asked him.

Zach shook his head. "No catch."

"What are we going to look for?" she said.

Zach thought quickly. He had no idea. One summer, he had suggested they look for kitsch. Americana. But Abby had told him that had been done. Overdone. Maybe he'd work on that. "I have a few ideas," he said. "Want to give your old man a chance?"

Hannah turned to see what Deirdre thought, but she had left, gone into the living room to finish getting ready.

"I don't know about that," Hannah said. "But I'll go with you."

Zach felt such relief that he had to lean against the wall.

"Okay," he said.

He thought that soon it would be the way it should have been all along.

YOU AND ME

"Well," Zach said, "it looks like we're stuck with each other."

Hannah didn't look at him. She just stared at the pattern on the floor. "Parquet," Deirdre called it. Tiny rectangles of wood, nestled together in a zigzag pattern that ran down the long hallway in the apartment.

"Just you and me," Zach said.

Hannah thought he sounded frightened.

All those summers, Abby had given balance to their days. Hannah had never held Zach's hand as they searched beaches and fields for objects, had never kissed him good night or told him her dreams. Abby had done all of that for both of them—kissed them, whispered to them, interpreted their dreams. Even in LA last spring, Hannah had felt odd around her father, awkward and uncomfortable. She was suspicious of him. She did not think she liked him very much.

Now here he was with this plan to take her with him, to Canada for starters. "Kitsch," he'd said. "That's what we're after." He'd added, unsurely, "A father-and-daughter team. Like Frank and Nancy." "Huh?" Hannah had said.

Zach looked around him, at the packed suitcases that crowded the hallway, the framed reviews and photographs on the walls.

"She was a real looker," he said, peering at a picture of Deirdre as Zelda Fitzgerald, all rhinestoned and feathered and fringed for the part.

"*Zelda*," Hannah said. She had memorized the captions and dates on all the photographs during her afternoons alone here since Noah had stopped coming.

"Starring Deirdre Falls Church," she recited. "The Music Box Theatre. October 17, 1962. Did you know that there's a Hirschfeld drawing of her dressed like that hanging in Sardi's? She must have told you that. She even showed me the stupid thing."

Zach nodded, still staring at Deirdre as a flapper.

"It closed after six performances," Hannah said. "She didn't tell me that."

From the living room, Deirdre's and Toby's voices were hushed and low. Soon, June would arrive and gather all of these suitcases and Deirdre herself, put them into the car, and head up to Williamstown. Zach tilted his head to try to hear what they were talking about in there. He wondered if they would try to stop him from taking Hannah with him. He had rights, he would tell them. Fatherly rights.

Jesus, Zach thought, this apartment is suffocating. The pictures seemed to have a life of their own, seemed to be breathing in all the oxygen.

He had only been here three other times. Once, that first summer he'd met Abby. Deirdre had whisked her out of the apartment on West Fourth Street in an NBC stretch limo and brought her back here. While Deirdre was taping, Zach had snuck in and he and Abby had spent the day in her twin bed with the antique wicker headboard. They had pressed close together, listening for footsteps or a key in the lock.

When they'd gotten married, Abby had insisted they come here the next morning to tell her parents. "They'll be happy," she'd said. "We're respectable now." But Deirdre had not let them past this hallway. He remembered how he'd seen this picture that day, too, how Zelda had seemed to smile down at him through dark pouty lips while the real Deirdre had stood, in a white silk bed jacket, frowning. Disapproving. Abby had gushed nervously, like a little girl, about the wedding, the suddenness of it, the romance. She'd even gone on about their dinner at Umberto's. "Extra garlic on everything," she'd said proudly. All the time clinging to Zach's arm. Toby had stumbled out, bleary-eyed and sour-breathed. "Well, well," he'd said, his trembling hand clutching Zach's in a sort of handshake. "This is just fine? Should we open some champagne? Celebrate?" He had looked slightly confused then. "Or maybe we should take them out somewhere special. Twenty-one or something." "That's a fine idea," Deirdre had said. "We'll call you both soon and set it up." They had never called, although Abby had insisted on staying home that night, and the next, to wait.

For years later, if Abby went to see her parents, she went alone, taking the subway uptown by herself early in the morning, meeting Deirdre for breakfast before that day's taping of *Day's Destiny*. Zach would find out later, through a casual remark about something Deirdre had said or done, that Abby had seen her. Sometimes, he'd know just by the troubled way she'd return home, sullen and insecure, asking, "Do you think I should cut my hair?" or "Am I fat? Should I go on a diet or something?" She'd buy diet books, health and beauty advice books, stories about personal growth. She'd try wearing lipstick

241

for a while, or a ruffled blouse. She'd eat yogurt, carrot sticks, broiled fish. Until, finally, after a week or so, she'd sigh, tuck the books away, leave a carton of low-fat pineapple yogurt forgotten in the refrigerator, and begin to relax.

If Zach answered the telephone when Deirdre called, she'd ask for Abby like he was the butler. "Get Abby for me, will you? That's a good boy." He'd told Abby after one of those calls that he would be happy if he never heard that voice again.

The last time he saw Deirdre had been one Christmas after Abby and Hannah had moved to New England. He had shown up in Vermont, at Abby's, to make amends for an affair he'd been having with a woman in San Francisco, a woman who had answered the phone sleepily one morning when Abby had called him. He had arrived on Abby's doorstep with boxes of hair ornaments that the woman had designed. A peace offering. Barrettes painted with tiny hearts and rainbows and tulips.

Hannah had not liked his gifts. She'd looked at them quickly, then shoved the box aside. But Abby had been delighted. "We'll wear some right now," she'd said, and pulled her hair back, clasping it with several painted barrettes. "It's like 'Gift of the Magi,' " she'd said. "Except I haven't sold my hair to buy you a watch fob." "So it's not like 'Gift of the Magi,' " Hannah had said. "Is it?" She'd lifted her hands to her head as if to protect her hair from Zach's presents. Abby had insisted, digging through the box, searching for the most beautiful one to seduce Hannah into wearing, to please Zach. To forgive him. At the bottom, she'd found custom-made barrettes, small white pairs with painted bluebirds on them and names painted in pink scroll in the centers. Kristen. Stephanie. Jessica. She had stared at them, puzzled, while Zach had asked, "How did *those* get in there?"

The next day they'd driven to New York to have Christmas dinner with Toby and Deirdre. "Well, well," Deirdre had said when she saw him, "look what the cat dragged in." Abby had squeezed his hand, had whispered that they would slip away after dinner. "Just you and me," she'd told him. "We can go up to the roof and look at the stars." But he had slipped off alone, after gulping down three glasses of champagne, after several people had come up to him, gushing, "So you're Abby's mystery husband!" After he'd had enough. He'd taken the last of his money and used it to get to Kennedy Airport and a flight back to California.

Today, when he'd shown up at Deirdre's and announced, "I've come for Hannah," it was the first time he had spoken to her since that Christmas Day.

"This apartment," he said, finally looking away from the photograph of Deirdre as Zelda. "It chokes me."

Hannah shrugged. "It's all right."

"I get claustrophobic," Zach said.

"Uh-huh."

Zach stared at his daughter, tried to imagine spending the summer alone with her. It seemed endless, hot and uncomfortable, her eyes always staring at him with disgust, or accusation.

"Look," she said, "I'm not thrilled about this either."

"About what?" he said innocently.

"You and me together. I mean, it's something I could live without."

"Thanks a lot," he said.

She just shrugged again.

Deirdre and Toby finally emerged from the living room, Toby staring down at his feet.

"So," Deirdre said in her most dramatic voice, "you two will go off into the sunset. I will go up to Williamstown and knock them dead in 'Night Mother'. And Toby will stay here and wait for his comeback. Maybe they'll film *The Return of Barney Miller*? Or *Kojack Two*. I rather like that idea. Would you shave your head for that, Toby? Paint a mole on your cheek? Do anything for art?''

Toby did not look up. ''Anything,'' he said.

''Neat little packages,'' Deirdre said. ''What we call in the theater *the resolution*.''

Toby said to Zach, ''You know, they're filming a lot of things right here in the Big Apple.'' He nodded his head enthusiastically. ''Buddy of mine has been in the last two Woody Allen movies. It's not just television. It's drama.''

''Sure,'' Zach said.

Hannah watched her father's face, waiting for him to smile his false smile, look over at her, and say, ''Change of plans. New resolution. Off you go to Williamstown.'' But when he saw her looking at him, he did not give her that phony smile. He did not back out. He just looked back at her.

Had she really pretended that he rode off on magic carpets, spaceships, giant birds? That Christmas when they'd come here, she'd realized that Zach was not magical at all, that he left on his own, walked out the door and into another life that did not include her or Abby. She had seen him do it right from this apartment, right out this door, before they'd even eaten the vegetarian casserole that Deirdre had had catered for dinner. Hannah had watched Zach's face change, had watched his eyes scan the crowd to make sure he could make his getaway. She had watched him walk out, and she'd followed him, hoping one final time that he would leave in a puff of smoke or a golden chariot, hoping that he was someone special and not the person she was afraid he was. But all he had done was to walk, fast, down the hall to the elevator. He had pushed the DOWN button, jabbing it three or four times, tapping his foot, anxious to leave.

There was no puff of smoke, no winged horses to carry him off to California. He left all by himself, because he wanted to. Hannah had stood at the high window that looked down on Broadway and watched as he hailed a Checker cab on the corner. She'd stood there and watched until the cab was long gone. Then she'd gone back to the apartment and told Abby, "He's left us again. He took off in a regular old taxicab." Later, Hannah had taken those stupid barrettes he'd brought them and thrown them away, dropping them into the garbage beside burned-down candles and glittery wrapping paper and scraps of vegetarian casserole. That was the year Abby had stayed away from him for a very long time.

Toby was saying, "Yessiree. Show Biz has returned to Gotham."

She wondered when Zach would make his announcement that he'd changed his mind. When he would turn around and walk out, take the elevator down and a taxi out of the city.

"So," Zach said, pointing to the suitcases, "which one of these is yours?"

Deirdre looked surprised. "No plot twist?" she said. "You're taking her with you?"

"We're going to Niagara Falls?" Hannah asked Zach. "For real?"

"Driving straight across New York State," he said. "Into Canada."

Hannah almost let herself get excited. "My stuff's in the study," she said. She didn't leave right away to get it. She thought that if she walked away from this moment, he would go away, that she'd come out, her suitcase in her hand, and find him gone.

"Do you need help?" he asked her.

She shook her head. Big deal if he leaves, she thought. What else is new?

In the study, she opened the bag that June had packed for her, fingered the bright orange Twiggy dress, the two outfits that Deirdre had bought for her at the Unique Boutique. Then she took them out and put them on the stiff-backed chair where Deirdre usually sat and memorized her lines. She did not even hear Deirdre come in until she spoke.

"What a month," she said. "Hasn't this been a month?"

"I guess so," Hannah said.

"What can I tell you, kiddo?" Deirdre said as she folded the orange dress, the clothes from the Unique Boutique. She put them back in the suitcase and snapped it shut.

From the hall they heard Toby talking loudly. "I knew Gary Cooper," he was saying. "The nicest man you'd ever want to meet."

"The nicest man," Deirdre said. "What does Toby know about it? What does he know about anything?"

Hannah shrugged. "What does anyone know about anything?" she said.

Deirdre laughed. "Not very much. That's for sure."

They stood there, awkwardly. "Well," Hannah said.

"So you're going to be a writer?" Deirdre asked her. "You think of really nice phrases. Keep writing them down. You know, I didn't have such a great childhood either. It makes you stronger, I think. I used to lie in that little bed in Virginia and dream about being a Rockette. Radio City Music Hall." She stretched her arms out and did a quick step, smiling a big Show Business smile. "Did I ever tell you I was first runner-up in the Miss Virginia contest? I was. I got a dozen roses and a satin banner and a hundred-dollar savings bond." She hugged herself tightly, glanced into the mirror, lifting her chin. A sad pose. "I could have been Miss America if I'd come in first."

Hannah nodded.

Deirdre said, laughing, "Off to Williamstown. I'll knock them dead."

"Sure you will," Hannah said.

"I always do, kiddo."

They hardly spoke the entire way through New York. It would have been Abby doing the talking, popping tapes into the tape deck, singing along or pointing out sights along the way. Just last year, as they'd followed the East Coast southward, Abby had shouted out each sign advertising a place called South of the Border. She'd read, laughing: "Chili today, hot tamale." It was Abby's job to do those things, and without her there was only silence.

Two hours outside of Buffalo, waking from a nap, Hannah said, "We don't even have any tapes." She pushed her fingers into the empty slot of the tape deck.

"Wait," Zach said, "I have one. In the glove compartment."

Hannah found it in the folds of a map of the Southwestern United States. Paul Simon's *Graceland*.

It played over and over, breaking the silence, until they finally reached Niagara Falls.

"Let's look at the falls before we go to sleep," Zach said.

"I don't care."

As soon as they stepped from the van, they heard the water pounding. They followed the sound to a railing where people stood, peering down.

"They're small," Zach said, disappointed.

Hannah didn't answer. She thought they were magnificent. She could feel them rumbling in her chest, her stomach.

"Victoria Falls," Zach said. "Now that's a waterfall."

"Why didn't we go there then?" Hannah said sarcastically.

"They're in Africa," he said. "That's why. You can't find kitsch in Africa."

"You could find African kitsch, couldn't you?"

"No, you could not," he said.

Hannah stretched her neck out, trying to feel the water's spray.

Around them, couples clung to the railing, oohing and aahing above the loud roar. A woman stood a few feet back, wringing her hands nervously.

"Watch it, Jeff," she said. "Don't lean over like that. Stand back here. You can still see."

A teenaged boy beside Hannah said, "No you can't, Ma. You have to look from here and down."

"Come on now, Jeff," the woman said. "Get away from there."

"What's the point of coming and not even looking?" Zach said to Hannah.

"I bet Mom would be afraid," Hannah said, happy to finally bring up her mother.

"Maybe," Zach said. "But she'd look anyway."

"Yeah," Hannah sighed. "She'd look."

The next morning, Hannah insisted they go and see the falls again before breakfast. They seemed, she thought as she stared at them, even more magnificent in the daylight.

"Dinky," Zach said, turning away, disgusted.

"Have you ever *seen* Victoria Falls?" Hannah demanded.

"They're bigger," Zach said. "Better."

"Fine," Hannah said.

They walked up the street to get some breakfast.

"What is it you're looking for here, anyway?" she

asked him, still angry. "Pieces of barrels people ride over the falls in? Pieces of people?"

"Please," he said. Then, "It's disappointing, that's all."

"So are we staying or not?"

"I don't exactly feel inspired," Zach said. "Abby always managed to find something special. To get me going."

"Well," Hannah said, "I don't even know what you're looking for."

He was looking for a way to forget his plans for them in Mexico. He had imagined bright-colored objects there, primitive shapes. Abby.

"Shit," he said as they slid into a pale blue vinyl booth at the restaurant. A sign on the window said: "Hungry Man's Breakfast. $1.99."

A bored waitress came over to them, banged a pot of coffee on their table.

"You want the special?" She drummed her pencil on her pink order pad, gazed past them through the window.

"Sure," Zach said.

The waitress brought them their food quickly, eggs and bacon and pancakes and hash browns.

"I hate breakfast food," Hannah said. She poured packets of sugar into her coffee, reading each one before she tore it open. Battleships.

Zach said, "I'm not even really hungry."

"You know where we should go?" Hannah said. "Graceland. Memphis, you know. Where Elvis—"

"Forget it," Zach said. "Do you know how hot it is in Memphis in the summer?"

"Fine," Hannah said. "Be that way. But Graceland has what you're looking for. Plastic busts of Elvis. Rubbings of his gravestone."

"Forget it," he said again.

She cut her pancakes into small pieces, humming the Paul Simon song "Graceland."

"I get the point," Zach said.

But she kept humming.

A woman burst into the restaurant. "A boy!" she shouted. "A boy went over the falls!"

Hannah stopped humming. "It was that one from last night, I bet," she said. "With the nervous mother."

"Don't be silly," Zach said, thinking the same thing.

"I want to go," Hannah said.

People were running out of the restaurant, down the hill toward the falls. There were sirens approaching, people screaming.

"Down there?" Zach asked her.

"No," Hannah said. "Away from here. I want to leave."

Zach stared at her. "Me too," he said.

Memphis, Tennessee, seemed like a very long drive.

Zach smiled at his daughter. "Let's go get Abby," he said.

Hannah's eyes widened. "Really?"

"We need her," Zach said.

Hannah smiled back at him. "We sure do," she said.

When they left the restaurant, they could see the crowd moving away from the railing. They could hear the constant roaring of the falls. Zach draped his arm around Hannah's shoulders. She didn't move away.

AT GOLDENS POINT

"Once," Hannah said to Zach, "I told my entire class that you were dead."

Zach focused on the highway. "Dead, huh?" he managed to say.

"Third grade," she said. Her voice was soft, confessional. "Mrs. O'Hara's class. You know, some father-daughter thing." She knew exactly what father-daughter thing it had been. A pancake breakfast. Estelle Padula's father had tried to break the world pancake-eating record, but had only managed to eat seven before he'd thrown up right there at the table. Hannah had wondered if having your father throw up in front of the entire class—practically the entire town—was worse than not having your father there at all. She had decided it was not. "I told them," she continued, "that you were driving through the Rocky Mountains in a snowstorm, trying to rush two people who were nearly frozen to death to the hospital. Your van tumbled off a cliff."

"What a noble way to die," Zach said. He tried to concentrate on the thick white lines on the road, but couldn't. Instead he imagined the van falling over a steep cliff. Tumbling through the snow.

"Ironically," Hannah added, "both of the people you were trying to save lived."

Then she was quiet.

Zach waited for her to say more, but she didn't. He gripped the steering wheel hard, like it was something valuable, until his hands ached. Only then did he loosen his grip slightly.

"I got in big trouble," Hannah blurted. "I had to write I WILL NOT LIE five hundred times on the blackboard and everything."

She was quiet again. She sighed and closed her eyes, remembering how one Saturday night last winter she had slept over Dara's house, in the twin bed across from Dara's, with the sandy, yellowish sheets, and Dara had whispered in the dark, "You'd better think of all your sins, because tomorrow we go to church and you can't receive Christ until you've confessed." A few minutes later, Dara was snoring asthmatically, hard noisy wheezes, while Hannah wiggled her toes among the cookie crumbs and gravel at the foot of the bed, worrying about her sins and church and receiving Christ.

The next morning, Dara's mother would not let them eat anything. "Cleanse yourselves, girls," she'd said, "so you can receive Christ." Hannah had followed Dara and her fat mother into church and waited in line behind them at the confessional. She had studied Dara's mother's soft white flesh. A tight necklace had seemed embedded in the folds of her neck, a scarab belt was lost in her stomach. Then she'd disappeared behind the heavy maroon velvet curtain and Hannah had heard her whispering her sins.

A boy Hannah had recognized from school had nudged her forward. "Move it, Plummer," he'd whispered. "It's your turn."

She too had disappeared then behind the heavy curtains. Inside, she'd sat on a small wooden bench, listening to an organ playing softly, wheezing like Dara, in the church. A small door opened and she'd made out the figure of the priest behind the screen.

"Hi," she'd said, wondering if she should tell him that she wasn't Catholic.

"Go on," he'd said. His breath had smelled like he'd just eaten lasagna.

Hannah had cleared her throat, then said, "You know, my father says he's a Buddhist."

"There are other people waiting," the priest had said. "What do you have to confess?"

She'd thought about movies in which criminals were held in bare rooms, a single light bulb burning overhead, while cops badgered them for confessions of rape, murder, kidnapping.

"I'm only twelve," she'd told him.

"No one," he'd said, "is sinless."

So she had confessed everything to him. How she sometimes hated her mother, wanted a different life, pretended her father was dead. She had blurted out everything and then run out of church, past Dara in her pale blue Sunday suit and the boy from school and all the people waiting in line who had probably heard what an awful person she was. She had run all the way home in the cold. When she'd finally gotten there, she'd found Abby still asleep and slightly hung over, but Hannah had climbed in bed with her anyway and hugged her and whispered that she loved her and really did not want any other mother in the world.

Somehow, since Zach had decided to go and get Abby, Hannah had felt the urge to confess to him. She had told him earlier that sometimes she liked to pretend she was someone else, someone whose parents were chic and caring, who lived somewhere exotic, like Paris. He had only nodded and said that he could understand that.

Now, his voice was quiet and he said, "I used to wish that too."

"What?"

His face in the fluorescent highway lights looked strangely yellow. "Dead," he said. "That my father was dead. Or at least someone else. Like Ward Cleaver."

"You have a father?" Hannah said.

Zach laughed. "What did you think? That I crawled out from under a rock?"

"Sort of," she said.

He laughed again.

Hannah's eyes narrowed, studying him. "And," she said carefully, "you have a mother?"

"I think that's how it usually works," he said.

"Right," she said, trying to imagine these parents of his. She pictured old, gray-haired people wringing their hands, waiting for him to come to them, standing in the door of a small ranch house in a fifties-type development. The smell of a cake baking lingered in the kitchen. They waited and waited for their son, long after the streetlights had come on and the houses around them had gone dark. "But he called," Zach's mother would say into the night, watching the street, hoping that this time he really would show up. "He said he'd be here." There would be a pot roast drying out on top of the stove, a casserole of vegetables growing cold beside it. Zach's father would smoke a pipe, and finally tell his wife they should just go on to bed. This house, these people, lived somewhere in the middle of the country. In Nebraska or Indiana. They followed football and the American Legion and planted trees on Arbor Day. They were, she realized suddenly, her grandparents.

"Did I ever meet them?" she asked softly. "Do they know me?"

Zach shook his head. "Well, Pearl knows about you. That's my mother. Pearl."

"Do they know Mom?"

Zach hesitated. "This summer we're going to meet her. And my grandmother too. The three of us will drive up to Seattle—"

"Seattle?" Hannah said, wanting to know more. She thought of Little Orphan Annie singing "Maybe," dreaming of her perfect parents out there, looking for her, waiting.

"You're from Seattle?" Hannah asked him again.

"Not Kyoto," he said. "Or India or even California." These were the things he used to tell her when she'd asked. He'd make up fanciful stories about stowing away on ships filled with silk and spices, of ancestors still far away in these magical lands. "Disappointed, huh?" he said. "Your old man is from Seattle, Washington."

But Hannah was anything but disappointed. She felt thrilled, excited. Like the Zach who had told her all those stories, and the man here beside her from Seattle, Washington, were two different people. She hugged herself tight. They would all go to Seattle. They would call from the highway and tell her grandparents they were on their way. She imagined that small split-ranch, the smell of chocolate cake, the two old people waiting for them at the door.

"Catholics confess, you know," Hannah told him at a McDonald's. "It makes them feel better."

Zach sipped his coffee. For the past hour she had asked him questions nonstop. What kind of job did his father have? What color was their house? Did he look like his mother or his father or a little of each? Her questions had made him wish he had never brought this up at all.

He had felt safer with the stories he used to tell her, with a father who was descended from a samurai, a mother who looked like Merle Oberon. He wanted to get to Abby before he worked all this out.

Hannah held up her milk shake. "Chelsea told me these are really liquid plastic."

He nodded.

Hannah slurped her milk shake. She closed her eyes. When I open them, she told herself, I'll pretend I'm meeting Zach for the very first time. At a party. She opened them and smiled at him.

"So," she said politely, "you're from Seattle."

"Look," he said. "Let's take this a step at a time. We'll get Abby and then we'll talk about all this. Seattle and my mother and anything else you want."

"Just tell me this one thing," Hannah said.

"No. Later."

"Is your father—"

"Are you ready?" Zach said, standing.

"Can't you just tell me this one thing?" Hannah said. She chewed a French fry. "You keep talking about your mother and stuff. Where's your father?" She imagined him, her grandfather, paralyzed, bedridden, old.

Zach let his mind wander, create its own endings. His father was a war hero, a gypsy. Hannah was staring at him, waiting.

"I never knew him," Zach told her. "Even my mother didn't. Okay? Enough?"

Her gray eyes hardened.

"Let's go," she said, draining her milk shake noisily.

"Hey," he said. "Hannah."

She looked at him with those hard gray eyes. "It's okay," she said. "We're not Catholic. You don't have to say anything."

*　　*　　*

The sign on the gate said: VISITING HOURS 9 A.M.–5 P.M.

Zach shook the gate. It rattled a little, but did not budge.

"It's not even 5 A.M. yet," Hannah said.

Zach stared through the bars, across the grassy hills where small white cottages dotted the lawn. She was in there somewhere, asleep.

"Do you know which one is hers?" he asked Hannah.

She pushed her arm through the bars and pointed. "At the crest of that hill."

"Are you sure?" he said.

Hannah sighed. "Yes already."

The air was still and hot. No noise, no movement.

Hannah was saying something about how he never believed her, how she always had to repeat the same things to him.

"Why don't you go and wait in the van?" Zach said.

"But—"

He ignored her, studied the gate instead.

"Fine," she said.

Her footsteps as she walked off sounded loud in the still morning.

Zach shook the gate again, then quickly scaled it.

Once on the other side, he looked back and saw Hannah standing beside the van, watching him. He gave her an "OK" sign, then headed away, toward Abby's cabin. The dew wet his sneakers as he walked. A bird sang, high and sweet. Zach stopped and rehearsed what he would say. His voice seemed to ring out in the quiet, even though he whispered. "I was in the neighborhood," he said. Then he thought that he should say something angry. "How could you leave me?" he said into the morning. Then he thought that what he should say was something true. "I love you," he said softly. "I'm sorry I didn't come when I said I would."

He took a deep breath and walked the rest of the way to the cabin.

The door opened before he knocked, as if she knew he was coming.

The sight of her took his breath away. Her hair was loose and her eyes were heavy with sleep. Zach opened his arms and took a step toward her.

She looked at him.

"Great," she said flatly. "Fucking great."

"Loony Beach," Abby said as she settled herself at the edge of the river. "That's what I call it."

"Crane Beach is nicer," Zach said, "but I guess this will do."

It was an old trick of his, to bring up old times, better times.

Abby would not let herself fall for his tricks. She didn't smile or respond. She traced squiggly lines with a short twig in the wet dirt.

"Who told you?" she asked him. Then, "Never mind. It doesn't really matter. Here you are anyway."

He could not find his voice. He opened his mouth, hoping for some rehearsed line to come out, but nothing did, except a sharp inhalation of air. The river smelled swampy. He could taste earth.

"I really thought I was losing it," Abby said. She stretched out on the grass, staring up.

Finally he spoke, his voice hushed. "I'm here now."

He did not expect her to laugh then, but she did, a short, hollow sound that could almost have been a moan.

"You," she said. She shielded her eyes from the sun, which was rising white and hot in front of her. She squinted to see him better.

"I lost me somewhere along the way," she said.

He bent toward her. "I did it," he said.

Abby let her hand drop, closed her eyes against the light, against his face near hers.

"I left Nina for good and I came for you like I promised."

Her eyes flew open. "Don't," she said. Her eyes teared now from the brightness.

Zach tapped his pocket. "I've got the tickets to Mexico right here," he said.

Abby held her hand up as if to stop something. It was Zach she was trying to stop. And herself. Despite all the weeks here, all the sessions and conversations and soul-searching, something inside her was yearning for him, reaching out to him. Something familiar and frightening.

She forced herself to conjure Dr. Kornbluth's face and voice. "Only you can make your life better," he'd said to her. "Only you can leave Zach and that old behavior behind." She tried to muster the determination those words had brought to her just hours ago.

But here was Zach, leaning toward her. If she reached her hand out just a little bit, she would be able to touch the curls of his hair, the side of his face. "Someday," everyone at Goldens Point had been assuring her, "you'll see him and feel nothing but a little nostalgia."

Today, Abby thought, is not that day.

He was going to kiss her. She thought, If I let him kiss me and I feel nothing, it will really be over. She thought, What's one kiss? And then she was doing it, kissing him and feeling everything all over again.

"You gave me a scare," Zach told her, his mouth over hers.

"Everybody needs to get away," Zach said later. "I understand completely."

Even as he spoke, tried to sound like everything was back to normal, he could tell that it was not.

"Hell," he continued, "I do it all the time."

Her back was to him and she kept drawing with that damn stick in the dirt.

"So," he said, "ready to break out?"

Her eyes were as gray as the river in front of them.

"I've got two more weeks here," she said.

Zach's heart quickened. "For what?" he said, trying to sound light.

The stick traced the same spots, again and again, wiggly lines, unconnected.

"All right," he said. "If you want to finish the . . ."

"Therapy."

"I'll wait. Hannah and I will wait."

"Hannah?" Abby said. She looked past him, toward the parking lot, as if she might catch a glimpse of Hannah there.

"I picked her up at Deirdre's," Zach said. "Ab, how could you leave her with your mother? I mean, really."

Abby jumped up, feeling like she was waking from a dream in which Zach had appeared at her door and the two of them had come down here by the river to make love. Suddenly, everything seemed very real—the hot sun, the smell of dirt and the Hudson, Zach beside her telling her what to do, making promises that he would not keep, telling her lies. If she walked away right now, Abby thought, she would not be making a mistake. She could even hear Jocelyn telling her that she had done something good by coming down here with him and walking away. "If you weren't stronger," she would tell her, "you really would have left with him."

Zach was telling her about Deirdre and Toby, how they had seemed when he'd showed up at their apartment.

"At least," Abby said, "they were there for me when I needed help. Where were you?"

He rose too now, and gripped her shoulders hard. "Let's start from now," he said.

Her head was swimming. She wondered how long she had waited for the words he was telling her. The two of them seemed so little standing here, the words so unimportant.

"I need for you to go away," she said, pressing her temples. "When I'm ready I'll tell you."

Zach frowned. This was not right. He felt afraid— afraid that if he walked away, he would never see her again, afraid of facing Hannah without Abby being with him. And, he thought, it had been fear that had kept him away from her for so long, until the ache for her grew too strong to ignore.

She started to walk away, up the hill.

"Wait," he called after her. "What about Hannah?"

Abby stopped at the top of the crest. She shrugged. "Take her home," she said.

"Home?" he said, confused.

"To Vermont, Zach."

She started to walk again.

He felt desperate. He thought, I should have brought her violets.

"And you'll come there?" he called. "In two weeks?"

"Yes," she said, without turning around.

Back in her cottage, with Jocelyn still asleep, Abby watched from the window as Zach climbed the hill and walked across the grass to the parking lot. He had his head down and his sneakers in his hand. She gripped the windowsill, to keep from running after him. She stared hard to keep from crying. "One, two, three," she counted silently, to keep from remembering the good times, the old times, the love she still felt. "Four, five, six."

He vanished from sight and in the distance, she heard the van start up and drive away.

Jocelyn stirred in bed. Abby heard her yawn and stretch.

"What's out there that's so interesting?" Jocelyn said.

Abby thought of telling her all that had happened this morning, of crying to her, of asking for help. But this time, she had to figure it out for herself.

She turned from the window.

"Not much," she said. "Not much at all."

THE IMAGE HE HELD

Hannah started to notice things about Zach. For one thing, she saw that he was old. His skin was the color of a September tan and there were dozens of little lines around his eyes. Sometimes, in a certain light, there were puffy triangles at the bottoms of his eyes. He told her it was from living hard and fast. Her mother, she thought, did not look nearly as old as Zach. Her face was smooth except for tiny crinkles that appeared only when she laughed. Or cried. Hannah pointed this out to Zach frequently. "Maybe," she told him, "you should slow down a little. In ten years you'll look terrible." He told her he'd take her advice.

She also noticed since they'd been together in Vermont that he was a good cook. Much better than Abby was. Although Abby had told her stories of meals Zach used to make for her, Hannah's memory only included things he'd whipped up on the road—hot dogs and vegetable brochettes on a small black hibachi that they sometimes set up at rest areas. Usually, she ate bags of potato chips or Doritos and refused things he'd cook there. But now, since it was just the two of them and they were at home, she ate the meals he cooked and listened to all the nutritional information he gave her. She even kind of liked to stand in the kitchen with him while he cooked. He never used recipes. Instead, he took handfuls and pinches of herbs and spices. "California cuisine," he told her. "Don't you mean Seattle?" she said. "No," he told her, "I don't."

Most of all, though, Hannah noticed that he was trying. He fixed broken hinges and screens, scrubbed the bathtub and sinks, cut the lawn. He filled empty Perrier bottles with lilacs from the yard, and even grew basil in a green pot on the windowsill in the kitchen.

He was not a big talker, she thought. Now that he had told her some of the truth about himself, he pretty much clammed up. Unlike Abby, who talked on and on about when she and Zach first met, and how in love they were, Zach remained private about things like that. At first, Hannah badgered him with questions. He told her that basically his life was dull. "That's why you make stuff up," she announced, but he only shrugged. Finally, as they ate his homemade whole-wheat pizza with eggplant and—at Hannah's request—goat cheese, Zach said, "If I tell you about my parents, will you stop with the questions?" She nodded.

He told her how he couldn't wait to leave Seattle and have adventures. To be away from a mother who spent more time mixing potions for inner peace than she did with him.

"The only thing I wanted," Zach said, "was to be someone interesting. Someone exciting."

Hannah nodded. It was not what she'd wanted to hear. She felt her genes inside her, creepy and weird. She didn't have a chance in hell.

The next day, he brought home a VCR. Every night,

instead of talking, they watched movies. He rented old ones that he had seen long ago. *Easy Rider. The Graduate. Goodbye, Columbus.* Hannah thought most of them were pretty boring, but she started to look forward to their nights together. The weather had grown humid, hotter. Zach bought little fans at Caldor in pastel colors. He rigged them up at different levels in the room so that he and Hannah were surrounded by whirring fans. At least once a night, the circuit breaker popped and all the fans would come to a halt. Zach would go down to the basement and fix them, calling up to Hannah, "Are they on?" She felt important then, like his apprentice, her eyes on all those light-colored fans—salmon and raspberry and sea-foam green—until they came to life and she shouted, "They're on, Zach!"

Although she didn't ask him any more questions, he revealed things about himself while they watched the movies.

"I took Beth Jarret to see this," he said, groaning, as *Bullitt* played on the television. "Her cheeks were as red as apples. People even called her Beth Appleton, as a joke. And her hair was so long she could sit on it. Really. We saw this at the Orpheum in Seattle, and during the chase scene we started making out and I missed the whole thing."

Hannah would just nod, pretending not to care when really she was enchanted by a girl with long hair and red cheeks, and by Zach.

Later, as she tried to fall asleep in her room, she'd hear familiar sounds from her mother's bedroom, where Zach slept. The sounds of Mary Tyler Moore and Alan Alda, the sounds of someone lonely trying to get through the night.

*   *   *

"Hi," Hannah said. "Is Chelsea home? This is Hannah."

Mrs. Kent's voice over the telephone sounded full of sympathy. "Hannah. How are you, honey?"

Hannah pictured Mrs. Kent, dressed in peach-colored tennis clothes, surrounded by her apricot walls, her marmalade drapes.

"I'm fine," Hannah said. "My father's here."

"Oh," Mrs. Kent said uncertainly. "How nice."

"We're having a blast. Last night he made bouillabaisse." It had tasted terrible, like salt and live fish. The clams and mussels had seemed to grow, like rubber, in her mouth. "It was great," she said. "Delicious."

"How nice for you," Mrs. Kent said.

"So," Hannah said, "is Chelsea there? I thought she might want to come over for dinner." Once, before the summer, Chelsea had asked Hannah, "Doesn't your mother ever cook?" They had been at Pizza Hut, where Abby always took guests of Hannah's, eating deep-dish pizza and drinking a pitcher of Coke. It had cost a fortune, and then Chelsea had ordered dessert too.

"She's up in Maine with Kate," Mrs. Kent said. "Visiting Kate's grandparents. You know, they live up there."

No, Hannah thought, I don't know that.

Mrs. Kent was chuckling. "They took the bus all by themselves."

Hannah pulled the phone cord so that all the curls turned straight.

"Oh," she said.

"They are having a ball! They called last night and told me they went to a restaurant and ate lobsters."

Hannah tried to laugh along with Mrs. Kent, but it came out like a sob instead, all choked-sounding.

Mrs. Kent stopped midlaugh. "Honey," she said, "are you all right?"

"Of course I am. My father's here."

"If you need anything—"

Gently, Hannah placed the receiver down.

Zach poked his head into the room, his hands full of grocery bags.

"I got swordfish steaks for tonight. Your friend's coming, right?"

"Wrong," Hannah said, pushing past him.

She went outside and sat on the grass. It felt sticky from the heat. She imagined Chelsea and Kate taking the bus to Maine, their parents sending them off with bags filled with Hershey's Kisses, apples, magazines, and gum. They had probably sat together, whispering to each other about the other passengers, singing songs loudly even after people told them to behave. At the other end, Kate's grandparents picked them up in an old reliable car. A Dodge Dart. Then they took them for lobsters and laughed along with them when they had to wear bibs. Every night, Mrs. Kent and Mrs. Sasser waited for the girls to call so they could tell them they loved them, to be careful and stay safe.

Hannah pulled her T-shirt away from her. It was her mother's, the one that said HANDEL WITH CARE. She pretended she was in Nice, or Monaco, on vacation from her parents' apartment in Paris. There were cool breezes, bouillabaisse, and grandparents and parents to call. She would write postcards to Chelsea and Kate. The front would show the Mediterranean sparkling below white villas and a blue sky. On the back, she would write a message. In French.

A large ghoulish shadow appeared in front of her. Dara. Scratching at her mosquito bites.

"Is he living here now?" Dara asked her. "My mother said they took your mother away with a butterfly net."

Hannah ignored her. She stretched out on the sticky

grass. It was white sand, she thought. And the ocean was right over there. She inhaled, smelled suntan oil and saltwater.

"I like your new haircut," Dara said. "It looks . . . European."

Hannah squinted up at her. "Like Jean Seberg?" Last night she and Zach had watched Jean Seberg and Jean-Paul Belmondo in *Breathless* and Zach had said she sort of looked like Jean Seberg.

"I guess so," Dara said.

Hannah smiled.

Dara giggled. "If he's an egghead."

"*Jean* Seberg," Hannah groaned. "A woman."

"Gene can be a man," Dara said. "Miss Know-it-All. Miss New York City. There's Gene Rayburn, Gene Simmons, Gene—"

"All right," Hannah muttered.

"Gene Martin—"

"It's *Dean* Martin," Hannah said. She stood up, her fantasy shattered. She wasn't in Nice. Or Monaco. She was right back in Vermont, in this dump of a house, talking to fat, stupid Dara. Inside, her father was chopping red peppers and garlic like a madman, trying to make up for her whole dumb life in two weeks.

"Stupid," she said as she walked toward the house. "Stupid, stupid, stupid."

"Wait, Hannah!" Dara called after her. "Come on. Stay outside."

Hannah kept walking.

"I can tell you things," Dara shouted. "I kissed Glenn D'Angelo right on the lips and he put his tongue on my teeth."

"Oh, brother," Hannah said.

She turned and faced Dara, who stood sweating and scratching in the hot sun.

Now that she had Hannah's attention, Dara started squealing. "I saw the Kirk Cameron movie five times." She clutched at the hem of her purple shirt. It had two round-cheeked chipmunks hugging on the front. "No," she shrieked. "I saw it *seven* times."

"Don't be stupid," Hannah said.

Then she ran into the house.

Now that Zach finally had Hannah off his back with those questions, he found himself settling into a routine. A routine that he found, surprisingly, almost comfortable. When he found it uncomfortable, he reminded himself that he was doing it for Abby. She would come home and find domestic bliss.

Every day he went to the small grocery store in town and bought whatever was fresh to make for dinner. A few nights ago artichokes had been four for a dollar and he'd steamed them with lemons and coarse pepper, then made a homemade balsamic vinaigrette to dip them in. Hannah had stared at them for a long time before she started to poke at the leaves. "Haven't you ever eaten an artichoke before?" he'd asked her. "No way," she'd said. "What the hell *do* you eat?" he'd muttered, demonstrating how to pick a leaf from the artichoke and then scraping it through Hannah's teeth. "Ring Dings," she'd told him. He'd looked at her, puzzled. "You know," she'd said, "they're round and chocolate with cream inside." "Trust me," he'd told her, knowing she didn't, not about most things anyway, "stick with artichokes." He'd pulled out the sharp quills then, and plucked out the heart. "Seems like an awful lot of work," Hannah had told him. "Ring Dings you just peel off the foil and eat."

Hannah. When she wasn't asking him questions, she was talking about Paris. If he could have chosen a daughter, he would not have picked her. He would have opted for one who, at least, liked him. Who liked good food. Who knew nothing of Ring Dings. But this was the one he had, and she frightened him a little. She acted a lot like him. Sometimes, when she talked, he felt like he had been tossed back in time, that out the window were the rainy streets of Seattle and that in the kitchen was his mother, stirring one of her potions, and that Hannah was him, a boy who asked questions with frightening answers, who dreamed of other places, places that were far away.

She liked to shock him. "Can you believe," she'd say, "that a five-year-old girl could give birth to ten-pound twins?" Or, she'd tell him that JFK was being kept alive in Uruguay. She'd challenge him to disagree. But he couldn't. He would, instead, look out the window to be sure that they were indeed in Vermont, not Seattle. He'd fight back the urge to hug her and tell her she would do best if she were just herself. "Zach," she'd say, "Bing Crosby's brain is in a hospital in Miami." She'd wait, her gray eyes penetrating him. He'd glance quickly out the window. He'd say, "Really? That's amazing."

These conversations usually occurred before he went into town, and they had become part of the routine of his day. Followed by grocery shopping and a stop at Movie Madness for videos. Hannah refused to accompany him on these errands, although at first she had. He always went to Charlie's Market, a small grocery store with narrow, crooked aisles and crowded shelves that ran to the ceiling and were crammed with cans, boxes, and bags. There was no order there—cat food sat next to soup, cookies next to bug spray. "This is ridiculous," Hannah had told him. "Mom always shops at the Price Chopper. It's better." She had grown impatient with his careful choosing of eggplants and tomatoes, his sniffing and tapping. "Zach," she'd said, "it's a vegetable. Just pick one and let's go." After that, she refused to go with him. "And play with lemons? Forget it."

So he left her at home, reading the *National Enquirer* or watching game shows. He did his errands, then went home and cooked. She never really watched him, just stood in the doorway, pretending to be bored. The first night she had offered him a stained copy of *Joy of Cooking*, but he told her he liked to wing it. After they ate, they watched the movies. Hannah usually fell asleep before the second one ended, leaving him feeling lonely and nostalgic. He would look at her, her head bent awkwardly as she slept propped on the couch, and be surprised at how much she looked like him. He would remember how earlier she had acted like him, and now here she was looking like him, and he would feel frightened, awed. He would feel like running away. But he would instead lean over and shake her brusquely. "Go on upstairs," he'd say. Then she'd stumble off to bed.

Zach tapped on a zucchini, pressed a few tomatoes, then added them to his basket. When he'd left to come to Charlie's, Hannah had told him that a headless woman was spotted in Vermont, looking for victims. He smiled, remembering how serious she'd looked when she'd told him.

"I never saw a man so involved with vegetables," a woman said.

He looked up, into soft brown eyes.

"You come in here every day," she said.

Zach nodded.

"I noticed," she said. She was very tall, and very thin, and her brown hair fell in tight ripples to her collarbone. She was dressed completely in white. "I noticed," she continued, "because not many men shop. Usually their wives do it. You know."

Zach nodded again. He found himself thinking of Hannah, her warning about a headless woman looking for victims. This one, at least, had a head. He picked up a bunch of broccoli and pressed it to his nose.

The woman examined his basket. "Looks like . . . pasta primavera?"

Zach dropped the broccoli into the basket. Suddenly, the narrow aisles, the too-packed shelves, seemed suffocating. Hannah was right. He should have gone to the Price Chopper. "I've got to go," he said, and pushed past the woman.

In the street, he took some long, slow breaths. The woman's skin, as he'd walked past her, had felt cool and he'd caught a whiff of Coppertone. He said to himself, "In five days Abby will be home." Then he said it out loud, softly. Then he escaped into the air-conditioned quiet of Movie Madness. He picked up the remake of *Breathless*. Something Hannah might like. With Richard Gere.

"The original is better," a voice said.

There she was, the woman in white.

"You probably think I'm following you," she said. "We just have the same route. I see you every day."

Zach put the movie back.

"I'm Alice," she said. She was holding *Pillow Talk*.

"*Pillow Talk?*" He laughed.

"I'm a sucker for Doris Day," she said. Her smile was wide, her lips long and thin. "And Alfred Hitchcock." She held up *Vertigo*.

Zach picked up the remake of *Breathless* again. "Well," he said, "enjoy."

She seemed to be waiting for something.

"Oh," Zach said. "Zach Plummer."

"So when I see you tomorrow I can say, 'Hi, Zach Plummer.' "

"Right," he said. Then, "Tomorrow I'll probably go to the Price Chopper."

At the door, she was beside him again.

"This is silly," she said. "I can't be subtle, I guess. I've been watching you every day and I think you seem interesting. I mean, you really buy some good food." She laughed, embarrassed. "I live right over on Park Place. Easy to remember. Park Place, like in Monopoly."

Her hands fluttered as she talked. Zach watched them dance to her neck, face, chest. Her breasts were flat, like a boy's, and he could see the nipples dark and hard against her white cotton shirt. He thought, "The question is: If I want Abby so bad, why do I want to go home with this woman Alice? Why do I want to see what she looks like without that white shirt, those shorts with the University of Michigan insignia at the thigh? Why does Abby's face seem blurred?"

Alice was saying that she made puzzles.

He pretended to be interested.

"Crossword puzzles?" he asked.

The man behind the counter cleared his throat. He was reading a tabloid. The headline shouted: HEADLESS WOMAN SEEKING VICTIMS UP NORTH.

Zach opened the door. "Maybe we should—"

"We could go to my place," she said. "I've got some cold Tecates."

The sunlight and heat outside were dazzling.

Zach searched his mind. "So," he said, "puzzles."

"Jigsaw puzzles," she said. "I custom-make them."

She seemed more relaxed now, her stride easy and long. Zach thought, "If I go home with her, no one will ever know." He thought of Hannah, her worried face. Be careful, she'd told him when he'd left. Right, he'd said. The headless woman.

"Like someone might want one for his wife," Alice

was saying. "They tell me things about her. She's from Ohio. She plays softball. She grows roses. I make her a puzzle in the shape of Ohio. I'll put roses around the edges, and a bat and ball. Whatever."

They had reached the van.

"This is mine," he said.

Alice raised one eyebrow.

"I—" He hesitated. "I'm married."

"How married?"

He shook his head.

"I'll see you tomorrow," she said. "I'll keep the Tecates cold."

Hannah wondered how she could have been so dumb. She had let Zach fool her. She had been taken in by his smile, his pesto sauce, his easy manner. She had let him feed her artichokes, place a leaf between her teeth and gently pull it out, leaving something delicious behind. She had almost believed he was going to stay.

On her bureau was a letter she had written to her mother on a piece of Gavin Berry's fancy paper.

DEAR MOM, THIS IS JUST A THOUGHT BUT MAYBE WE SHOULD LET ZACH STICK AROUND. FOR A LIT-TLE WHILE, PEUT-ÊTRE? THAT'S FRENCH FOR MAYBE. WHAT DO YOU THINK?

The paper had bumpy flecks on it, like tweed, so her handwriting came out like a little girl's.

She tore it up. And threw it away.

Zach was having an affair with Alice Petrie, the woman who taught crafts every other Monday at school. The woman who made them tie-dye T-shirts and taught them to make wind chimes out of Dixie Cups and rocks. The woman who the boys said had no tits. But as Alice Petrie had stood with Zach beside his van, Hannah noticed how she most certainly did have tits, tight little ones not unlike Hannah's own. Alice Petrie had smiled at Zach through her long skinny lips and Hannah had been able to make out the word "tomorrow" as clear as anything.

She had gone to Movie Madness on her own, to rent movies to surprise Zach with. She had even ridden her old bike with the bent wheel rim all the way there, wobbling noisily. In the store, she had asked the man behind the counter to recommend a good old movie. "A classic," she'd said. He'd suggested *Adventures in Baby-sitting*. "That's not a classic," she'd told him. "And it's not old." "Look," he'd said, "there's some ghoul heading this way. I got no time to be Siskel and Ebert." He'd tapped the newspaper. "I know all about it," she'd told him. Finally, she'd chosen two movies with James Dean, figuring if he was in them, they must be classics.

It had been so hot that she'd stopped at the drugstore for a soda, and when she'd walked out she'd seen Zach and Alice Petrie walking down the street together, acting all familiar, slow and easy as old friends.

Other women were Zach's downfall. She had heard her mother say that once on the telephone to someone. Deirdre said it was responsibility he was afraid of. Right now, Hannah didn't care which it was. She just hated him.

From downstairs, Zach called to her.

Maybe, she thought, she should just leave on her own. She could go to Paris alone, and work as an artist's model. After all, she looked like Jean Seberg. She unfolded the map of the Paris Métro that she'd bought at the thrift shop in town one day while Zach was squeezing his stupid vegetables. She read the stops out loud, to comfort herself. *"Les Halles. Gare du Nord."* The words felt funny on her tongue.

She thought about really being there, seeing the Seine, the Eiffel Tower.

In five days, her mother would be home.

"Big deal," she said. They would probably spend the rest of the summer driving around with Zach. Then fall would come and he would go and this whole summer would have been a total waste. She had had her own heart broken, had been left behind while Chelsea and Kate went to Maine, while her mother got her act together, while Zach had an affair with Alice Petrie.

"Zach," she said out loud, full of contempt.

She could smell garlic and vegetables. So what? she thought. He knows how to cook and his eyes are blue and he knows everything about old movies. That was probably the same way he had fooled Abby.

"Despite what you think, Miss Ring Ding," Zach said from her doorway, "vegetables are not good if they're soggy. They lose all their nutritional value that way."

Hannah carefully folded her Métro map, following its creases. One thing she had learned all these summers was how to fold a map.

"This is great primavera," he said.

Feed it to Alice Petrie, she thought.

"Hey," Zach said. "These are really good."

She looked at him out of the corner of her eye. He was holding up the two James Dean movies.

"The Saint Marks Cinema used to play these as a double bill. One of my favorite combinations."

Hannah still ignored him.

"He only made three movies, you know. Do you know what the other one was?"

"Did you take your wife to the Saint Marks Cinema?" Hannah said. "Remember her? My mother?"

"Okay," Zach said, "what's going on?"

"You tell me, you . . . you. . . ." she struggled for the word, knew it started with "adult."

"What?" he said.

"Go tell it to Miss Petrie."

"Miss Petrie?"

"I saw you!" Hannah shouted. "You couldn't even wait five days until she got home. We're never going to be a real family like Chelsea's. Like everybody's."

She did not want him to see her crying, so she pushed him away, punched at him. He grabbed her wrists and told her to stop. But she couldn't. She hated him too much. And Miss Petrie and her mother and herself. All she wanted was to go to Paris. To be someone else. To have a different life.

Zach watched both James Dean movies and the remake of *Breathless* while the pasta primavera hardened in a pan on the stove and Hannah stayed locked in her room. He thought that Richard Gere looked ridiculous. He thought that this night, these five days, would never end. He thought that perhaps there was no way to please anybody but yourself. He went upstairs once and knocked on Hannah's door, calling to her sweetly, but she did not answer him. "Fuck it," he said to himself.

He left the house, thinking of Alice and her puzzles and the smell of Coppertone that came off her skin. Park Place was a short street, with only four small, identical houses. Capes, with slanted roofs and aluminum siding and carports. The first one he came to had a sign in front: PUZZLED? The sign itself was a jigsaw puzzle, with spidery cracks against a white background. As he walked up the path to the front door, he saw Doris Day and Rock Hudson glowing from the television screen inside. They were talking on the telephone, Doris all pink pajamas and stiff blond hair.

A brass nameplate above the mailbox said PETRIE. Zach hesitated before knocking. That was it. Petrie. Hannah had somehow seen him talking to Alice in town today. For a moment, he considered leaving, going back and explaining everything to her. Not just about today and Alice luring him with the promise of cold Tecates, but all of it—that day in the park in New York when he'd first seen Abby and how afraid he was of her love, of messing up, of doing it wrong. Hannah had told him that his true stories were more amazing than the ones he made up. He could, he thought, go home and tell her some true stories. He could tell her about all the people he'd used to get even one lousy showing at a gallery. Or about Nina, the way he'd lied to her too. He could go home and tell his daughter how as a child, he had dreamed of faraway places also.

But he knew he would do none of these things. Instead, he knocked on Alice Petrie's door. And when she opened it, dressed in baby-doll pajamas just like Doris Day's, he smiled at her and said as if it was a joke, "I'm puzzled. I need to figure some stuff out."

Alice leaned against the door. A can of Tecate was sweating in her hand and she lifted it and pressed it to her face.

"You smell like you've been to the beach," he said. "Like Coppertone."

"I use it," she said, "to keep my skin soft."

Zach did not think that it could get hotter, but it had. When he got back it was almost dawn and the sky was a hazy yellow, rippling from the heat like a mirage or a dream. The television was still on, all static and overlapping with the voices from the next channel in the distance. He did not even turn it off. He just went upstairs and lay on Abby's bed, trying to figure out what to do.

The quiet and the heat made his mind feel muddled. The smell of Coppertone clung to his skin. Perhaps, he thought, he should sneak away now.

He imagined getting in the van and driving away alone as the sun rose and Hannah slept alone here. When he visualized it, and thought of Abby coming home and finding him gone, he got an ache in his stomach. No, he told himself, he wanted to stay.

I Love Lucy came on and Zach tried to think of just that, of Lucy and Ethel staging a show at the Copacabana while Ricky was sick.

"You've been gone a long time," Hannah said.

Zach could barely make her out as she stood in the doorway.

"I know," he said.

"You always let us down," she said. Her voice sounded very young.

"I know," Zach said again. "I was just thinking that too."

She stepped closer. He could see her face shining from sweat, and her T-shirt sticking to her. Her arms and legs looked fragile, thin.

"She tells me the story about the day you met like it's a fairy tale," Hannah said.

"It isn't," he said. "Not really."

"You tell it then," Hannah said.

"I don't know," Zach said.

"I guess to you it wasn't much of a story."

He looked at the television where Ricky was just noticing Ethel among the dancing girls. Ricky's eyes bulged. He slapped his forehead.

"I guess it was summer," Zach said. "And I was walking through Washington Square Park, watching all the street performers. Jugglers and people like that. I always liked jugglers. Anyway, all of a sudden I heard this beautiful music. Violin. And I followed it across the park to see who was creating this amazing music. I remember thinking she looked beautiful and helpless, both at the same time. I stood beside her and it took all my energy not to reach out to her and brush a strand of hair from her face. Then when she finished—I guess it was Mozart, a violin concerto—I told her that she was beautiful." He laughed a little. "And I said something very romantic, very fairy-tale-like. I said, 'Can I buy you a beer?' "

He waited for Hannah to say something. But she didn't. She just stood a few feet away from him, still and quiet.

Zach said, "The rest, as they say, is history."

He felt like Hannah could see right through him. That she could tell which parts of his story were true and which were lies. He had left out the part about the lines he had fed Abby that day, the stories he'd told her so that she would like him. And he'd left out how standing there beside her, he'd wondered what she would look like naked, and how he could find out. And that the image he most held about that day was of later, in the White Horse Tavern, sitting across from her and hoping that she was the one who would save him.

Hannah spoke then, her voice so filled with sadness that he felt that same ache in his stomach that he'd felt when he'd imagined leaving here tonight.

"Zach," Hannah said. "It was spring. And she was playing Vivaldi."

THREE-LEGGED HORSE

"A DEIRDRE FALLS CHURCH," Abby read out loud. "TUR-KEY, AVOCADO, JACK CHEESE, AND SPROUTS ON HEALTH BREAD."

"And they're fabulous, kiddo," Deirdre announced. "Trust me."

Abby turned from the restaurant counter and watched her mother approach. Deirdre was dressed in flaming, almost blinding, red silk—pants and oversized shirt—with a just as bright pink-and-orange scarf.

"We'll have two, Maura," Deirdre said to the girl who sat behind the counter chewing grape bubble gum and reading *On the Road*.

Deirdre scanned the small room and her face flickered with disappointment when she saw that the only other customer, an old man slurping clam chowder and wearing a Red Sox cap, did not look up when she arrived. But then she focused on Abby, took her by the shoulders and said, "Let me look at you." Silver bracelets tinkled gently on Abby's arms. "I believe you have lost a few pounds," she said.

Abby started to shake her head no, but Deirdre had already turned away from her. "Isn't she gorgeous, Maura?" she said. "And a concert violinist, too." She gave a big wink to Abby when she said that. Deirdre's eyelids were dusted with shiny green shadow.

"Yup," Maura said, without looking up from her book.

"I want to hear everything," Deirdre said as they took their food to a small wooden table. Someone had carved the word ZEN into it, and Abby pushed at the letters with her thumb, as if to rub them off.

Deirdre sipped her coffee. "Caffeine," she said. "Damn bad habit."

"There are worse ones," Abby said. Only three days earlier she had awakened with a thought: Why didn't her mother leave Toby? She had rushed to Dr. Kornbluth's office and stood in front of his desk, with the sun so bright it looked like fake sunshine in a bad movie, and asked him the question. "Why doesn't she leave him now?" she'd said. "What's the point?" "Maybe," he'd told her, his voice drowsy, "she's afraid of being alone." Abby had laughed. "You don't know my mother."

Facing her now, Abby had a different thought. She thought, as she watched this powdered and rouged face, listened to the strong voice, that maybe Dr. Kornbluth had been right. And maybe it was she who didn't know her mother very well.

"I could be like Toby, I suppose," Deirdre was saying. "Now that's worse."

Abby leaned toward her mother. "I thought I'd come to see the show tonight," she said.

"Great! Fantastic! What a treat. Why, you haven't seen me perform since—"

"It's been a while."

"Ah, kiddo," Deirdre said. "You're going to make it just fine, aren't you?"

Abby forced a big smile. "Do you think the daughter of Deirdre Falls Church could ever *not* make it?"

Deirdre threw her head back and laughed. "You said it. We're survivors, you and me. And Hannah too."

Abby sipped her coffee. It was flavored with cinnamon and too sweet.

Deirdre was talking about Hannah, but Abby couldn't really listen. Her mother's lines seemed rehearsed, like ones she had said in a play long ago. Had they always been that way, old and worn, someone else's words, with Deirdre just reciting them? Abby saw herself as a young girl, dressed in a long black skirt and eggshell-white blouse, holding her violin in its case as if it was the only thing that mattered, waiting outside Lincoln Center for her mother to arrive for a concert. She remembered watching a Checker cab pull up and Deirdre seemingly float out of it, her dress blue velvet, her head held high, her eyes greeting an audience that had been meant for Abby but had turned to Deirdre instead, whispering her name in hushed voices filled with awe, asking for her autograph. Abby could still see the streets, wet from a quick rain shower, reflecting the lights of Lincoln Center. She could still see her mother stealing the show from her as they walked past the bubbling, lit fountain. "Knock 'em dead, kiddo," Deirdre had whispered to her as she'd squeezed her arm. Another old phrase.

Tonight, she would go to the play and watch as Deirdre did what she did best—act. Be a different person, one who led a life perfectly written and orchestrated by someone else. She would act out emotions that she could then leave behind. And she would get all of the applause. A review that hung on the wall in the hallway of the apartment in Manhattan said: DEIRDRE FALLS CHURCH TAKES THE SHOW FROM EVERYONE!

Deirdre was talking now about this show, *'Night Mother*, and how when she walked on the stage, before she uttered a word, audiences burst into applause.

"I bet you're really wonderful," Abby said.

"I am," Deirdre told her. "I'm terrific."

Tourists crowded the streets of Williamstown. Deirdre passed through them, an imposing figure in her bright red silk. Abby heard the whispers, caught fragments of sentences. ". . . Dulcinea Day." "I saw her on Broadway in . . ." "She still looks incredible . . ."

"You didn't even touch your sandwich," Deirdre said. A mother's lines.

"It seemed strange eating something with your name," Abby said truthfully.

But Deirdre laughed. "Next time I'll get you a Christopher Reeve. You'd bite into *that*, I bet."

They stopped in front of the theater, pausing at the marquee.

"Sold out, you know," Deirdre said. She pressed her fingertips to the sign, just below her name. Her voice grew quiet. "What would you think if I retired?" she said. "If Toby and I moved to Palm Springs. Or the south of France? Someplace quiet."

Abby touched her mother's wrist. "Mom," she said.

Deirdre let her hand drop. "Ha," she said. "I'm not ready for that yet."

Abby caught her breath. "I almost believed you there for a minute."

"Nonsense," Deirdre said, and started to walk to the still-empty theater.

Inside, it smelled of sawdust and lemon-scented cleaning solution. Abby remembered how, when she was a little girl, her parents used to take her to rehearsals. She would sit right up front and watch them read their lines from bound scripts, moving stiffly across the stage from one taped X to another. Then, on opening night, Abby would be in the front row again, perfectly dressed and her hair braided, watching in amazement at how smoothly they spoke and moved, like a miracle had occurred.

One summer, at a theater like this one, she had watched as Toby flubbed his lines, over and over, during a rehearsal of *Private Lives*. Each time he did it, he'd laugh stupidly and say, "Need a little more oxygen to the brain, I guess." She remembered how his hand had trembled when he took a coffee cup from a stagehand and sipped from it greedily. It might have been the first time that Abby realized that Toby was not really drinking coffee. When Deirdre had started her best scene, Abby had yawned loudly and walked out. She had gone behind the theater and played her violin loud and fast. Bluegrass. Until Toby had come out and asked her to keep it down. "We can't even think in there," he'd said. "We all want to start square dancing."

Now, Deirdre climbed onto the stage and Abby was struck by how small her mother looked up there alone.

"You know," Deirdre said, "I always wished Toby and I had done *Streetcar*. Together, you know. I always thought we'd be terrific in that."

Abby stood at the foot of the stage, looking up at her mother.

Deirdre struck a pose, head back, back arched. When she spoke, her voice was Southern, pure Mississippi delta. "I have always depended on the kindness of strangers," she drawled.

Abby could see a New Orleans street on a hot summer night, French latticework on the balcony, lacy shadows.

Deirdre dropped her pose and laughed. "I always did want to play Blanche DuBois," she said.

A few hours later, the theater was full. Abby sat in the front row, her hands folded together, her heart beating fast. The lights dimmed and the crowd grew instantly quiet. There was a pause, a moment of expectation. A man in the back coughed. Then silence again until the curtain rose and revealed the lit stage. A kitchen and living room.

Deirdre entered stage right.

She did not even speak her first line before the audience burst into applause. Abby found herself joining in, clapping for Deirdre Falls Church, for all the performances she had given, for the one she would give tonight.

Deirdre stood, frozen like a statue, until the applause died. Then she moved to the kitchen, opened a cupboard. She was no longer Deirdre Falls Church. She was a mother with a desperate daughter. There was no sound. Then Deirdre spoke her first line, perfectly.

"Jessie," she said, "it's the last snowball, sugar. Put it on the list, okay?"

Zach imagined that Abby would call from somewhere along the Taconic Parkway. She'd tell him she was almost home. He had his response ready. "I'll meet you at Nellie's," he'd say. And after they ate Nellie's greasy hamburgers and French fries with malt vinegar and drank Rolling Rock beer, he'd play Patsy Cline on the jukebox, take Abby into his arms, and dance across the tiled floor. When he thought about it, he could almost feel Abby's calloused fingers, almost smell the cheap strawberry shampoo she used.

He did not know if he could do it, if he could be all the things she wanted from him. But in his fantasy, that didn't matter. All that mattered was Patsy Cline singing while he and Abby slowly spun across the floor. Everything else was fuzzy and unimportant. That dance, that moment, canceled out the rest.

But, like most dreams, this one didn't come true.

Instead, she walked into the house late one night while Zach sat watching *Breakfast at Tiffany's* and Hannah slept sitting up at the other end of the couch. She had fallen in love with Holly Golightly, and they had watched the movie for the past three nights. This time, when she fell asleep, he didn't try to wake her.

The tiny fans were all still in position, but the weather had finally broken and so they were turned off, standing around the room like planes ready to take off. He didn't even hear Abby come in, so captivated was he by Audrey Hepburn on Fifth Avenue.

He was startled to see her there, standing in the living room, and jumped up quickly, waking Hannah, who stood too, confused.

"Did it end?" Hannah asked sleepily.

Abby pulled on the overhead light, blinding everyone for an instant.

"Hey," Hannah said.

Zach felt awkward, a schoolboy on his first date. "You didn't call," he said.

Abby shrugged, awkward too. She felt confused by this scene of domesticity. She could be a wife walking in to announce dinner, a mother calling her daughter for bed.

Hannah, awake at last, saw her mother for the first time.

"Hey," she said again.

"I have this great plan," Zach said, struggling to keep his fantasy intact.

"Zach," Abby said.

His voice was excited. "We can still do it. We can drive to Nellie's now."

"Nellie's," Abby said.

"*Now?*" Hannah said.

Abby rubbed the top of Hannah's head. "You cut it all off," she said.

Hannah moved from beneath her mother's hand. "Isn't it *très?*"

"Why don't you go upstairs," Abby said to her.

"But I want to go to Nellie's," Hannah said. "I want chili."

"We're not going to Nellie's," Abby said, looking at Zach.

Abby motioned toward the steps slightly with her head. "Go on," she said quietly.

Hannah stamped her foot, then reluctantly walked away. If she was Holly Golightly, she thought, she would do something special right now. Something unexpected and delightful. But she wasn't. She was just Hannah Plummer. After all of this, that was the one thing she was sure of, the only thing she really knew.

Abby kept staring at him, hard. As if she was memorizing his face. He wished she would stop.

"You're ruining my great fantasy," he said.

He felt like she knew that he wasn't sure if he could stick it out. His night with Alice had proven that to him. When he had left Nina, he had been so sure. He had felt as if he had really decided something. Everything was topsy-turvy now. Abby had not been waiting for him. He had tried to make everything right while she was away, and he had failed.

He tried again to make the fantasy real.

"You and me," he said, "slow dancing at Nellie's. To B-12." He added, " 'I Fall to Pieces.' " Once she had told him that song made her think of him, but now she said nothing.

"I can't sell you on this, can I?" he said.

He had a very real sense of things coming to an end, a realization that soon he'd be leaving here alone, that he wouldn't be coming back. His hand pressed his stomach, tried to ease the ache that was back.

Abby flicked the cord of the light on the end table beside her. The lamp had a plastic fake Tiffany shade and pieces of it had melted off, leaving blank spots in the red and blue and yellow rectangles.

"You fixed this," she said.

"It only needed a new bulb," he said. "I'm a real Mr. Fix-It, huh?"

"One of the things I think about a lot is your eyes. Isn't that strange? To sit and spend hours a day remembering how blue your eyes are?"

Maybe, he thought, if he could tell her a lie, that he was ready to change and work it out, to stick around forever. Maybe then she wouldn't look at him like this.

He started to tell her stories. She just sat and listened, her back straight, her hair pulled into a tight ponytail. She looked like she was about to give a violin concert, about to raise it to her and stroke its strings.

"Hannah," he said, "has this fascination with her roots. She even wants to go to Seattle and meet my crazy mother. I told you she was crazy, right? Into channeling and flower power. *Real* flower power, I mean. We don't have to go to Mexico this summer. We could do the Pacific Northwest."

She flinched when he said "this summer," but still she did not speak.

Zach thought, Why are we sitting here like this? We're supposed to be in each other's arms. We're supposed to be dancing at Nellie's.

The night before, after watching *Breakfast at Tiffany's*, he and Hannah had watched *Summer of '42*. Zach had been struck by the movie, by the way he seemed to have missed teenaged days like that, the quaint nervousness, the timidity and wonder. He had felt nostalgic for a time he had never even known. But sitting here now beside Abby, he was feeling all those things. Nervous and frightened and amazed.

"Or you know what?" he continued, telling himself to tell her what she wanted to hear. Tell her they would go to Big Sur and renew their vows, really try at being married, have more children, act responsible, fall in love again. "We could focus on California. Inverness, Mendocino."

She looked away from him finally, focused on the hands folded in her lap.

"Focus on California," she said so softly he wasn't sure he'd heard her correctly.

"You'd love Inverness," he said. "Famous for its oysters. Do you . . . do you like oysters?" Why didn't he know if she liked oysters? This was ridiculous.

Her eyes, when she looked at him again, were soft, and gray, the color of smoke.

It hit him then, like a punch.

"You're not coming with me," he said.

She shook her head. "No."

"What do I have to do to change your mind?" he asked her.

She laughed, a sad laugh. "You would have to stop being you. You would have to keep all of your promises. And you can't do that. I know that you can't."

He told her the truest thing he'd ever said. "I love you, you know."

"The funny thing," she said, "is that I do know that."

*   *   *

They both watched Zach go.

Hannah stood upstairs in her mother's bedroom, looking out the window. He was not a father who would send for her at school vacations, or call her on her birthday. Someday he'd drop by, or call if he was near, but that was all. She had told Chelsea once, "My father sucks." But standing here, watching him go, she did not feel that way at all.

Abby stood at the kitchen door. So many times, she had hidden from his partings, sat in dark rooms or under the cool sheets of her bed, anything to not watch him leave. It had been a superstition, as if watching him made it more real. As if it made it certain that he would not come back.

This time, she stood straight and faced him. She lifted her hand in a small farewell wave. Before he'd walked out, he'd held her close, and her heart had quickened and hope had risen in her that he would change his mind and stay and be what she wanted him to be. But then he had released her and walked out.

At the door to the van, Zach hesitated. The dawn was wet and misty, the sky streaked with palest pink. Why couldn't she just run out that door and climb into the van with him? They could drive anywhere, nowhere. But she lifted her hand and waved goodbye.

Abby strained against the screen door, into the near-light of morning, to catch a final, real glimpse of Zach. She wanted to see, as if to confirm, the blueness of his eyes. But she couldn't from this distance, and had to rely, for a long time to come, on her memory of them. Years later, perhaps, he would pass by where they lived, and would call from a pay phone somewhere close, and she'd meet him for coffee at a diner. It would be awkward. She would feel nervous at the familiar pounding in her chest, at the excitement he still brought to her. But she would notice that his eyes were not quite so dazzling as she'd remembered, their blue not nearly as vivid.

When the sunset on the back of Zach's van had completely disappeared from sight, Hannah ran down the stairs to her mother. She expected to find her, as she had in the past, sitting in a darkened living room, with a bottle of wine, crying to herself.

But this time, Abby stood at the kitchen door, looking out.

For a minute, Hannah thought he had turned around and come back. She ran to the door, too, and peered over Abby's shoulder, but there was no one there.

"We could go to Paris," Hannah said. "I know the subway there pretty good."

The morning sun was bright now, and full. A cool breeze, with the hint of autumn in it, rustled the curtains in the kitchen where Hannah and Abby sat eating Ring Dings at the table.

"I was thinking of something a little more realistic," Abby said.

"Paris *is* real," Hannah said. She would send Noah a postcard of the city at night, lit up and beautiful. There would be a real French postmark on the back, a smudged Eiffel Tower and the date in blurry French.

Abby stood, wiped her hands on her shirt. "Go upstairs and pack everything that matters."

Hannah thought of her room, the crooked shelf and unfinished Snoopy rug and creased map of the Paris Métro. None of it, she decided, mattered very much.

"Well," she said, "if we're not going to Paris, where are we going?"

Even though her voice sounded strong, Abby's hands trembled slightly as she spoke.

"I was thinking we could relocate," she said. "Go

back to New York. Upstate. Jocelyn plays the guitar, you know. Years ago she pretended to be Joan Baez and played in coffeehouses in the Village. Folk stuff."

"No," Hannah said. "I didn't know."

"If we find a third," Abby said, "we could become the new improved Three-Legged Horse."

Hannah studied her mother's face to see if she was serious. She decided she was.

"Mom," she said, "I think we've got everything that matters."

"Not quite," Abby said.

Abby left the room, and when she came back she had her violin. She held it close.

"Now we do," she said.

When they drove away from the house, neither of them looked back. The sun was bright and high above them, and the road, once they left the gravelly driveway, seemed full of possibilities.

Dara stood on the corner in her frog T-shirt.

"Hey," she called to them.

Hannah stuck her head out the window, felt the cool air on her.

"Au revoir," she called as they sped away.